HOW TO LOSE YOURSELF COMPLETELY

HOW TO LOSE YOURSELF COMPLETELY

PETER BOGNANNI

A Rock the Boat Book

First published in the United Kingdom, Republic of Ireland and Australia
by Rock the Boat, an imprint of Oneworld Publications Ltd, 2026.
Published by arrangement with Balzer + Bray, an imprint of
Macmillan Publishing Group, LLC

ISBN 978-1-83643-300-2
eISBN 978-1-83643-301-9

Printed and bound in Great Britain by Clays Ltd, Elcograf S.p.A

The authorised representative in the EEA is eucomply OÜ,
Pärnu mnt 139b–14, 11317 Tallinn, Estonia
(email: hello@eucompliancepartner.com / phone: +33757690241)

Oneworld Publications Ltd
10 Bloomsbury Street, London WC1B 3SR, England

For Junita, with love and gratitude

Grief is just love with no place to go.
—Jamie Anderson

ONE

You wake up on a moving bus somewhere in northern Minnesota, and for a few seconds you think he's still alive. This happens almost every day when you're awake, but you haven't yet opened your eyes. That's when you see him. Slouching in a doorway. Eating olives from a jar. Sitting next to you on your bed in the heat of summer, reading a Choose Your Own Adventure book. You can see it all so clearly. His lanky body sprawled on the bed. His eyes searching the page as he tries to make it through the last chapter without meeting a bad end. But before he does, and before you can ask him if he's real, your eyes flash open to a pink sunrise blurring past your window, and immediately, you remember where you are.

You are on a school bus you boarded this morning in the parking lot of your old junior high. And judging by the road noise, this bus has seen better days. The constant drone puts your thoughts in a blender, and it takes you a second to get your bearings. You are not in your old room. You are not with your brother. You're in a seat by yourself, fists clenched in your lap, and your cheek numb against the cold glass of the window. Outside, a line of jagged pines cuts through the rising sun. Inside, it's hard to see much of anything, even your fellow passengers.

They must have been there this morning, but it was pitch

black outside, and you were distracted by your dad, who was there to make sure you actually got on the bus. It was so dark he almost did a face-plant as he helped you with your new sleeping bag and survival gear. He isn't the world's most coordinated guy even in broad daylight, and he couldn't even hug you without accidentally stepping on your foot. You were okay with the hug, though, which broke a quiet tension that had haunted you on the drive over.

You were less happy when your dad decided to speak.

Because what he said was:

"Just try. Okay, Case?"

This was not the right thing to say for two reasons.

One, it implied that you haven't been trying to feel better since the funeral. And two, it suggested that you don't usually try at things. Both of which aren't true. You want more than anything to feel better. And you try way too hard at most things. You once heard anxiety described like a duck moving across the water; on the surface everything looks smooth, but beneath, it's all frantic motion. This sounds about right to you, so maybe all your dad has been seeing is the surface and not your little duck legs, paddling for their very lives.

You managed to swallow your anger, though, and moments later you were sad as you watched him shuffle back to his dented Prius with the bumper sticker that reads FOLLOW ME TO THE WAFFLE HOUSE! He gave you a half wave before getting inside, and he seemed hesitant to leave, which was odd since this whole thing was his idea. Your mom had to work early at the hospital today, but she made your favorite dinner last night and refolded the clothes in your bag. Just thinking about all your shirts in there, sitting in perfect squares, is enough to make your throat catch.

Sometimes when you're up late, your mind doing its usual laps, you think if you don't start to feel better soon, you'll have to live with your parents for the rest of your life. This is comforting at first. Then you remember the way they scream at each other over the deafening drone of the coffee grinder in the morning, and how your dad still walks around in his briefs, which have a number of see-through patches in the back, and you feel like you would probably slowly turn into a very different person if this was your fate.

The bus goes around a bend in the road and a blinding ray of sun cuts through the windshield, setting the air aglow. But, still, it's hard to make out your fellow travelers behind the row of tall seats. The only thing you know about them is that, like you, they are in high school, and like you, they are willing to go out in the middle of nowhere for weeks with total strangers to confront their overwhelming anxiety and try to find a reserve of strength to overcome it.

Adventure Therapy.

That's what it's called.

The phrase made you laugh out loud the first time you read it on the website. You imagined yourself whining about your life as you rappelled out of a military helicopter and hacked through a dense jungle with a machete. The specifics of what you're actually going to do have been kept secret, but there are pictures of canoes and overgrown hiking trails on the FAQ page, so you know it's going to be something outdoorsy, and something that counts as an "adventure."

But that could be anything, really.

Using a public bathroom can be an adventure with your condition.

"Excuse me."

A disembodied voice sends your thoughts dissolving like thinning mist, and it takes a second to realize that the words are being directed at you.

"Do you have a Klonopin?"

"What?" you say.

The face that greets you is fuzzy in the half light, but the voice sounds like a guy's. And, sure enough, the longer you stare, the more the rounded silhouette of a short afro comes into focus. Then a pair of retro, brow-line glasses.

"Klonopin. It's a central-nervous-system depressant. Do you have one I could borrow?"

His voice is soft with a slight quaver, and you can't tell if he's being condescending or just as clear as possible about what he needs.

"I know what it is," you say. "Just . . ."

"Just what?" says the voice.

"Did you really come on an anxiety trip and forget your meds?"

A frustrated sigh.

"No, I've got, like, half a Walgreens with me, but it's in my duffel under the bus. I usually keep a lucky one in my pocket, but today I forgot. Go figure. Anyway, I . . ."

"I'm a Xanax person," you say.

"C'mon, man. What is this? Amateur hour?!"

You are momentarily quiet at this judgment. It has never occurred to you that people might have such strong feelings about nearly identical sedatives.

"Sorry, sorry," he immediately says. "I'm a little edgy. Moving vehicles aren't my thing. And I usually have my support animal, but he couldn't come. Which is why I need the . . ."

He clicks his tongue and trails off and then seems to actually look at you for the first time.

"I'm Troy," he says.

"Case," you say.

He extends a sweaty palm, and you shake it before he yanks it away. He's silent after that, and you remember that before you stopped going, your therapist was always telling you to ask questions. People like being asked questions, she said. It plays to their vanity.

"So what is it?" you say.

"What is what?"

"Your support animal."

"Ah," he says. "Right. You mean Turbo. He's a wiener dog. Thus, the shirt, I guess . . ."

He points to a white ringer T-shirt with bright blue ribbing around the neck and sleeves. You have to squint to make out the faded letters stretched over his skinny chest, which read: THE GRASS IS GREENER UNDER MY WIENER.

"Oh," you say.

"Yeah," he says. "I'll snag one, by the way."

"One . . ."

"Xanax. Sorry. Sometimes I forget the whole context thing. But I'll take it, you know . . . if the offer's still on the table."

You dig into your pocket, where you feel the familiar ovoid contours of the pill. Sometimes all you need to do is just dip your fingers into your pocket and touch the edge and you start to feel a little better. Still, it doesn't feel good to fish this little talisman out of your pocket now to give it away.

"Thanks, man," Troy says when you hand it to him.

Then, instead of swallowing it, he quickly chews it into a paste, a trick that only the professionally anxious know makes it kick in faster (at the expense of the worst aftertaste imaginable). After that, he salutes you for some reason and disappears behind the wall of his seat again.

Outside, the sun turns the air a chalky white and it begins to rouse a few more of your compatriots. You hear a yawn or two. The telltale candy-rattle of a pill container. And that cartoon-bubble-popping sound a phone makes when a message goes in or out. Once you reach your destination, deep in the Boundary Waters, your phones will no longer work, so it makes sense that people would be using them while they still can.

You don't want to use yours, though.

Not because you have no one to text—you still have a few loyal school friends, even after your months of isolation—but because you know if you get your phone out now, you'll just look at pictures of your brother, Sean. And, if you do that, the suffocating guilt will almost certainly return and you might even start crying. Right now, you have a chance, however short-lived, to be the guy who doesn't cry first on the therapy trip.

So you keep your phone in your pocket. But because just thinking about all this is making you feel bad anyway, you decide to get up and walk slowly to the bathroom at the back of the bus, where you close the old accordion door and look in the mirror.

"Wherever you go," your therapist once said, "there you are."

It was the name of a book or something. You never read it,

but the phrase stuck with you. And here you are in this bathroom: same floppy haircut you've had since freshman year, and the same lost expression on your face. You take a breath and try, just for a moment, not to think of your brother, who, ironically enough, actually liked the outdoors. Hiking. Fat-tire biking. Cliff-diving. He was always trying to get you out of the house, and he would have been beside himself with excitement at the thought of a wilderness mystery trip.

If he were here right now, he would surely be punching you in the arm and telling you, with his face too close to yours:

"C'mon, Space Case. Get out of your head!"

You draw one long breath—in through the nose, out through the mouth—and flush the toilet in case anyone outside somehow wants to prove you didn't really go to the bathroom (yes, this is actually the kind of thing you worry about). And then, while you're splashing water on your face and trying to shake the feeling that coming on this trip was probably a terrible mistake, you suddenly hear a voice from somewhere else on the bus.

It's too distant to make out any words, but you stop anyway, water dripping from your forehead into the tiny basin below. Even though it's far away, and even though there's a door separating you from the sound, you know immediately whose voice it is. It doesn't seem possible, but it's one you know very well. A voice you used to hear almost every day before things went terribly wrong.

A voice you were sure you would never hear again.

TWO

The bus is braking when you step out of the bathroom, and you have to steady yourself against the wall to keep from lurching forward into the seat of an Asian American kid in an all-white tracksuit who immediately gives you a death stare.

"Watch it, NARP," he mutters, and then returns to squeezing a tennis ball so hard that his knuckles could cut glass.

You don't know what *NARP* means—though, really, how could it be good?—so you turn away and look toward the front of the bus, trying to catch a glimpse of the person you expect to be there. But all you see is the view out the windshield and what looks like the last truck stop at the edge of human civilization. It's an orange box of a building with diesel pumps and a hand-painted sign that says FERG'S SMOKED FISH.

You glance at the seats up front, but you don't find her there either. Only a ruggedly handsome man in a red snapback, who is slowly getting to his feet. You know from the prep materials that his name is Silas and that he's some kind of therapy-nature guide. There was another guide with him in the photos, a short muscular woman with red hair, but you look around and you can't find her anywhere. Meanwhile, Silas fishes something out of the pocket of his vest. It's a palm-size rectangle, and when he removes the plastic case, you can see it's a cassette tape. One he promptly feeds into the bus's ancient stereo system.

He doesn't look old enough for cassettes, which means it's either his parents' or he got it just because this bus has a tape deck. Either way, after a long, high-frequency hiss, out come the first few notes of a song.

And unfortunately, it's a song that you recognize.

You know it from a radio station that your dad liked to listen to at full volume on the way to your therapy appointments. It's called "Country Roads," and it's by a guy named John Denver, who looks, you remember, like a friendly shop teacher in spectacles.

Everyone on the bus is silent, holding out for some kind of explanation. And when the chorus kicks in and shop-teacher John starts yelling about "mountain mamas," Silas starts walking slowly down the aisle of the bus, shaggy brown hair spilling out of his backward hat. You sit back down and watch him. He is tan and has a chipped front tooth, which somehow makes him even more masculine and good-looking. And before anyone can ask him what this has to do with therapy, he doubles down and starts to sing along in an enthusiastic and totally off-key voice.

"Take me home! To the plaaaaaaaaace I belong!"

He's not dancing, thankfully, but he's looking at each of you directly in the eye, daring you to say something about all of it. When you don't, he motions to the bus driver, who gets up and turns down the music.

"Adventurers!" he shouts.

Blank stares all around.

"Who among you . . . would like me to turn off this song?"

Five hands shoot up, including your own. That's how you know how many of you there are.

"I will consider it!" he says, his eyes scanning the seats. "But first I want reasons."

It takes a second for everyone to weigh the cost-benefit of stopping whatever this is versus speaking publicly. Finally, Troy stands up behind you and cups his hands over his mouth.

"THIS SONG IS NOT GOOD," he says.

This gets a few laughs.

"That's subjective, brother," says Silas.

"No, it's not," mumbles this girl a few rows in front of you who's practically burrowing inside her lavender hoodie.

"Okay, Fran, okay. What else you got?" says Silas.

At this, Fran-the-hoodie-girl goes silent. There's another spell of quiet. Only a few seconds probably, but anxiety tends to stretch uncomfortable moments like taffy. Then another girl, the one you couldn't see before, stands and speaks.

"I don't like watching you listen to it," she says.

And there, finally, is the voice again.

It's low and a little monotone, with a high note at the end of the sentence that sounds like she's asking a question even when she's not.

"Aha! Now we're getting somewhere!" says Silas. "Why not?"

To this, the girl says something that you don't hear, probably because your heart is now pounding in your temples. When she's done speaking, though, Silas smiles and turns back to the group.

"Did everybody hear Diana?" he says.

You all shake your heads.

Diana.

You have to fight to get a breath.

"Well, I'm not going to repeat all that. But, basically, Diana is embarrassed for me and it is causing her extreme discomfort. Like, a *bunch* of discomfort. Does that sound familiar to anyone?"

Nobody nods. Especially not you because the name *Diana* is now stuck on a loop in your whirling brain, and a pit in your stomach is threatening to swallow your whole body.

"Case!"

You feel yourself jolt upright in your seat. It's possible you make an unflattering noise of some kind when you do this, but you don't hear it over the cranking gears of your own internal machinery.

"Yes?"

"Yes, what?" says Silas.

It takes you a few seconds to remember what the question was.

"Yes," you say again. "It . . . uh . . . sounds familiar to me. And yes, I'm super embarrassed for you."

He stares at you and shakes his head. His eyes stay locked on yours, and you can also feel four other pairs of eyes stuck on you now.

"Well, that's bad news," he says. "Because that's not going to work for us."

"What isn't?" says the tracksuit guy.

"Embarrassment, brother! We have to find a way to get rid of that real quick."

Silas motions to the bus driver, who turns the song back on.

"On this trip," he says over the jangly music, "we're going

to be together for a long time, trying to make some progress on this thing we're all struggling with. Everything we do is going to be kind of embarrassing. The sooner we can be open with one another, the more progress we're going to make. You understand?"

A hand goes up.

"Yes, Fran?" says Silas.

"No offense. But wasn't there supposed to be, like, another therapy person on this thing besides you?"

Silas nods.

"Yes," he says. "There was. But unfortunately, she had a medical emergency and she can't make it on this trip. So it's just us, adventurers. And I'm here to tell you: We are enough. We are enough!"

You hear his words, but he might as well be speaking underwater. So you close your eyes and give in to the zoning your brain is so fond of, and when you come to full consciousness again, your ears pulsing, chest tight as a drum, everyone is getting off the bus. You have, it seems, been given permission for one last pit stop.

You don't really want to move, but curiosity about Diana pulls you from your seat. And as you head toward the thin rectangle of daylight at the front of the bus, you finally see her clearly, just a few feet away. Her jacket has the same row of safety pins near the collar. Her curly hair still hangs barely over her eyes. You stop, and then you just stand there with your arms at your sides. She doesn't block your path, but she doesn't exactly move out of the way either.

She did the same thing every time you met her in the hallway of your house, usually when she was leaving Sean's room, spritzing on perfume to cover up the weed smoke or tucking her shirt back into her jeans. And if you happened to meet eyes with her, she often gave you the same deadpan expression she's giving you now, and she never, ever got out of the way.

"Hey, Case," she says.

"Hey, Diana," you say.

THREE

You will never forget the way you met her because of two things. One: It was your sixteenth birthday. And two: You were on the roof of your garage. The two were related. You'd decided long ago, after a childhood birthday party where only two people showed up, that you would never again risk the humiliation of a great big blowout fiesta with a guest list a mile long and enough food to feed the neighborhood. From then on you kept birthdays painfully low-key:

German chocolate cake with your family.

Maybe a movie.

And then a little time alone (sometimes, to be completely honest, with an old *Playboy* magazine you found in a box of your dad's stuff from college) reflecting about the last year, which was usually—let's keep being honest—a highlight reel of various cringeworthy things you said and did in key situations, played over and over again by the relentless sadist who lives in your brain.

It wasn't the world's greatest tradition. But at this point, you were sticking to it for lack of anything better. On the night you met Diana, the cake part of the evening was done and you were full of sugar and familial support. You'd watched a movie earlier that day, so you were on to the reflection bit, crawling up on top of the garage for a little stargazing.

This was a new thing for you, in part because you were afraid of heights, and had been since you were a kid. But recently your therapist had told you about exposure therapy, so you were trying, occasionally, to expand your "window of tolerance" for high places. Also, you had just gotten a new app called Pocket Planetarium that alerted you to various astrological events, and all day it had been going completely apeshit, excited beyond belief about the Draconids meteor shower that was set to begin in the next fifteen minutes.

To be clear: You did not care that much about the Draconids meteor shower. What you mostly cared about was distracting yourself from the fact that another year of high school was beginning and it was already evident that nothing much was going to change. As sure as the meteors would soon radiate from the constellation Draco, you would undoubtedly spend your days radiating social anxiety, and looking on from distant parts of the galaxy while other people had memorable experiences.

Like that very night, for example. Just across the moonlit lawn, in his bedroom, your brother and some of his friends were having an impromptu party. The shades were pulled, but you had seen the crew earlier, a few guys from his diving team and an unfamiliar girl or two, their pockets sloshing obviously with contraband as they lumbered into Sean's room. Even from the roof, you could hear the occasional "Shut up, bro!" echo against the garage, while you tried not to think about the fact that it should probably be you having friends over.

Where are the goddamn meteors? you were thinking when the strange girl crawled out of Sean's bedroom window. At first you thought it was one of his buddies from the team. They weren't exactly the most risk-averse group of guys you'd ever met, and jumping out of windows was absolutely on brand. But then you saw a girl's leg straddle the windowsill and a small body drop to the ground and it was clear that whoever this was, they were not doing this on a dare.

"Ow. Screw a kangaroo!" she said. "My ankle."

Sean poked his head out the window.

"I said you could go out the front. My parents are sleeping!"

The girl gave him the finger and brushed herself off.

You turned over onto your stomach then, your body shaking slightly, and looked down the slope of the roof just as she stepped into the light from the upstairs window. All you saw was dark curly hair and a baggy jean jacket, and it wasn't until she looked up and spied you on the roof that you understood why she was there. Initially, she hadn't looked like Sean's type exactly—girls who spent most of their time in yoga pants, posting carefully staged selfies taken in forests. But when she moved closer, it was clear that she was, like the others, very beautiful.

"Dude," she said, standing right below the roof. "You startled me. What are you even doing up there?"

Then she started laughing really hard, which was how you realized she was probably kind of hammered. This was not uncommon. Sean, for all his sports conditioning and boy-next-door charm, smoked and drank quite a bit, and so did most of the people he spent time with. He had recently come into your room at 3 A.M. on a Tuesday for help cleaning a scorched sauté pan. Eventually it came out that he had tried to make cookies "faster" on the stovetop.

"I'm watching the Draconids," you said because you never, ever said the right thing, so why should you start now?

This started her laughing again, and she had to lean against the garage to keep her balance.

"Hold on," she said. "That sounds awesome. I'm coming up."

The thought of her falling sent a jolt of anxiety through you. And you were about to tell her about the pile of firewood around back that she could use to get a leg up. But before you could get the words out, she jumped up, grabbed ahold of the gutter, and began to hoist herself toward the roof. You nearly left your body watching her hang there, but it was impressive upper-body strength, especially given her state. She managed to get a foothold on a windowsill, and in what felt like seconds, she was lying flat on her back only a few feet away from you.

"All right," she said. "Okay . . . I think I get it now."

"Get what?" you said.

"Why you're up here. I thought maybe you were peeping in people's windows. But it's kind of nice like this. Stars and stuff."

She burped incredibly loud then.

"Oh my god," she said. "That feels so much better."

You weren't sure if you were supposed to laugh, so you stayed quiet. She didn't seem to mind. It wasn't often that you were this close to a girl, and you had decided that the best strategy for not embarrassing yourself was to say nothing that you absolutely didn't have to. She seemed content with this until something must have occurred to her.

"Wait a second," she said. "You're Case, right?!"

"Yeah," you said.

At that point, she punched you hard in the arm.

"I just ate some of your cake."

"Thanks?" you said.

"No offense," she said, "but this is how you're spending your birthday? Alone on a garage?"

You sighed.

"I guess that was kind of offensive," she said.

"It's okay," you said. "I get it. It's not the world's most exciting place. But it's kind of a tradition to spend it . . . with myself."

She nodded.

"Okay, respect," she said. "I'm not great at being by myself, personally. Which is probably why I was just in your brother's room even though it's clear he barely remembered my name. He does have good taste in whiskey, though. Cutty Sark!"

She burped again. Then she sat up, her hands flat on the shingles behind her, and closed her eyes. She had dark eyebrows, a little unkempt compared to most girls your age, and they connected when she frowned.

"I don't know if I'm ever going to see you again, Case," she said then, "so I'm going to tell you something."

"Okay," you said.

"That dude in there really loves you."

"Who, Sean?" you said.

"Yeah, he wouldn't shut up about you. How smart you are."

"That's not really . . ."

"Did you actually skip two grades?"

"Well, one, and then some specific subjects . . ."

"Do you really write his papers for him?"

"I consider myself more of an editor."

"One more question," she said.

"Okay."

Her eyes went a little glassy and she looked back at the house.

"Is he nice to girls?" she asked.

But before you could answer, she looked up and her eyes went wide.

"HOLY SHIT! I just saw a UFO! In real life!"

You felt a squeeze on your leg then, and when you looked down, her hand was clamping onto your thigh. You knew it was probably just instinct on her part, a gesture born out of shock, but nonetheless, a charge passed through your body in that moment that left you breathless. Her nails were sharp even through your jeans, and they pinched your leg.

"Meteor shower," you managed.

"What?"

"Comet debris. It . . . According to my app, it burns as it enters our atmosphere. And then . . ."

You waved toward the sky, and another one arced by on cue, like a tiny sparkler someone had tossed javelin-style through the night. She didn't say anything. She just watched the sky now, and you saw maybe a half dozen more, flying pinpricks trailing light so quickly they were gone before you were even sure you'd seen them. Then everything was static again, all the stars fixed in their right places, and she was staring at you with a very different kind of look on her flushed face.

"Wow," she said. "Okay. That was actually kind of amazing. You're like a star wizard."

She finally seemed to notice her hand on your leg, and she gently pulled it away.

"Yeah," you said. "That's actually my nickname. Star Wizard."

She laughed.

"Not so bad for being alone on a garage, right?" you said.

"Only you weren't alone," she said.

She seemed completely sober now, like the meteors had zapped her of something. She looked at you again, and it felt like she was going to say something else, but you cut her off.

"He's nice," you said.

She didn't ask for any additional explanation. She knew what you were referring to.

"Hmmm," she said. "It's sweet that you would lie for him."

And before she disappeared beneath the lip of the roof, she gave you one last smile that appeared genuine.

"Happy birthday, Case," she said.

And you thought, after she left your sight, that this would probably be the last time you saw her. She didn't seem like the type to keep coming around—too interesting—and Sean got bored of people pretty quickly.

But, amazingly enough, this was not to be the case.

Diana, as it turned out, had staying power. And before long, she had done what few others had managed to do: achieve girl-friend status with your fickle brother. Which meant you *would* see her again over the next year until they broke up only weeks before he died. At which point she would call you every night at exactly ten o'clock for nearly a month, and you would never pick up, not even once, even though you wanted more than anything to do just that.

So she never called again.

FOUR

"So . . . ," she says now, outside the truck stop.

She's scuffing the bottom of a hiking boot against some pea gravel.

"So," you say.

And it seems like this might be it: the underwhelming extent of your reunion. Until she looks at you quizzically, one dark eyebrow arched. You can't tell if she's surprised you're on this trip, or that you have nothing to say for yourself. Time has suddenly gone geological, and you have approximately an eon to ponder some things.

Like the fact that it's been since the funeral that you saw her. And that you barely recognized her there because she had cut her hair and dyed it blond. Now it's growing back and she's done nothing to disguise the roots, so her dark curls are flecked with gold at the ends. Neither of you is saying anything, but since you are a born anxious silence-filler, you eventually point to the bus and say the first thing that pops into your head, which is:

"What are the odds?"

What you mean is: What are the odds we're both here? Or maybe what you mean is: What are the odds that any of this should have happened at all? Actually, you're not sure if even *you* really know what you mean, so you don't blame her for not responding right away. It's hard to read her expression. Frustration or confusion. Maybe anger.

"Yeah," she says. "I guess."

Then her voice kind of dies. There's no high note at the end like usual. And there's none of the familiarity or intimacy it once held. She just turns around and heads toward the truck stop.

"See you on the trail, Case," she says.

She has the same swaggering stride—even grief hasn't touched that—but when she gets to the glass doors of the building, she stops for a moment to look at her reflection and carefully moves a hair behind her ear. It looks almost like she's scared to go inside, to cross the threshold of a public place—which you can definitely identify with. Finally, though, she opens the door and steps through, and you watch the glass swing shut behind her, and then your brain just kind of shuts down entirely.

This has been happening off and on in the past half year, this freefall of "disassociation," as your therapist called it. Basically, when things get too overwhelming for your nervous system, time seems to disappear and you feel outside yourself until suddenly you are you again and the fugue just drifts away as quickly as it descended.

"Why are we just sitting here?!" you ask to no one in particular.

Somehow, you are back on the bus. Fran, who has re-disappeared into her hoodie, points a long grim reaper–like finger toward the window behind you. And when you look out into the copse of towering pines beyond the parking lot, you see the kid in the white tracksuit marching back to the bus with Silas behind him. If you didn't know better, you'd think it was at gunpoint.

"Sporty made a run for it," says Troy.

The first thing you notice is that the once-pristine white track-suit is no longer pristine or white. It is an abstract-expressionist canvas of mud spatters and grass stains. Troy lowers his window, and the guy's voice comes through clear as can be as he stomps closer to the bus.

"I keep telling you, I'm not supposed to be here!" he says. "This isn't for people like me. It's for . . . *those* people!"

His cheeks are pink, either from the emotion or a recent sprint or both.

"I hear you, Will," says Silas. "I'm listening. And I'm sorry that's how you feel. But I can't leave you at the smoked-fish place. I just can't. The train has left the station, brother. There's nowhere else to take you."

At this, Will puts his head in his hands for a moment, like he needs to hold it in place. He runs both hands through his shiny black hair. Then the whole bus watches as he trudges onboard. His eyes are wet, and you try not to meet them. Instead, you risk a look at Diana sitting at the front of the bus, and you find her looking back at you. And that's the moment when the reality finally sets in:

She's going to be on this whole trip.

Another thought comes quickly on the heels of that one, and it's surprising how clear it is. *You should have made a run for it like Will.*

This was supposed to be an escape from your life, but your life, it seems, has followed you here. And as the bus pulls away from the last public place any of you will see for some time, you know it's too late to get away. You are all a version of Will right now. Sitting in a ruined tracksuit. Trapped in your seat. Scared and powerless to change whatever is coming next. Which is unfortunate because things are already feeling strange.

And the next strange thing happens only hours later at the lodge.

FIVE

You've never been in a lodge before, so you don't know if this one is representative of all lodges, but it looks like it was made of Lincoln Logs about two hundred years ago and it's infested with spiders. Fishing spiders to be exact, which are very large and got their name because they can walk on the surface of a lake and kill small fish(!). Troy saw one in the shower and has vowed that he will not bathe again until he returns to his fumigated house in the suburbs. The spiders, however, are not the strange thing.

The strange thing happens later, when everyone is asleep.

You, of course, are not asleep. This is partly because seeing Diana has done weird things to your brain. But it's also because you don't sleep anymore. At least not consistently. For much of each day, you can keep your grief and panic at bay with distractions. But at night, after your parents have gone to bed and the house is monastery-quiet, there's nowhere else for your brain to go but to him. Sometimes to the accident. Other times, you just land on small moments.

Like the time when you were six and you were running after Sean in the sprinkler, trying to do the same karate kick he was doing, and you slipped on a patch of wet grass and broke your ankle. You blacked out almost instantly from the pain. And all you really remember after that is looking straight up at the limbs of the big oak tree and then closing your eyes and coming out of surgery to the bright lights and sounds of an operating room.

When you were finally awake in your hospital bed, Sean was next to you, his leg also bandaged up. You were scared he was hurt too until your mom told you that Sean had the nurse put some bandages on his leg so you wouldn't feel alone. You thought maybe he was just doing it for the day, but instead, he sat with you that way for the next week, watching movies and drinking those little hospital capsules of apple juice with the peel-off lids.

You're thinking about this, trying to focus in on his ten-year-old face. The missing tooth he lost when he got pushed into the water fountain at school. And the freckles that appeared on his nose in the summer. You've almost successfully transported yourself back to those days, when you hear a noise next to you.

The sleeping bags are all in a circle on the old pine floor, so you think, at first, it might just be someone turning in discomfort. But when you open your eyes and your vision adjusts to the dark, you see somebody tall.

Silas.

He's still wearing the same clothes as earlier, down to his hat, and he is looking around to see if anyone is awake. He doesn't notice you because you're not moving a muscle and your eyes are 90 percent closed. But they are not *all the way closed*, and you watch as he goes over to a duffel bag and starts yanking things out of it, tearing it apart like he's hunting for something.

He's quiet about it, but meticulous, opening each compartment and sticking his hand inside. He does this a couple of times, but it seems like he's coming up empty. Finally, he zips the bag and just stands there in the dark. Obviously, he's looking for something, but what could it possibly be? You go down a list, trying to keep your mind focused so you don't move.

Toothbrush?

Toothpaste?

Steroids?

Jock-itch cream?

Night-light?

That's as far as you get before you see him reach out and scoop an object up from the floor. You blink. It's another bag. And this time, it's definitely not his. It's Diana's bag. You recognize it because it's covered in safety pins just like her jean jacket. He unzips it and rifles through it, leaving no corner untouched. And for some reason—okay, fear—you don't stand up and ask him what he's doing.

You are technically part of the "troubled-teen industry" now, and maybe random bag searches are just part of the deal. He has his hand around something, and he's about to pull it out when you decide to take action. So you tense all your muscles and you . . .

Clear your throat.

Okay, so it's not the bravest thing you could do, but it actually works because he immediately drops the bag and whatever was inside and looks in your direction. You close your eyes all the way. You try to swallow, but your mouth is parched, and you feel like you might start coughing any minute. You open your eyes again and see Silas take a step toward you. And right when you think maybe you should just stand up and run out of the lodge forever, you hear a scream from across the room.

At first, you're sure someone has been axe-murdered, because that's what happens in the woods, isn't it? But you quickly see that it's Troy, and he's having some kind of night terror. He's shaking and covered in sweat. He can barely breathe. And Silas, who was so close to you only seconds ago, is by his side in an instant, parting the crowd of bleary-eyed recent sleepers and putting a hand on Troy's back. There's no hint of the intensity that was in his search just moments before. In fact, the voice he uses to talk to Troy is easily one of the calmest things you've ever heard in your life.

"Hey," he says. "Hey, Troy. Look at me."

Troy is not responsive. But Silas focuses on him anyway.

"Troy, listen to me. You don't have to do anything else but listen right now. Can you do that for me?"

Troy nods, and you take a second to look around at the others, half in their sleeping bags, a safe distance from the fray. You want to tell Diana everything that just happened with her bag, but she's too far away. And when you turn back, Silas is looking directly into Troy's eyes.

"I need you to understand that you are with friends," he says. "And there is nothing to be afraid of. Your body is just going through a series of checks to see if you're in danger. But you're not. So now we're going to breathe. Can you breathe with me?"

You look down and see that your hands are shaking. Troy takes a full breath. A bead of sweat runs right down the middle of his nose and drops onto his lip. Then he says one word.

"Turbo."

"What's that, brother?" says Silas.

"He needs to take his heart pills."

"Who?" says Silas.

"My parents aren't going to remember," Troy says. "And then

he's going to get sick again. It happened before and he was super dehydrated. I thought he was going to die."

"I'm sorry," says Silas. "I just don't . . ."

"HIS DOG!" yells Diana. "TURBO IS HIS DOG, MAN! WAKE UP!"

Everyone turns to look at her. She has a T-shirt on. A faded red shirt that you recognize instantly as Sean's. It's from the ice cream place where he worked one summer and was fired from for giving away free cones to just about anyone who knew who he was (and some people who didn't). You're staring at it, but everything is hitting the fan with the Troy situation and you have to look back.

"He got sick before," he says. "He has heart disease, so he has to take the pills. But my parents won't remember . . ."

"That's not going to happen," says Silas. "Turbo is fine. Turbo is cool. Everything else is just the anxiety. Don't let the anxiety decide what's happening."

Then Silas is full-on holding Troy's hand. And he's doing it super comfortably. You're not sure you've held another man's hand since you were six years old. And you're wondering why that is . . . Why don't people just hold hands? It's very comforting. You are so impressed by this that you almost forget what you saw earlier.

Almost.

Because that is when you look at Silas's face and find him not looking at Troy as you assumed he would be, but staring right at you. It's not for long. Probably just a glance in the scheme of things, but you know in that moment that he saw you. He saw you watching him with the bag. It's clear.

What is not clear is what it means.

So you take this opportunity to edge your phone gently out of your pocket. *It wouldn't be hard to call your parents.* That's the thought that pulses through your brain. Your contacts are right there, glowing from your pocket. Your thumb hovers over the number for the landline your parents refuse to get rid of. You're ready to tell them this didn't take. Come get you. They might be disappointed, but you're sure they won't be surprised.

Your dad has been laser focused on fixing you since your brother's death. He'll probably just find somewhere else to send you. But your mom, who thinks that nothing bad will ever happen again if she can just keep things perfectly organized and in her field of vision, will be happy to have you safe in the car.

You inch your thumb down, but when you finally press the number, nothing happens. You stare at the phone, waiting for the screen to show the call going through. It's only when you press the call button again that you think to look in the right-hand corner where those tiny, all-important bars—the ones that signify the possibility of contact with the outside world—remain as hollow and dim as your prospects for escape.

"Okay," says Troy, sniffling. "I think everything's okay."

SIX

There's only one dream you remember from your restless sleep that night. You and Diana walking by an ocean, arguing over the color of the water. "Blue-gray," she says. "Green," you say. She shakes her head. "We need a tiebreaker," she says, and then you both go quiet because even in this dream, you know who the tiebreaker should be. Who it's always been.

Under your feet, the ground is crunching whenever you take a step. For a moment, you're sure you're walking on bones, and you can feel a sense of horror creeping through your body, but when you look closely, they're just seashells, all broken and fragmented, like the serrated teeth of some prehistoric creature. Diana is walking in front of you, but every once in a while, she turns back to see if you're still there. The waves crash and foam. You try to catch up. You finally make it to her, but when you reach out to take her hand, you open your eyes instead.

"Up! Up! Everybody up!" says Silas in a faux-cheerful voice. "Day one starts in fifteen minutes! Gather your gear and roll out!"

You look up through unfocused eyes and see him cupping his hands over his mouth. He starts making trumpet noises.

"Day one of what exactly?" says Fran from somewhere inside the depths of her sleeping bag. "You haven't told us freaking anything. We could be going on a death march, for all we know!"

Silas ignores this comment. He throws open the doors to the lodge and slips through them without a sound. He does this before you can make eye contact to see where things stand, so you look around the room instead. You can't make out much except the twisted cocoons of sleeping bags until you finally catch some motion to your right where someone's doing push-ups with the syncopated motion of a piston.

It's Will, of course. His form is impeccable, and he's counting them off in what you assume is Korean, his face bright red. "Hana. Dul. Set. Net." He just keeps going. Past ten. Twenty. Thirty. They look like they're never going to end. But, finally, he transitions into a handstand, his body perfectly perpendicular to the ground, before launching himself back onto his feet, where he dips down and rolls up his sleeping bag with precision.

Then he turns to face the room, where everyone is now awake and unabashedly staring at him. He brushes a lock of sweaty hair from his forehead.

"What?" he says.

Troy is the first to speak.

"What do you mean *what*?" he says. "Are you in Cirque du Soleil?"

Will smiles, but it's dangerously close to being a smirk. He turns his head sideways to crack his neck in a way that sounds painful.

"Stillness is death," he says.

He waits for this to sink in. It doesn't seem to.

"For the body," he says. "You guys might as well be eating a bag of doughnuts and mainlining a milkshake, lying there like that."

"That would be more fun than listening to you," says Fran, who emerges, having seemingly slept in her hoodie, though now there are some strands of faded pink hair sticking out. "Also, have you ever *had* a doughnut? They're really good."

Will rolls his eyes. He turns around to go, and that's when you finally hear Diana's voice from the back of the lodge.

"Hey," she says. "What's a NARP?"

Her voice is softer than you remember, but it still cuts through the room with some of its old power.

"What?" says Will.

"You called Case a NARP. I don't know what that is. Can you tell me, please?"

His jaw flexes.

"A NARP," he says, "is a non-athletic regular person."

Then he smiles again.

"So, you know: basically all of you."

His sleeping bag is rolled so tight it looks like it might implode from the pressure.

"Says the guy who couldn't outrun Silas," says Diana.

If this makes Will angry, it doesn't register on his face.

"It's not terrain I'm used to," he says plainly. "And I didn't have the right shoes. Otherwise, I would be gone, bro. Believe me."

"Why did you come here, then?" you ask before you can think better of it.

He's quiet for a few beats.

"His dad tricked him," says Fran.

Will shoots her a death glare.

"Sorry, man," she says. "I saw you in the parking lot. Your dad lied to you. I heard you yelling at him. That's super messed up."

"Wait," says Troy. "Where did you think you were going?"

For a moment, Will seems to consider answering. Then the vulnerability in his face disappears. His brow smooths.

"At least I didn't choose to be here," he says. "At least I have an excuse. You guys brought this on yourselves."

Then he too walks out the door and into the lusterless morning, leaving the rest of you to exit your swaddles. When you're done packing up, you wait a second for Diana, hoping she'll tell you why she stood up for you with Will. But, as usual, she's gone. Which is no surprise. She was always good at disappearing, leaving nothing more than a hint of perfume in the hallway after she spent the night in your brother's room, a ghost of something girlish in a house of boys.

When you head out, she's out there too, walking toward the lake like the rest of you. You're still half asleep as you follow the herd, but you open your eyes wider when you reach the water. In all of your brief life, you've never seen water like this. This is not a city lake from back home, clogged with beer cans and a sheen of boat oil. This surface is so clear it looks like a mirror. And the old-growth cedars towering above you reflect upside down on the water along with an endless sheet of ice-blue sky. You can't look away until you kick a pebble into the water, and the ripples swirl it all into a Monet.

You've never been much of an outdoors person—aside from a little stargazing on the garage, you are more likely to be blowing up digitally rendered parts of the natural world in a video game than enjoying it in real life—but even you can admit that this place is different. It's untouched.

Pristine.

The word seems to echo in your head as you watch the water. This place is pristine.

"Five days!" says Silas, bringing you back.

His boots plant in the muddy shore in front of you. Behind him is a row of sleek, bright yellow canoes that look like giant bananas made of Kevlar. They're laid out, half in the lake, half out. There is one, you quickly calculate, for every two of you.

"That's how long we have to get to the first drop point for supplies. We have exactly enough food and water to get us there, but if we don't make it on time, we're gonna be hungry."

Your gear is piled in front of you, the essentials you were told to bring, and okay, sure . . . a bit more, but there isn't much food in there. Now you know why: Apparently you have to earn your food?

"If we don't find the drop point," says Silas, "we're going hungry."

A nearby canoe lists in a breeze.

"And if animals get to our food before we do . . . ," he says.

A mosquito's scream dopplers around your ear. You swat it away.

"Let me guess," says Fran. "We go hungry?"

Silas points at her and touches his nose.

"What is this, the marines?" asks Troy, pushing up his glasses. "Why didn't we just bring enough food for the whole trip?"

"Because it would be too heavy to carry," says Silas. "And because it's a challenge. But I know you're capable."

Troy actually laughs at this. Then he takes his glasses off and defogs them. His eyes look bloodshot, and you're guessing he didn't sleep much after his episode last night.

"Capable of *what*?"

Silas takes a step toward him.

"Capable of anything, brother," he says. "If you can do this thing we're about to do, then you can do anything. Period. And if you can believe in yourself here, then you can believe in yourself when you're suffering. That's how this works."

Silas is speaking with an air of finality, but Troy is not having it. He's sleep-deprived and looks uncomfortable in his hiking clothes. He didn't use the toilet because of the spiders.

"Sounds like the marines," he says. "And there's not a great history of the way they treat Black and brown people in the army, by the way. I'm not going to break myself any more than I'm already broken for your sadistic enjoyment, man. I hope you know that."

He pauses, looking out over the water. Everyone is quiet, watching him. Including Silas.

"Besides," Troy adds, asking the question we all want to ask: "How do you know this works?"

Silas sighs. Precious time is being wasted. He collects himself, though, and he looks at all of you, not just Troy.

"I know because I did it myself," he says.

He nudges a canoe with his boot.

"When I came on this trip twelve years ago, I was having ten panic attacks a day, and there wasn't much that I could do to stop them. I couldn't be around more than four people at a time. I couldn't drive a car. There were songs I couldn't listen to because they made me too anxious. Let me say that again, my friends: I had to avoid *songs*. I would leave the room when they came on.

And movies with anything tense? Forget it. I was crossing new things off my list every day that I couldn't do. Sound familiar?"

No one speaks. But no one denies anything.

"And listen: This trip didn't change everything. But it started the process. It can work. It does work. But you have to be willing to challenge yourself and see what you can do. Any more questions?"

He doesn't wait for any this time. And he doesn't do anything to acknowledge your stunned expressions, but you sense a shift among your troops, a slight bend toward Silas.

"Now," he says, "if we're ready, can we move on to lesson one?"

He pulls out something you have only previously seen in movies. The object is round and attached to a small rectangle. And if you aren't mistaken, it looks like a . . .

"Compass. This is a compass, guys. Most of you probably know that. Regardless, it is your friend. But you have to know how to use it. So let's talk about true north versus magnetic north, shall we?"

Everyone looks rapt. But you don't hear much of what Silas says because someone directly behind you is whispering into your ear.

"Don't look," they say, and for a second you don't know who it is.

You start to turn around.

"Don't turn around," they quickly add.

"But . . . ," you say, a little too loudly.

And when she shushes you, you finally know. You know that

shush. And you also know that this is the closest you've been to her in months. You didn't even hug her at the funeral, a fact that brought you to tears on the way home. But now she is right next to you, and you feel that same familiar warmth through your body. Like nothing has changed. Even though you know it has.

"Don't you think we should be listening . . . ?" you say.

"Shut up," she hisses. "Something is not right, Case."

Your name in her mouth lets you know that this is no joke. She's only said it a handful of times so far, and it was almost always laced with disdain.

"I saw something," she says.

Her voice is so quiet, but she's close enough to your ear for you to hear it clearly. And for you to hear the touch of fear in the sharp inhale that comes after her final word. Because you don't know where else to look, you look down at her feet, in a pair of brand-new hiking boots she bought, presumably like the rest of you, only because she had to.

They're brown and drab and look like they could climb a mountain by themselves, but she has replaced the unbreakable laces with a pair of bright yellow ones that look like they belong on some retro high-tops. For some reason, the image of those laces nearly makes you tear up, though you can't explain why.

"What?" you whisper. "What is it?"

She pauses.

"He was . . . crying."

Relief lowers your shoulders.

"I know," you say. "Everyone saw him. He misses his dog. You were the one . . ."

"No," she says. "Not Troy."

She looks straight ahead, and you follow her gaze right to the face of your fearless guide. It takes a second for this to get through.

"This morning," she continues, "when no one else was awake, he was crying and talking to himself behind the lodge."

You can't help it: You look very closely at Silas now. He is going on about a concept called "declination," and he's half smiling as he points to something on the compass, his chipped tooth prominent beneath his upper lip. Your eyes move toward Diana's pack this time, the canvas bulging in all kinds of strange places.

It seems you're not the only one whose anxiety led them to overpack. To a person, your packs are full to bursting. Yours has a collapsible whisk inside. A collapsible whisk! Because, apparently, your type-A mom was under the impression that there was going to be an omelet bar in the absolute middle of nowhere. Diana must have these nonessentials too. It strikes you as funny suddenly, and you stifle a laugh.

"You have a lot of crap," you say.

She isn't expecting this. She looks down at her pack. Then at yours.

"So do you," she says.

"We have baggage," you say.

You finally turn around, and for less than a second, you see her smile. This is the one thing you've always shared, no matter how hard things got. The same stupid sense of humor. But the smile is short-lived, and it's quickly replaced with a look of complete exhaustion.

"What do we do, Case?" she whispers.

And the look in her eyes, one of pure question, is a lot different from the Diana you used to know, the one who always seemed
to know what to do. She knew what Sean should wear when he
was elected to homecoming court but didn't really care about it.
She knew what to do when his car battery died past curfew. She
knew how to make a device that eradicated the smell of marijuana
smoke when you blew through a toilet-paper tube full of dryer
sheets. The Diana you knew before always seemed to understand
these things intuitively and live free of the constant worry that
made your every moment so tiresome.

Which means right now, standing steps away from this lake,
on the verge of a mission for survival, she must be feeling pretty
bad. Maybe even worse than you. She isn't used to all this. She's a
rookie. And she's asking you for help.

"Hey," you say, not really paying attention to your volume
anymore. "Listen. About the funeral. I . . ."

"Screw you, man," she says right away. "We are not getting
into that right now—"

Then she stops speaking. She does this because Silas is standing right in front of you, staring at both of you in silence. Neither
of you noticed his approach, but he's definitely standing there
now, so close that you can smell his organic deodorant. And he's
definitely not happy about the interruption to his TED Talk
about how not to die in the woods.

"Diana," he says slowly. "Case."

Neither of you moves.

"Do you guys have something you need to say to me?"

Diana chokes her half-bleached hair into a nervous ponytail
and lets it go. She cracks her knuckles. Then she looks at you, her

eyes closing to half-mast, and suddenly, she adopts a strong accent with a rising intonation and says:

"Molimo vas."

Silas's anger promptly shifts to befuddlement.

"What was that?" he says.

He doesn't understand. Of course he doesn't.

But *you* do.

That's the thing.

You actually understand what she's saying.

SEVEN

You don't remember when exactly the lessons started, but you remember where you were: a Perkins Family Restaurant off the highway, across from a car dealership. It had a broken claw machine, green vinyl booths, and a crew of chain-smoking servers who came mostly from a nearby halfway house. It was the place Diana took Sean to do homework over bottomless pots of coffee and Mammoth Muffins, and the occasional cigarette in the parking lot.

You were asked to tag along, mostly so you could do Sean's calculus (to his credit, he paid handsomely). But Sean was a rising star on the diving team, and when he was in season, he transformed from a late-night studier to someone who kept the hours of an aging retiree. His dream was to be recruited by a D1 school, and in the past couple of years, this had begun to seem more like a possibility. Starting in his junior year, coaches turned up at his meets, conspicuous in their school-branded half-zips, recording his every pike and tuck on their phones. So when Sean turned in at nine thirty like your grandmother, you and Diana started making the expedition to Perkins on your own.

After she'd spent enough time sitting around Sean's room, watching him play video games and doing other things with him you preferred not to think about, she would kiss him good night and walk across the hall to knock on your door.

"You fly. I buy," she'd say each time, and you would grab the keys to the ancient Toyota Corolla you and Sean shared.

Diana didn't have a car, and though she explained it away by saying she was scared of driving, eventually you figured out that she just didn't have the money. Your family wasn't exactly rich either, but you were middle class enough to have an extra beater car for you and your brother. It had a passenger-side door that wouldn't shut all the way, and a tire pressure light that was always on, but it could make the two-mile drive to an American casual dining chain that never closed.

The first time you went without Sean, it was a little weird. He was a big presence in any room, and it was his steady commentary and running jokes that usually kept the party going. He was effortless with people and always had been. He even developed an unlikely bond with a server there named Geoff who was at least fifty-five years old, had long stringy brown hair, and always read sci-fi novels on his breaks. Once, while you were finishing Sean's problem set, he and Geoff had a twenty-minute conversation about the painter Hieronymus Bosch, a person, as far as you knew, who Sean had never heard of.

"Maybe you should be dating Geoff," Diana said when they finally came up for air.

It was a ridiculous joke, and the smile on Diana's face was a playful one. But Sean immediately responded with:

"Maybe you should be dating Case."

His face gave away nothing, and it was hard to tell if it was just a friendly jab or if there was some tender spot lurking behind the comment. It was true that you and Diana seemed to have more in common sometimes. You were both on the quieter side, happy most nights to laugh at Sean's jokes and listen to his half-baked fan theories about TV shows he liked. You were both more academically minded. Diana, despite her retro punk-rock image, was gunning for a scholarship due to her financial situation. And for you, school was the only thing you'd ever been good at. If anything, the two of you were too similar. The key difference, of course, was that old problem of genetics.

In short: Diana and Sean were beautiful. They were beautiful together. They were beautiful separately. If you put them in designer clothes and walked them around Los Angeles with a small dog, people would easily believe they were famous. That wasn't true for you in quite the same way. You weren't bad looking, but things were only just starting to arrange themselves into a pattern that another person might find attractive. If anything, you were a work in progress.

So even though there was some truth to Sean's suggestion, both he and you knew it was absurd on its face that Diana would choose you over him. Which is why he didn't care that you escorted his girlfriend to get a greasy breakfast a couple of nights a week. He was even happy, he told you once, to see you spending time with a girl, something that didn't happen all that often. And because of this lack of tension, you also felt unusually comfortable around Diana.

At first there was silence to fill, and you tried half-heartedly to sub in for Sean, making jokes about the names of menu items and mufflerless cars roaring by on the highway. But eventually, you realized you didn't have to spout nonsense all the time and things got easier after that. You did homework. You drank bad coffee. You listened to the pop hits of the nineties that were piped into the dining room at the request of no one. *I don't wanna be a fool . . . in your game for two!* And you occasionally asked questions, including one night when you saw her writing something in her notebook in an unfamiliar language.

"Whoa. What's that?" you said, pointing at the flowing cursive script.

Diana picked up her pen and looked down at what she was writing, like she was surprised anyone had noticed.

"Oh. Just Cyrillic," she said.

You waited for more, but that's all she said. The word was vaguely familiar, but you weren't sure if she wanted to talk about it. So you just said:

"Oh."

She started writing again, and you watched her pen dip and scrawl over the page. It was kind of mesmerizing, and eventually you couldn't help yourself.

"Okay, but *why* are you writing in Cyrillic? And how did you learn it?"

She sighed, and put down her pen before you could say anything else. Then she looked at you for a second like she was wondering if she could trust you. It was very obviously an assessment: How many two-egg combos did you have to have with someone before you could tell them about your actual life? Eventually, she poured herself a cup of coffee from the almost-empty pot, and you watched the dark grains swirl to the bottom.

"I'm living with my baba right now . . ."

"What's a—"

"*Baba* is Serbian for *grandma*. Anyway, she's super big into our heritage, and she said she'll get me a new phone if I learn the Cyrillic alphabet. So here we are."

She gestured to the page.

"Ah," you said. "That's cool. But why can't you just ask for one for your birthday?"

She emptied two packets of stevia into her coffee and stirred it with her finger. Then she licked the coffee off.

"Baba grew up in northern Minnesota on the Iron Range, okay? She killed chickens with her bare hands. She lost two husbands to mining accidents. She doesn't believe in birthday presents, Case. She believes in hard work . . . and drinking brandy."

Diana started in on a letter that looked like an *O* with an *I* in the middle of it. She smiled to herself.

"I'm kind of getting into it, though. She teaches me swear words if I can learn to spell them right. And it's like a whole new universe opening up for me."

"Okay," you said. "Let's hear something."

"What?"

"Swear at me," you said. "Hit me with your best shot."

She barely hesitated. She furrowed her brow and pointed a finger right at your face.

"Idi u kurac!" she yelled, and then started laughing. A few people from other tables glanced over at you, clocking the disruption. None of them appeared to be Serbian.

"What did you just say to me?"

"It's the best."

"Tell me!"

"It's actually the best."

You waved your hands impatiently.

"Okay, so there are some technical differences in translation, but it basically means: Go back in your dad's balls!"

Right as she said this, Geoff set down the food, a tattered copy of *Dune* poking out of the pocket of his baggy black pants.

"Oh my god, I'm so sorry, Geoff!" she said. "Not you. You can stay outside your dad's . . . I mean . . . you don't have to crawl back in there."

She started laughing again. Geoff grimaced and backed away and did not check on the two of you for the rest of the night.

It became a tradition after that. Each time you went to Perkins, she would teach you a Serbian swear. Which is how, in time, you learned to tell people to have sex with their mothers, their dogs, their goats, their ponies, and oddly enough, their bread. Oh, and the sun. Go f#$% the sun! You also learned how to tell people where to go: to the devil, back inside their mother, to hell, and any other terrible place you could think of. And on one memorable night, when it was snowing and the highway was deserted, you told an unsuspecting man who cut you off in the parking lot that he must have boned a hedgehog's back last night, making Diana snort with laughter.

"Your pronunciation is so bad!" she said, and collapsed against your shoulder, where she stayed for the rest of the drive home, falling asleep as you steered the Corolla slowly through the falling snow.

When you got to your house, you drove around the block two more times before waking her up. You told yourself it was so she could get more sleep, but you suspected, as you passed your house for the second time, that it might be about the feeling of her head against your body. She reached into your pockets sometimes to take things, and once she had grabbed your hand when a car honked at her. But something about this was different. And for the first time on one of these nights out, you thought of Sean asleep in his bed.

So you closed your eyes, took a breath, and gently woke her.

She didn't seem bothered by where she was, but it was past her curfew, so she immediately called her grandmother on her old cell phone. Whenever this kind of thing happened, there was always one phrase she said over and over again. Molimo vas. As in: "Molimo vas, Baba. Another half hour and I'll be home." Or: "Molimo vas. I don't want to hear about this anymore."

It was the word *please*, she finally told you. But the way she used it—it was always an urging for something. For her grand-mother to show some leniency. It was a rare time when you heard her get emotional, a window into something a little darker in her home life. And on this night, when she hung up the phone and an awkward silence fell over the car, you finally asked her why she didn't live with her parents. Where were they?

At that, she reached out and grabbed your hand and said the words softly.

"Molimo vas."

As in: *Please, Case. Don't ask me about that.*

And just like that, the closeness she'd just shown you was gone.

EIGHT

The words are still fresh in your memory. Even though it's been half a year since you sat in the usual booth for your final lesson, you recognize them instantly when Diana says them out loud to Silas. And that first phrase is the key that unlocks the others. It's not just the words, though; it's the memory of her saying them, and how content she seemed just hanging out with you, drinking endless cups of coffee and grabbing at the table in fits of laughter.

You also remember the way it felt to be there. How safe. And how you never seemed to have panic attacks on those nights, even if you'd had an especially anxious day. Like there was a spell over the roof of that green-awninged restaurant and the Serbian words were a secret charm that kept your nervous system at bay.

Both Silas and Diana are looking at you now. Diana because she wants you to do something, and Silas because he thinks Diana has completely lost her mind and he's hoping you can provide some kind of an explanation. So you attempt to pull it together for a moment. But this time, a familiar tightness in your chest begins. A tingling in your temples.

"Um, yeah," you say. "So I do have a question, actually . . ."

The air is quiet, chirps and buzzes of the woods occasionally filling the space. Above you, the sky is so blue it seems to soak into your skin. Everything around you suddenly feels so immense.

You're stuck right on the edge of a panic attack, so you shuffle around in your mind for one of your therapist's tricks. Eventually you find one. Just describing five things you see. Rooting your body in the now. That's worked before.

A single cloud reflected on the surface of the lake. One.

"Okay. What's your question?" says Silas. "We don't have a lot of time here, Case."

A tiny water strider bug, balancing right on top of the water. Two.

"Well . . . ," you say.

A frayed lace on Silas's left hiking boot.

You're at three, but it's not working. You desperately search around for another detail, trying to focus in on one tiny part of this lush wilderness. Instead, time slows and the air around you gets thick and soupy. You feel that old disassociation starting in, like you're watching everything happen to a stranger. Finally, when the sweat starts to bead on your forehead, you know it's happening. You're now in a full-blown panic attack.

Diana watches you as you melt down into an awkward crouch, breathing heavily.

"Hold on. Wait a minute. Calm down, Case," Silas says. "Is this about the bags?"

Your labored breathing immediately comes to a halt.

Not because you're feeling better. You still feel terrible, but it's like he read your mind.

"What bags?" Fran says.

"Yeah," says Will. "What bags?"

Silas adjusts his snapback.

"I'll be honest with you guys. Case saw me going through some bags last night."

"What?" says Fran. "Why?!"

Silas takes a moment. He looks at all of you.

"Because we need to watch out for one another," he says.

"What the hell is that supposed to mean?" Will says. "By spying on each other like a bunch of creeps?"

Silas runs a hand over the one-day stubble on his neck.

"Look. We're not going to make it through this alone," he says. "We need to see one another. And if something's wrong, if someone's off, we need to be honest and talk about it. Do you understand?"

"No," says Fran. "I don't. Why were you going through our shit?"

Nobody says anything for a minute; then Silas turns to Diana, who is avoiding eye contact. The buzzing in your ears continues.

"Diana, do you want to tell Case why I was going through your bag or should I?"

Diana, in turn, is silent, her lips sealed tight. When Silas speaks again, it's calm, seemingly without judgment.

"I thought I smelled something strange, so I was checking it out. Sure enough, I found some alcohol in Diana's bag. Which, as you all know, is against policy."

Everyone is looking at Diana now. It's hard to tell what they're thinking, but in case there's any judgment, she heads that off at the first pass.

"It was an airplane bottle!" she says finally. "That's, like, one shot. For sleep. Like that's so different from Ambien, you hypocrites."

Silas finally seems to notice that you're on the ground, and he extends a hand. You're trying to put all this new information together, but it's hard in this state. You're not thinking about anything clearly.

"Thanks for speaking up about the bags, Case," says Silas. "I'm sure that wasn't easy."

You look at Diana, but she's no longer meeting your gaze. Your mouth is so dry, which always happens after an attack, but the idea of fumbling in your pack for a drink of water right now is unimaginable. You feel yourself calming a little. And then, because you don't know what else to do, you finally take Silas's hand and he pulls you to your feet, looking you right in the eye.

"All right," he says. "Everyone in the boats!"

NINE

It should come as no surprise that no one in your group knows how to paddle a canoe. Still, it's kind of astonishing what a disaster it is. People going forward. People headed bass-ackward toward the shore. People spinning in slow circles like upended beetles. It would be hilarious if you didn't need to accomplish this to get food, and if you weren't one of the worst offenders.

You're in a boat with Fran, who sits in front of you just holding her paddle across her body like a lap bar on a roller coaster. Her hood is finally down, revealing pink hair that looks much brighter in the sun. Fran, as it turns out, does not like being bad at things, and in the face of this current humiliation, she has gone completely silent and immobile—"dorsal," your therapist once called it. This leaves you to thrash around, trying to point your vessel toward the open water. You look for Diana, and you see her in a canoe with Troy.

Something is still bothering you about Silas's revelation, and you're not completely sure what it is. Maybe it's just that Diana was desperate enough to bring booze on a therapy trip, which seems like a layer of not-okay you didn't sense from her until now. But there's something else too, something that you can't put your finger on. You look around for Silas, and see him paddling behind you.

"STOP!" he shouts suddenly. "Everybody, stop!"

And for the first time, you see him laugh. It's a full-throated one, and you're pretty sure it's *at* you rather than *with* you, though it doesn't seem cruel. More like a pharaoh watching in amusement as his servants try to build a pyramid out of old busted rocks. His face remains calm, and he paddles by, barking out orders in a cheerful tone. Will sits quietly behind him.

"Okay, listen up, people! You need to rotate your torso! Don't paddle with your arms! Look at me, Troy! Use your whole upper body like this! Keep the paddle in your field of vision! Synchronize with your partner! Diana, that means you!"

Silas keeps at it, but as he drifts farther from your boat, it gets harder to hear him. And all you pick up is:

". . . paddle shaft even with the keel of the boat . . ."

You want to make a joke about Silas's "paddle shaft," but you don't know Fran very well yet, and you're not sure how she'll react to your fifth-grade sense of humor. She might think you're harassing her. So instead, you look away and try to speak in a completely neutral voice, saying:

"So maybe I could paddle on this side if you just want to—"

Fran hocks something up and spits it into the lake, which you guess is her response to your suggestion. Then she automatically switches to the other side and stabs her paddle in the water like a murder weapon.

"So," she says, "what's with you two anyway?"

She puts her hood back up and doesn't turn around. Her sweatshirt of choice today is jet black, doubling down on the grim-reaper look, a raised paddle her proxy scythe.

"What?" you say. "Who?"

But she ignores you completely.

"I mean, I get it," she says. "I think *I* might already be in love with her. The hair alone is grounds. But she hasn't even looked at me, so I'm guessing she's not into girls. Or she doesn't know she's into girls yet, and I love myself so I will not be taking on that project."

"Are you talking about Diana?" you ask.

"Um, yeah," she says, splashing up some water with her paddle. "You guys can't go thirty seconds without looking at each other. I'm not going to turn around, but you're probably doing it right now."

You're quiet at this. She stops paddling and finally looks at you over her shoulder. There must be a chastened expression on your face, because her voice instantly changes.

"Sorry," she says. "I'm not great at small talk. We don't have to talk about her if you don't want to. I guess I'm just jealous you guys are so close already."

Because she's not paddling and you are, the canoe is now going sideways.

"Case! Fran!" yells Silas. "Synchronize! C'mon!"

You both plunge your paddles back in the water, on the same side at first, then you alternate again. You look around for the others, but you're all scattered across the lake now. Diana and Troy are easily forty feet behind you, though Troy actually appears to be paddling, albeit kind of half-heartedly.

"It's not what you think," you say.

You're about to add more, to tell her about Sean. It wouldn't be hard. The words are so simple.

She dated my brother. He died.

But it's more complicated than that, so nothing comes out. Then an awkward-enough pause opens up that you feel compelled to fill it.

"She actually kind of hates me right now."

The word *hate* lodges in your throat, and you have to swallow it down.

"Psssht," says Fran. "That's no big deal."

She's rowing faster now, and it's hard to keep up.

"What do you mean?"

"Hate you can work with," she says. "Hate means they care. Indifference is what you have to worry about, my gangly friend. And that's what *I'm* getting from our lady at present. If she could look through me, she would. I would trade places with you in a minute! Hate is . . . that's a possibility."

You turn around again, and Diana's canoe has made up some ground. She and Troy are actually announcing their sides out loud.

"Left. Right. Left. Right."

"I know her. From before," you say.

"I suspected," says Fran. "Were you guys close?"

From across the river, Diana paddles faster, getting into the rhythm.

"Yeah," you say.

And you can tell Fran wants more details, but that's when you hear Silas again from up front.

"Adventurers, are you ready?" he says.

His question hangs in the air until, finally, Troy takes a break from his deep concentration and provides the necessary response.

"Ready for what?"

"Your first group challenge!"

Fran turns around and nearly hits you with the grip of her oar.

"What did he say?"

"Something about a challenge," you say.

"Ugh," she says. "What is this? A reality show?"

Beside you, Troy and Diana have actually pulled even with your canoe. You look at Troy this time, and he has an expression on his face like the one when he first asked you for a pill. He's breathing hard, and his glasses start fogging up. He goes to wipe them, and when he can see again, he immediately drops his paddle into the lake. It hits the surface with a splash and starts to float away.

"Troy!" says Diana. "What the hell? I think we're going to need that!"

But he's not moving. He's not moving because he sees what's ahead. And when you finally look away from his terrified face and see for yourself what's coming, you freeze too. You don't drop your paddle, but you can see how one might. This is definitely a paddle-dropping kind of moment.

Because what's ahead are some swirling rapids, and you are heading right toward them. You've never seen actual rapids before. And while these are relatively gentle by movie standards, there is still a very real current whipping along, and they look like they could probably kick your ass.

The lake is feeding into a river, and the water where they meet is churning, sending foamy white splashes up in the air. A couple of rocks obstruct the path, and water just pounds them, erupting over the top in waves. It's hard to tell how close you are, but you're definitely moving faster than you were before. No one's even paddling anymore, but it doesn't matter; the water is moving, so you're moving.

Silas is talking again, but you can barely hear him through your shock at what's coming.

"Life is going to throw things at you that you're unprepared for," he says in what can only be described as "loud therapy voice."

Your boats funnel closer as you approach the river.

"That's what life is, really. A bunch of stuff you're unprepared for. Control is an illusion. But you can learn to handle it, guys. It's possible. Sometimes you just have to let the current take you."

You all pull closer to the rapids with each word.

"Jesus Christ," says Fran. "You can't paddle us backward, can you?!"

You stick your paddle in the water to give it a try, and the power of the water almost rips your arm off. It's kind of shocking how strong that force is. Fran has to reach back and grab you by the shirt to keep you from going ass over teakettle. And when you look back up, you're only a few feet away from the start of the rapids. Fran yells something as the current sucks at your boat, but it's hard to hear.

"WHAT?" you say.

"I SAID I REALLY HATE METAPHORS!"

For a moment, you think everything might be okay. It doesn't look like too long a stretch before the safety of the next lake. It's just a little speed, then you'll coast to a stop on the glassy surface beyond. You raise a fist in the air to try to embrace it all, and that's the exact moment when you feel the crash of another canoe careening into yours.

Then everything goes dark.

The world sounds like a vacuum roaring through your ears, and when you open your eyes, you're underwater and you can see the white rapids swirling above you. Your life jacket is trying to tug you up, but the current is making it hard. Also: You have never been colder in your entire life. You spot someone near you, kicking toward the surface, and you start to swim.

As you get closer, you see it's Diana and you reach out for her. You both pop up at the same time, your life jackets up around your ears, and your packs floating around you like lily pads. An upside-down canoe drifts by and you half-heartedly reach for it, but its destination clearly has nothing to do with you.

Fran pops up next, sputtering and swearing, but seemingly okay. Then you hear screaming from behind you, and you all turn at once.

"Oh god," says Diana. "Troy's on that rock."

Which is true. Troy is definitely holding on to a rock, water pulling at him from all sides. You know right away what you're supposed to do in this situation. But your brain protests. You're too numb to move. You try to swim forward, but the current is strong and your limbs are slack. Maybe from the cold. Maybe from panic.

"Guys!" yells Troy. "I'm not a strong swimmer."

You want to help him, but you feel drained. Empty of life. The water pulls you toward the shore, and a half-hearted attempt to move forward almost sends you back under. You turn around and Diana can't get there either.

"Hold tight!" she yells to Troy. "We'll get you from the shore!"

She looks at you and nods.

"It's okay," she says. "Just let go."

You both stop treading water and try to let the current carry you. You look back at Troy one more time and find him gripping tight. His strength is impressive, but it's unclear how long he can hang on. Then you spot Will and Silas on the nearby bank. They're moving quickly. Silas is rushing to an outcropping near Troy's rock, Will trailing him. And as you all watch, Silas carefully reaches over the water and holds a canoe paddle out to Troy, who looks at it like it might as well be a pool noodle come to rescue him.

Silas is yelling something you can't hear. And gradually, Troy peels a hand off the rock and reaches for the paddle. He misses the first time. Then he extends a little farther and grips it hard. He closes his eyes and lets go of the rock completely. For a second, you think he's going to get swept away, but Will grabs the paddle too, and the two of them manage to tow him to shore, where he sits stunned in his soaking-wet clothes.

Somehow, you make it to the muddy bank and claw your way up through the cattails. Diana moves up ahead of you, and you watch her squeeze her hair, trying to get the water out. Her boots are squelching water, and her pants are stuck to her legs. She's just as soaked and humbled as you, and you know there's nothing she would rather do than get into some dry clothes or lie in the sun. But instead, she walks over to Troy.

He doesn't look up. Still, she sits next to him. You can't hear what she says, but you can see the care in her face. And you see her mouth something encouraging. Troy blinks and eventually he nods. She pats his shoulder and stands up, and then she looks back at you for just a moment before heading toward Silas, who is already working on a fire. He's got blankets from his canoe, and he's handing them out. Diana takes one and throws it over her head, bundling herself like a papoose.

You shiver and hug yourself for warmth. In this moment, you feel total defeat. You were hoping that just being out here on the trail might miraculously unlock some ability to act brave in tense situations. But that does not seem to be the case.

Wherever you go, there you are.

You turn to Fran, who still looks shaken, and you say:

"You were right."

Fran blinks. Her memory of your talk seems long gone at this point. She pulls off a boot and dumps out about a pint of lake water. It spatters on the rocks.

"About what?"

"Me and Diana."

Something clicks in her eyes.

"We weren't together," you say.

Then you close your eyes.

"But I was in love with her."

TEN

That night, shivering in your river-dampened sleeping bag, you dream of Tennessee. Specifically, a dark highway in Tennessee. Lit-up billboards for pecan farms and megachurches. Fields of abandoned machinery. It was the last trip you ever took with your brother, the whole family crammed into a van for a cold-weather pilgrimage to Florida.

Your parents drove most of the way, arguing about exits and forcing you to listen to true-crime podcasts that seemed to get more and more violent the farther south you got. But when the sun went down, they handed the keys to Sean and fell asleep in the back seat. So it was just the two of you up front, headlights carving out a path through the night, your parents snoring behind you, too tired to wait for the cheap hotel in Chattanooga.

The trip had been sprung on you by surprise. Your mom had been working overtime at the hospital, and there was some extra money for once. Not enough to fly, but enough for a room someplace warm if the old Honda Odyssey could make it. Also, the mood in your house had been low lately.

Sean had been favored to win State this year. Nearly everyone who wrote about local sports had him as a lock. But on the day of the tournament, in one of his preliminary dives, he attempted a reverse three-and-a-half somersault and scraped his head against the board. The place went silent. There was blood in the water. He managed to get out of the pool on his own, but he was immediately taken to the hospital for stitches and ended up missing the biggest recruiting opportunity of the year. He was devastated, and you barely saw him in the weeks afterward, as he recovered from his concussion. Part of you suspected that this whole family journey was a cheer-up-Sean mission.

"Sunshine and strip malls aren't going to heal Sean's head," said your dad when your mom suggested the trip.

"Well," she said. "A little vitamin D can't hurt! Not sure about the strip malls . . ."

What went unmentioned in that conversation, like most other conversations in your family, was just how severe your anxiety had been lately. But your mom was definitely aware. You had taken more mental health days in the past month than you'd ever taken before, and on two different occasions, she had caught you downstairs around 3 A.M. walking circles around the living room arguing with yourself. Your anxiety was always worse in the winter, so you could chalk it up to the seasons, but even you knew there was something else going on.

Namely, you had realized your feelings for Diana, and the guilt was tearing you apart. Last week, when you got home from another night of Serbian vulgarities at Perkins, you had even tried writing a letter explaining it, telling her all the reasons why you didn't want it to happen, but how it *had* happened anyway, and how you knew nothing could or should come of it, but that keeping the secret might be killing you. Sean, who was having trouble sleeping on his stitches, found you writing late at night, and asked what you were doing. "Nothing," you said, and quickly closed the notebook.

Even *thinking* about telling Sean made your whole body feel like it had been drained and filled with battery acid. Especially after his recent disappointment. How could he see your feelings as anything other than a breach of trust at the worst possible time? But now here you were, side by side with him, nothing but silence and the open road ahead of you for the next half an hour, and it felt like there might never be a better time to confess your sin. So why couldn't you open your mouth?

About twenty-five miles from Chattanooga, you passed a school bus painted bright pink with four deflated tires and a sign in the window that read COLD BEER AND BIKINIS! It sat near an exit for a small town, with an arrow painted on the side, imploring you to take a detour and seek your fortune in Fairfield. Right above it, however, was a looming sign for a small church that read SURRENDER TO JESUS in all caps. You looked over at Sean to see if he was clocking this, and he cracked a smile.

"It's going *down* in Fairfield tonight!" he said, and in spite of the ball of tension in your chest, you laughed.

Your dad, who had been lightly snoring in the back seat, let out a high-pitched snort, which got you going all over again. And you could feel your nervous energy starting to relent.

"What if we just parked in the lot of the bikini place and waited for them to wake up," you said. "We could hide behind the car so they'd think we're inside!"

Sean smiled.

"I don't know. They might actually be happy," he said.

"What do you mean? Why?!"

He looked straight ahead at the road.

"They'd think you were feeling better."

You were quiet for a moment after that. You didn't even know Sean was aware of your recent anxiety spike. He always seemed so absorbed in his own world, especially lately. It shocked you to know he'd been paying attention.

"You've had a lot going on," you said. "I didn't think you noticed."

"Are you kidding me?" he said. "Look at your leg right now!"

You glanced down to find your right leg bouncing like a rabbit's. You didn't even bother trying to stop it.

"I know you, Case," he said. "It's those twin vibes."

This is something he joked about when you were young. Around the neighborhood, even though you were two years younger, he told everyone you were twins. Then he dared the kids not to believe it.

"I'm fine," you said.

"You don't have to lie to me," he said. "You can lie to everyone else if you want to. But I don't care. You can be honest with me. And you can be miserable if you want. You don't have to pretend."

The word *honest* jabbed at you, and for a moment, you were on the verge of telling him everything. Maybe he'd just laugh it off. *Of course you fell in love with her! She's beautiful! Now let's figure this out.* But still, you couldn't do it. You were so afraid of truly disappointing him that it made the whole thing seem impossible. So instead, you asked him a question.

"Where have you been since the tournament?"

Then it was Sean's turn to get quiet. He looked in the rearview mirror at your sleeping parents. You're not sure why; they were two of the loudest, most obvious sleepers in the world. But it let you know immediately that something was wrong.

"I've been meaning to tell you," he said quietly. "I just haven't found the right time."

You watched his hands tighten on the wheel.

"I met somebody."

Your leg stopped.

"What? You mean . . . like, a girl?"

"It's not what you think, okay? She works at the ice cream store, and we just became friends. I've been picking up some extra shifts since I can't practice, and she's fun to pass the time with. But the thing is . . ."

"She's interested in you," you sighed.

It was a familiar story.

"I didn't think she was! And then there was this day when my head actually felt clear for once and we were daring each other to go in the Deepfreeze and close the door, and she just followed me in and kissed me."

This was the way Sean always described his interactions with girls. He never claimed to have any power. Things just happened, and it was as if he wasn't even in his body to experience it.

"So what happened after that?"

"We've been hanging out after work sometimes. Making out in the parking garage. Just talking in her car. I was pretty broken up about State. All the work I put in for that one goal, and then it was just gone. It passed me by and no one even seemed to care, like maybe it wasn't important in the first place. She listened, and I guess it felt kind of nice."

His face was hard to read, and you couldn't tell where he was going with this. But if history was any indicator, you had a hunch.

"So you're breaking up with Diana, then?"

For an awful moment your heart soared. A camper van passed by with a bike fastened to the back, its front wheel spinning madly. Sean exhaled, and when you looked back at him, it seemed like he was about to cry.

"Sean?" you said.

"No," he said.

"No . . ."

"No, I'm not breaking up with Diana."

He exhaled again and blinked.

"Last night, we were sitting in her car, the girl's car, and she was putting her shirt back on and I just kind of had this moment of clarity about the whole thing. Like: What is *wrong* with me? I don't get what I want in diving, so I just go out looking for the next thing. The next little thrill that's going to get me out of my head. I get so itchy sometimes, you know, like I can't even be in my own skin! Does that make sense?"

You nodded.

"And listen," he said, "it would be fun to keep making out with this girl in the freezer at work, but she doesn't know me or even really *like* me that much probably. But Diana . . ."

"She knows you," you said.

"Exactly!" he said. "And she's real. She doesn't take any shit from me. You probably think I'm an idiot right now that I'm finally getting this. But I didn't use to care. I didn't care if it was real. I think I might care this time."

"I don't think you're an idiot," you said so softly it was barely audible.

"Well, I am!" he said. "I've been screwing up what could be this beautiful thing. And you've been doing so much to cover for me. I was putting everything into training that I hardly saw her. And where did that get me? Meanwhile, you've basically been keeping her happy. That was such a kind thing to do, Case. She probably would have left me months ago if it wasn't for you. And I just want you to know that when we get back, you don't have to do that anymore, okay?"

He put his hand on your shoulder.

"You've got enough going on, man. You don't need to be taking my girlfriend out. That is just above and beyond! You don't have to be a saint."

You watched a tear roll down his cheek. He sniffled and smiled.

"God, it feels so good to tell someone about this," he said. "You're the only person I can talk to about it."

His right hand was still on your shoulder, and you wanted more than anything for him to take it off. But there was no way to do that without having to explain yourself. So you let him keep it there, while, inside, it felt like your lungs might not be able to take in a breath ever again. Your heart was shattered. And if that wasn't bad enough, you felt terrible for feeling the heartbreak. Your pain itself was a betrayal.

Having said what he wanted to, Sean took a moment to collect himself, then turned on some music, and the two of you drove without speaking for the next twenty-or-so miles until you finally woke your parents and ate Memphis-style ribs at a little restaurant near your hotel. And though you were near silent at dinner too, no one else really noticed, and they all laughed when the server told you that snow had swirled down from the mountains last week and caused fifty-three fender benders in an hour because people didn't know how to drive on it. You didn't laugh, though. You knew why they crashed.

They just never saw it coming.

ELEVEN

"The worst has happened," announces Silas the next morning.

You're all huddled together near a crackling fire, started hours ago with nothing but birch bark and a flint. Your campsite is on a sandy landing with a view east through some white pines toward a sherbet-colored sunrise. You're so unused to views like this, they don't quite seem real yet. Like someone could flip a switch and it would all disappear. You're wedged between Will and Diana, who has yet to speak to you this morning.

Breakfast is "Cowboy Casserole," a meal made entirely of canned beans, BBQ sauce, and bacon.

"Who knew cowboys were so into diabetes and heart disease?" says Fran.

But no one is complaining. It's food. And it's warm. And as the amber light from the rising sun warms your skin, you are gradually thawing after a cold, damp night. In fact, all of this might actually be pleasant if it weren't for the fact that you all almost drowned yesterday.

"It's over," he continues. "Nothing else that we do is going to be worse than what we did yesterday. And guess what? You all made it. You're here. You just got a little wet and scared, but you're still here."

"I hit a rock," says Troy through a mouthful of beans.

"Okay. That wasn't ideal," says Silas. "But you made it here too. And actually, you did a pretty amazing job holding on to that rock. You were like a barnacle on that thing, brother!"

"I would like to officially announce that I pissed myself," says Fran.

Everyone stops eating for a moment and stares at her.

"Just now?!" says Troy.

"No!" she says. "No. While I was in the water after the rapids! I peed in the river. From fear."

"Perfectly normal response," says Silas.

"Cool," she says. "I'll remember that. Peeing in a river is normal."

It's quiet then, and there's only the sound of spoons scraping against campware, and the pop of trapped steam bursting out of some newly added firewood. Meanwhile, you wait for the protest.

Last night, everyone went to bed still too shocked to get mad. But now that your basic needs have been met, you expect to hear at least one person say they won't go on. Troy, for sure. Maybe Fran. Even Will. But instead, everyone just eats, squinting into the sun. You can almost see the fight leaching out of the group as they shovel overly sweet beans into their mouths.

"Today should be relatively smooth paddling," Silas says. "No rapids. But we have a fair amount of river to cover to get to our next lake and stay on schedule. So let's finish up and get our packs in the boats!"

Silas stands up then, and for a single moment, he seems unsteady on his feet. Only a couple of you notice as he reaches out for a tree and then seems to get his balance. It all unfolds so quickly, and then he just keeps walking as if nothing happened.

Eventually, you do the same, watching him all the while. And though you all seem a little hesitant to start paddling again, finally everyone gets in their boats and pushes off from the shore.

The day that follows is punishing. It starts off okay—you and Fran even manage a rhythm of sorts—but the pain begins after an hour or so. A pinch in your shoulders that moves in a circuit up your neck and down your back. By late afternoon, the temperature has risen and your body is one giant inflammation. It feels like every muscle you have has been stretched like Silly Putty and smushed back into a pulsing, amorphous ball.

By the time you finally find the trailhead in the early evening, your crew is looking rough. Your canoes crunch over the smooth stones beneath the clear lake water and nestle against the wet gritty sand of the shoreline. The campsite is up a small hill, and a stand of shedding birch trees grows diagonally out over the water. You all take long drinks from your water bottles and slump out of your boats.

Silas, sweaty and red like the rest of you, sits you in a circle at the top of the hill. You expect him to build a fire and maybe start some dinner, but he doesn't. What he does is slowly take the baseball hat off his head and toss it on the ground near you, where it skids into the dirt.

Everyone examines the hat. It's the first time he's taken it off, and he looks different without it. Older and younger at the same time. But you don't have much time to study him because next he reaches into his pocket and pulls out a small bundle of yellow minipencils held together with a rubber band. He also grabs some scraps of paper. He passes the pencils around and waits patiently until you all have one. Then he starts writing in slow, careful script. When he's done, he folds the tiny sheet in two and gives the paper a little flick.

It lands squarely in the hat.

"Ladies and gentlemen," he says. "Welcome to Fear in a Hat."

Fran stands up straight, cracking her back.

"Fear in a what?" she says.

"Hat," says Silas. "Fear in a Hat. That's the name of the activity."

He scratches at his hat hair. Then, finally, he sets about starting the evening's fire, laying out his tools like a surgeon.

"It's a little cheesy," he says. "I'm not going to lie. But it's a way to get us talking about our anxiety. Basically, you write down a fear and toss it in the hat. Then I read them anonymously. The idea here is that we get used to sharing and maybe we feel a little less alone in all this."

He spreads out his tinder and strikes at his flint. Then he watches while each of you jots a word or two on your paper. Everyone, that is, except you. You get as far as holding your pencil, but then you just kind of stare at the paper. And eventually you fold it in half and place it, blank, in Silas's hat without making eye contact. The timer sounds the moment you let go.

"Okay," he says, scooping up the hat. "Moment of truth. I'm just going to grab one here."

He closes his eyes and reaches into his worn ball cap. You can feel your pulse accelerating. You're afraid that he's going to pick your blank paper and know it was you. And then you'll have to make it right by revealing something. You look around and see the same tensed eyes and tight mouths that must mirror the look on your own tired face. The ridiculous fact of the matter is: You are all afraid of Fear in a Hat.

"And it looks like I have . . ."

He pauses a moment for dramatic effect. Then:

"Sushi."

"Sushi?" says Will immediately. "What is this stupid game, man?"

"Will," says Silas, "that's not helpful, brother. We have to be respectful of people's fears here. Okay? We don't need to editorialize."

Silas starts reaching in the hat for another fear, but just when his hand goes in, a voice stops him.

"Wait a second."

It's Fran.

"No more comments," says Silas. "I think it's best if we keep going. Don't spend too long on each one."

"No," says Fran. "That one's mine. I wrote *sushi*, and I was wondering if I could say something about it."

Everyone's quiet.

"We don't have to do that tonight," says Silas.

But Fran looks insistent. For the first time since you've seen her, she isn't wearing a hoodie, and it's like seeing a turtle without its shell. But it's also harder to ignore her when she's not hiding.

"All right," says Silas finally. "If you want to talk, then I want to listen."

"Okay," she says. "Thanks."

She waves some smoke from her eyes and adjusts her legs. She looks right at Will.

"I get that it's weird, okay?"

Will looks down at his boots.

"It's raw fish. It's not going to hurt me. I understand that. But . . . my parents are divorced."

She stops, and for a moment, you think that's her entire explanation. Her parents are divorced, so she's afraid of sushi. But you hold your tongue, and eventually she starts in again.

"And when they were together, they never wanted to go out to eat. We didn't have a ton of extra money, so that was part of it. But it's also because they couldn't stand each other and they knew they would have to sit five feet apart all night if they went to a restaurant.

"So, on my birthday last year, of course they both want to take me to dinner. Separately. And because it's still a big deal to go out for me, I do this dumb thing and I say yes to both of them. Like somehow if I say yes twice, their yeses will combine and we'll actually just go out as a family like we used to.

"Of course, this would never happen because they are children. It's got to be two dinners. Two separate dinners. I know this deep inside, but I stupidly tell them both to take me on my actual birthday, so I can feel like I'm with both of them."

She laughs then, but it's not a happy laugh. It's a laugh of defeat. A laugh at the power of self-sabotage.

"You probably see where this is going. My birthday arrives, and my mom takes me to this BBQ place we like, and we're having so much fun, I actually forget and eat, like, thirty pork ribs. We have a contest to see who can eat the most and whose face can get the messiest. But then when it's time to go, it suddenly hits me: *Oh no*, the second dinner! And sure enough, when we get home there's my dad waiting in the driveway.

"And I'm too embarrassed to tell him what I did. Instead, I just go to another dinner with him. He takes me to this sushi restaurant, and he orders this giant platter while I'm in the bathroom. Then when it shows up, I already feel so full that just looking at it is making me feel nauseous. And my dad always hated wasting food when I was growing up, so I feel like I'm going to have to eat it anyway. But it looks so bad. A buffet of misery. And when I reach for the first piece with my chopsticks, everything just shuts down.

"I can't move my arm any farther. And then I have the worst panic attack I've ever had. I run back to the bathroom, and my dad doesn't understand why I won't come out. And eventually, a female sushi chef has to come in and get me, and she brings a single tampon. She's holding it like a baton. And man, I wish that a single tampon would solve everything. But it's slightly more complicated than that. I open my mouth to tell her, but nothing comes out, so instead, I just take the tampon and start crying. Then I'm in the bathroom, crying, and holding a tampon. And that's why I never want to see a piece of sushi again."

She brushes the hair out of her eyes and looks into the fire. And it takes a second for you all to realize she's done. You don't quite know what to do with the feeling that's lingering. It was just a simple story about a restaurant, but you've actually never heard someone tell one like it. About the way a simple thing can go so wrong because of the anxiety. And how that feeling can hold you hostage. It's a story that could easily have been yours.

"Is anyone going to say something?" asks Fran.

Silas adjusts the hat on his lap. He looks uncomfortable all of a sudden. Distracted again, but this time it's like there's a restlessness. There's a tapping sound, and you realize it's coming from his foot. People are just starting to notice it, when someone finally speaks.

"Yes!" says Diana. "I am."

Fran looks surprised to hear from her. Diana stands up, and with a sleeping bag draped over her shoulders, she looks like royalty, or maybe some benevolent deity. Her face glows from the bottom up.

"Okay . . . ," says Fran.

Diana walks around the fire until she gets to where Fran is sitting. Then she looks her in the eye, and says:

"Thank you."

It's clear that Fran doesn't know what to say, so she just smiles. Diana doesn't move. Something has happened, though you can't say what it is at first. Even Will looks somewhat chastened and contemplative.

"Yeah, thanks," says Troy, the fire glowing in his smudged glasses.

Someone has been vulnerable.

Maybe it's as simple as that. For a moment, you feel like you could say something if you had to. Maybe not about Sean yet, but just about your anxiety. About how hard it has been, and the shame spiral that won't stop tugging at you every morning when you wake up. You wonder if other people are feeling this small moment of relief. It's a kind of lightness. Which makes it all the more strange when Silas empties that hat, puts it back on his head, and says:

"I think that's enough for tonight."

It's an odd reaction, particularly given that he's been talking about how you all have to risk intimacy, how he wants everyone to be honest with one another. It doesn't make sense that he would cut things off right now.

"Why?" says Troy. "We didn't get to my fear yet."

"We have a long day tomorrow," he says.

You only see Silas's face once more before he puts out the fire, and you see it in the brightest light of the glow. There's a sheen of sweat where there wasn't before. He closes his eyes, and a drop slides off his right eyebrow and into the flames. And before anyone else asks a question, he tips a canteen upside down and pours cold water onto the blaze. The hissing sound is deafening as the water hits the coals, and the smoke is white as a cloud. You watch for him once it has faded a bit, but he's already walking to his tent, and the world has gone dark.

TWELVE

You wake up once in the night because you think it's morning. There's a bright, pearly glow outside the tent that you're sure is dawn. But when you unzip the flap and peer through the opening, you realize it's just the fire. Someone has brought it back to life, and it glows in the pitch dark like a beacon. There's a single body, just visible through the top of the flames on the other side. You hope it's Diana, but when you walk close enough to see the night keeper of the fire, you see Silas, huddled under a blanket.

He's half in shadow, half in light, but even with your limited visibility, you see his face and it looks calm, though his teeth are chattering a bit. You're about to say his name, but the cool night air seems to steal the words when you open your mouth. You realize then just how chilly it is, even with the fire nearby. The breeze goes right through your sweat-soaked pajamas, and you feel the cold travel through your whole body. You're about to turn around and go back when you hear his voice.

"Are you ready?" he says.

When you glance at him again, he's just looking into the fire—nowhere else, and it's hard to tell, actually, if he's even speaking to you.

"Um. Ready for what?" you say.

There's a long pause, during which you hear only the wind and the crackle of the fire. Then he looks up, just for a moment, but there's a smile on his face.

"The devil's loot," he says.

At least that's what you think he says. It's hard to hear him over the wind.

"What was that?" you ask.

He's looking at the fire again, and he waves you away with a single hand. You just stand there for a moment, waiting to see if there's more. But there's not more and you're officially freezing now, so you take one last look at his glowing face and then you walk back to your tent. It's an odd moment, to be sure. But you're barely awake by the time you crawl back into your sleeping bag, and you don't remember closing your eyes again.

And you don't remember any dreams.

You only know that when you wake again, dry-mouthed in the actual morning, to the sound of light rainfall on the top of the tent, it takes you a second to realize the panicked voice you're hearing outside is real.

"Guys! Wake up. Guys!"

Everyone is up in seconds, and while your tentmates scramble for the flap and emerge into the clearing, you hang back and sit completely still in the empty tent. There is some murmuring that you can't make out, then a clearer question.

". . . Well, then, where is he?"

You know who they're talking about immediately, but you're trying to delay the moment when it becomes real. Because as soon as it becomes real, your brain will start up the old familiar machinery, and your nervous system will explode. You don't get much time, though, before you hear a familiar voice.

"I don't know."

It's the same voice that you heard on the phone the night of your brother's death. The same voice that wished you a happy birthday on the roof of the garage a million years ago. It's the voice that has been, in recent months, the only one you wanted to hear, but also the one that you couldn't bring yourself to ask for.

"Guys," she says. "I think Silas is gone."

The light sprinkles you heard against the tent are turning into a real, cold rain, and when you finally emerge, you can feel the icy sting of the drops on your neck and hear them hitting the canopy of leaves hanging above you. The drops sizzle when they hit the coals of last night's fire. You look around, and among the hangdog faces of your fellow adventurers, you see no sign of your leader. His tent is gone and so is everything inside it. No pack. No gear. Not even his hat. You look toward the water, and sure enough, one of the canoes is gone too.

"Hold on a second. Where did he go?" Fran says, a manic current to her voice.

"Don't freak out," says Will. "It's early, bro. He's probably out catching a fish or something. Outdoorsy people are super weird like that. They're always horny for the morning."

"I've been up for two hours," says Diana. "And I haven't seen him. Also, why would he take his tent?"

Nobody asks why Diana was awake. Most of you have some kind of insomnia. The only thing that matters is the fact that he's been gone so long. Everyone gets really quiet; the only audible sound is a series of deep breaths coming from Troy, who is trying to get some oxygen in his lungs. He has his eyes closed, and he's working so hard to keep calm and meditative that it looks like he's hyperventilating. His wiener dog T-shirt is slowly getting soaked and showing his skin in sodden patches. You're thinking about speaking, when Troy pipes up again.

"I knew it," he says between gasps. "I knew it!"

"Knew what?" says Will.

Troy grabs his own head and shakes it back and forth.

"Don't you get it? This is all part of it!"

"Part of what, Troy?" says Fran.

Her pink hair is wild from a night of bad sleep, and her eyes are so bloodshot they look completely red.

"The therapy!" he yells. "It's more immersion stuff. Like the rapids! He's throwing us in the pool again. Only I didn't sign up to be thrown in the pool. I can barely swim."

He starts walking around then, kicking things, sending pine cones skittering into the woods, until he finally seems to tire himself out and sits down. Will and Diana are staring at the place where Silas's tent once was. Diana still looks shocked even though she was the first to know about this. Will is harder to read, his stance a little more rigid.

"He said something about the devil," you say finally.

And everyone immediately turns toward you.

"WHAT?!" says Troy. "What about the devil?"

"I don't know," you say. "He was mumbling. It was windy."

"Oh, c'mon. Don't be paranoid," says Will. "He can't leave us in the woods with nothing. That has to be against the rules or something."

"Not if he's a devil worshipper!" says Fran. "What if this is all for a big sacrifice and he's going to, like, make us get naked and drink goat's blood or something? Then eat us!"

"Fran," says Will. "Enough."

Troy stands up.

"How much research did you guys do on this whole experience?" he says. "I was reading about all kinds of kids on these wilderness-therapy trips. They starve, get hurt, even run away or die. You trust your parents to figure out if this is one of the good ones? I don't! Mine were desperate to do something with me. They would have sent me to a cult if it was legal."

"A devil-worshipping cult!" says Fran.

Will shakes his head.

"You guys need to chill the eff out," he says. "He's coming back. I was just in the canoe with him yesterday, and he was telling me how much he loves these trips. How they help him as much as they help us."

"Help him with what?" says Fran.

There's an edge to her voice, and for some reason, it's this question that finally makes Will flinch a little. Fran seems to be asking it honestly, but it doesn't sound great after it leaves her mouth. You feel your body shiver again, this time from the big, cold drops soaking your shirt. It's impossible to ignore the rain now, and finally you see Diana move toward the girls' tent. There's water running down her face, and she doesn't even brush it away. When she gets inside the little dome, she hugs herself deeper into an oversize sweater and lies down.

"We don't know," she says from inside. "That's the truth, right? We don't know if he's coming back. Or if this is some kind of a test. So what can we do?"

Troy starts to sniffle.

"Oh Jesus," says Will. "Pull it together."

You expect Troy to wander away, or suffer in silence. But instead, he gets up and walks right over to Will, his skinny soaked frame only inches from Will's muscular chest. He just kind of breathes in Will's face for a moment, and Will tries not to look weirded out, but an uncomfortable smile betrays his true feelings.

"I'm just going to say this once to you," says Troy.

Will blinks.

"Wake up."

"Dude, seriously, if you don't . . ."

"This is all really happening," says Troy. "And you need. To. Wake. Up."

Will steps slightly closer to him, and all of you are just waiting for this to jump the rails. It wouldn't surprise you in the least if they fell on each other, screaming and flailing. Your money is on Will, but there's a look in Troy's eye that makes you wonder. For someone who needs a support animal, he doesn't seem very scared right now.

You take advantage of the brief pause in their standoff to walk toward them. You put a hand on both of their shoulders. You're hoping to ground them, but the contact doesn't have the intended effect, and both of them try to jostle you out of the way at the same time. First Troy knocks into you with his shoulder, which sends you bumping into Will. Will bounces you back, and you trip, somehow sending all three of you to the ground. The back of your head glances off a rock, and when you put your hand over the spot, you feel the contours of a small cut.

"What the hell, guys?" you say.

"Hey!" says Diana.

"Nice going, Will!" says Troy. "Maybe you can help our situation with pure bro anger."

"Guys . . . ," says Diana.

"You push like a NARP," says Will. "Do you know that? That was the NARPiest push I've ever seen."

"I think my head is bleeding," you say.

"GUYS!" yells Diana, now right behind you. "SHUT UP AND GET IN THE TENT RIGHT NOW!"

Nobody moves until a flash of lightning forks through the sky above you, seemingly inches from the tops of the pines. It's followed by the loudest thunder clap you've ever heard in your life. It sounds as if the sky itself is calving like a glacier. When you look up, a pitch-black cloud is moving toward you, casting a darkness the way a giant spaceship does in a UFO movie.

Within moments, you're all in the tent, packed together, breathing one another's morning breath and trying to zip the flap closed, like somehow, this little nylon pod in the middle of nowhere can keep you safe from whatever Mother Nature is about to unleash.

THIRTEEN

The rain picks up first. It pounds the tent in a flurry of punches, one blow after the next. Then the wind kicks in, screaming through the trees and sending the tent fluttering like a broken kite. If there weren't five of you sitting on its floor, your flimsy shelter would be twenty feet up a tree right now. The lightning too is like nothing you've ever seen. It strobes in extended flashes, making any movements inside look like stop-motion animation. In the midst of everything, you are all speechless. There is no time to argue anymore; only time to huddle together and try not to die.

It seems so easy, all of a sudden, to be killed by an indifferent world. And in this moment, you wonder how *anyone* is still alive. Outside, you hear the cracking of what sounds like a tree limb, and you brace for the impact you're sure is coming. "Teen's Head Crushed by an Enormous Branch," the headline will read. "He Tried to Get Better at Life, and Life Destroyed Him with a Falling Tree." You hear it crash to the ground somewhere else that's not your body.

You close your eyes then, and you try your best to disappear.

And you keep your eyes closed. You're not sure how long. Somebody is yelling. Someone else is crying. You can't tell the voices apart. You only know that when the rain finally starts to ease up, your face is hot and covered in sweat. And you feel someone's fingers gently pushing your hair around on the back of your head.

"I think it's okay," says Diana. "Not so bad, actually."

Her voice is soft. You turn around, and her face is close to yours.

"What are you talking about?" you ask.

Your body is pulsing with adrenaline.

"Your cut."

You had forgotten about the cut, but now that she's dabbing at it with a T-shirt, you can feel the sting again. Her body is near to yours, and she smells like campfire and vanilla shampoo from two days ago. The rain has completely stopped, leaving behind an eerie soundlessness punctuated only by dripping. There are tears in your eyes, but you're not sure if it's because of the pain or her fingers in your hair.

Others gradually unfold from their fetal positions, and rise like the kids in your childhood theater class when you had to pretend to be flowers growing. In a daze, they leave the tent, one at a time, wandering out into a new world. But Diana doesn't go. Instead, she stays next to you.

"I saw him last night," you say.

"Where?"

"By the fire. He was saying strange things."

She dabs at you again, and when she brings the T-shirt down, you see it's covered in dried blood. If you were home, you'd go to your mom, the nurse who's never off duty, but here, in this moment, there are no adults to help you pretend the world is safe.

"Do you think he's coming back?" you ask.

More than anyone else's, it's her opinion on this that you want to hear. She knows how to read people. Or at least she used to.

"You know what I think?" she says finally. "I think we can't keep doing this."

"I know!" you say. "That's the whole point. Without him—"

"No," she says. "You and me. We can't keep pretending."

"Oh," you say. "That."

"Is that really what you want to do out here: just pretend we're strangers? Pretend that Sean's not gone, and that you didn't abandon me when everything was at its worst? Is that your plan, Case?"

She pulls her hands away and brushes them together. You don't want to look at them and see your own blood.

"I don't know," you say.

"Just tell me right now if that's what you want to do, and I'll cut you loose. I can do that. I've been doing it my whole life. Just tell me."

"Diana . . ."

"You really hurt me."

You take a breath.

"I'm sorry," you say. "I just . . ."

You want to say more, but nothing comes out. And while you try to build the courage to continue, there's a commotion outside, a chorus of rapid voices. You hear the crunch of footsteps moving closer to the tent. Diana doesn't look away from you, but you're still unable to speak. She reaches up to her face, and just before someone tugs open the tent, she wipes away what must be a tear from her own cheek. Then Fran dips her head in. She looks at the two of you funny, then she regains her composure.

"Guys," she says. "I think you need to see this."

FOURTEEN

At first you don't even notice Troy.

You're too busy wondering how you're all still alive. There are trees down around you, maybe five or six, just snapped like matchsticks. And one of your canoes is lodged in some brush fifty yards away. It looks like someone picked it up and flung it there in a tantrum. All the while, Troy stands patiently before you. He doesn't say anything, but eventually when you finish surveying the broken landscape, you look at him and you see what he's holding.

A small white circle.

It looks like a cap.

The cap to a pill bottle.

Only there is no bottle.

"It's gone," he says.

"What's gone?" says Fran.

"My Clonazepam."

And because you have a PhD in anxiety, you know this is the official name of Klonopin, his sedative of choice. Fran reaches out and takes the cap from him.

"What do you mean? You're already out?" she says.

"No!" says Troy. "I shouldn't be. I think . . ."

"What?" you say.

"I think he took it."

Fran's hood is down, but she tugs hard at the strings.

"Are you sure they're not in the tent?" she asks.

"Take a look yourself," says Troy.

Fran strides right by you back into your shelter.

"Can you check for mine?" you ask. "It's in the very front pocket of my bag."

You listen as she riffles through things, the duffel whistling across the tent's nylon, and the clump of your clothes hitting the ground. She stops only to huff out angry breaths. Then, finally, it all goes quiet and she speaks.

"Your Paxil is still here, Case," she says. "But no Xanax."

"I don't understand," says Diana. "Did he just take the sedatives?"

You're about to posit a theory, but your thoughts are scattered by one of the most horrible noises you have ever heard in your life. It starts as a kind of high-pitched keening, like a teakettle boiling over, or a siren going past, but gradually it morphs into a full-on primal scream.

"Jesus!" says Diana. "What the hell is that?"

All you can do is plug your ears, and eventually you look up and notice that it's coming from Troy. It's astoundingly loud, enough to make your ears ring, and it is not stopping. If anything, it is getting louder and more terrifying by the second.

"Troy!" comes a familiar voice. "TROY!"

Will is screaming in Troy's ear, but it's like Troy's gone catatonic. He won't make eye contact. You feel a hand on your shoulder, and you turn to see Diana.

"Case," she says into your ear just loud enough to be heard. "Can you please make him stop doing that?"

You nod, but you're not sure how you're going to deliver.

"TROY!" you try. "PLEASE!"

It doesn't seem like he would have much oxygen left, but still, on he goes. Birds scatter from the downed trees. Everyone is plugging their ears. You walk slowly over to Troy, one ear against your shoulder, one covered with a hand, lumbering like an ogre. You don't get too close, but close enough to make direct eye contact.

"TROY!" you try again. "YOU CANNOT DO THAT ANYMORE! IT'S KILLING US!"

Miraculously, he stops, and the moment of silence is like the absence of life itself. A brief void you get lost in. Then he takes a breath and screams again.

"WE'RE ALL GOING TO DIE!"

Only he extends the last word so that it's ten syllables long.

Something more like: "DIEEEEEEEEEEEEEEEEEEEEE!"

You put a finger to your lips, and you hold it there until the *die* finally dies out and you're left just staring at each other. You're shocked that it worked, but maybe there was something in your gesture that made Troy feel like a baby again. Or maybe he just ran out of air.

"We might," you say. "Okay? We might! But if we're all going to die, then I want to do it in peace."

At that, he sits on the ground. He's wearing no shoes, you notice, and he hugs his chest with thin arms. His glasses are dotted with raindrops. The aftermath of the storm has brought a chill. He must be freezing, but he doesn't shiver.

"He left us with no supervision," says Troy in a raspy whisper. "And he took my Klonopin."

"But . . . ," says Will.

"He's not coming back!" says Troy sharply.

You try for a moment to think of anything other than your medication. And what it's going to be like with no ammunition for the worst attacks. Your SSRIs, whether it's Paxil, Prozac, or Lexapro, they keep you even. But it's the benzos like Xanax that fight fire with fire when the anxiety takes over your entire body. Silas has taken the only way to quell your brain's full-on rebellion.

"We have to find him," you say.

"What do you mean?" says Will.

"There's no other choice. Maybe this is some kind of cold-turkey, scared-straight thing like Troy says. Or maybe we've truly been abandoned. But in the end, it doesn't really matter."

"It definitely matters," says Fran.

"No," you say. "I mean, either way we have one objective."

"And that is . . ."

"To make it to the drop."

"But we don't know where we are," Troy starts. "And when you're lost . . ."

"We don't have enough supplies!" yells Diana.

She's walking toward you, dragging something across the rocky ground. It's a cooler, carving its way through a thick trail in the dirt. She lugs it into the center of the group and tips it over onto a patch of grass near the shore, and you all stare, mouths open at the meager contents scattered before you. Some almond butter, some hummus powder, dehydrated beans and lentils, oats, and a few granola bars. There are also a couple of pans to cook with, but that's about it.

It was supposed to be enough food for five days, but you're at the beginning of day three and it doesn't look like much. You and Sean could have polished this off in an afternoon.

"This was supposed to get us through half the week?!" says Will. "In what sadistic universe? My brother ate better at weight-loss camp."

"Silas must have taken some food," says Fran.

Of course.

"Okay," says Troy. "So, we're screwed. But don't you think someone will come look for us?"

Diana huffs.

"Our families think we're going to be out here for weeks," she says, sitting on the empty cooler. "It could be a long time before they even start looking."

Silence. The nearby lake reflects the passing clouds as the last of the storm finally dissolves into a light fog. A few lingering drops make rings that slowly fade in the lake's surface.

"I'm with Diana," says Will finally. "It's not smart to stay here and just eat through our supplies. We need to move toward a goal. Something."

"Why can't we just go back the way we came?" Fran says.

"The current is moving in the opposite direction," says Will. "Besides, we went through a chain of lakes. Do you remember the way?"

Diana walks to one of the tents and starts pulling up stakes to take it down.

"But how are we going to find the drop point?" Troy says.

Diana shrugs, and you watch her yank on a metal stake, and the left side of the girls' tent deflates a bit. Fran gets up and goes to rescue her pack before the tent collapses. She hugs it to her chest.

"Also, what are we going to do with all this crap?" Troy adds.

"Portage it," says Diana.

"What does that mean?"

"Portage: to carry a boat and its cargo between two navigable waters," Diana says as if reciting from a teleprompter. "Didn't any of you guys read the pamphlets they sent?"

"We have to carry all this?" says Will.

"And a canoe," says Diana. "We have to put the canoes on our shoulders when we're not using them. That's why there's a portage yoke."

Everyone looks at her.

"I read it in the pamphlet," she says. "Now, c'mon. Let's get moving."

Nobody shouts their agreement, but nobody challenges her either.

You leave the group for a moment and walk back over to the extinguished fire, the last place you saw Silas. You sit down in his spot.

Why was he out here so late?

Why wasn't he already leaving? What was he planning? And what did he say about the devil? You kick at the stones that make the fire ring and curse yourself for not confronting him when he was being so weird. Just another moment when you failed to act out of simple fear and discomfort.

When you get up, you notice something on the ground. Something very small. A soggy scrap of paper like the kind you used to play Fear in a Hat. At first that's what you think it is. A leftover from the game. But when you reach your hand down and unfold the slip of paper, it doesn't seem like a fear. Instead, it reads, in blue pen, blotched by the rain:

One day. One hour. One minute.

You don't know what it means, if it's part of a poem, a song lyric, or something else entirely. You turn around to say something, but everyone is busy packing, and you're not sure what to say about it. It's just a soggy scrap of paper. So you put it in your pocket and try to focus on gathering your stuff. Still, while you're walking back to your tent, you reach your hand in and touch it one more time.

It's not the first time someone you know has left a paper trail.

FIFTEEN

There was no note after Sean died. He never had the chance to write one. With Sean, all the writing came before. Only a week after he told you about cheating on Diana, you watched as he came home to his room and tore down all the photos of his favorite divers from the corkboard above his desk. He'd been collecting them for years, building a collage of heroes, and they were gone in seconds. In their place, he started tacking up handwritten mantras.

It began with bad self-help clichés, cribbed from social media. *Lean toward love! Be your own light!* But he soon progressed to the Buddha: *One is not called noble who harms living beings.* Sean had always been impulsive—going all in on obsessions—but this overnight enlightenment was a lot even for him. Where there were once photos of toned Olympic athletes piking into turquoise swimming pools, there was now a self-help mood board.

You weren't sure what to think about it. Part of you wanted to give Sean the benefit of the doubt. He was, it seemed, finally waking up to the way he'd gone through life so far, taking what was given—compliments, trophies, girlfriends—without much gratitude or giving in return. He'd been consumed with diving since he was ten, and now that his goal had slipped through his fingers, it was like it had never existed. A clean reset. You wanted to support him. You wanted to encourage him on this new journey—whatever it was—but you also couldn't shake the disappointment you felt after what he'd told you.

And you couldn't stop thinking about what it meant for Diana.

Because it soon became clear that, in spite of all the quotes about love and compassion, he had no intention of telling her what he had done. When you eventually got up the guts to ask him if he was going to confess, it didn't even seem to occur to him. And this was a problem. Because once you were back home, Diana started coming over again, and you found you could barely look at her. Knowing what you knew, you literally couldn't make eye contact without turning away. And of course, she instantly noticed how weird you were being.

"What's with you?" she said one night when she saw you in the hall.

You had been sneaking to the bathroom, trying to avoid just such a chance meeting, when she came coughing out of Sean's room, reeking like incense. It took her a moment to catch her breath.

"I don't know what happened to you guys on that road trip, but I am not a fan," she said. "I understand he's going through it right now, but if he keeps talking to me about what I'm 'manifesting,' I'm seriously going to lose it. And then there's you . . ."

"*What?*" you said.

But even you didn't believe your attempt at feigning innocence. For once, you tried to look at her, but you were only able to hold your glance for a second. She looked a little different. She'd cut her hair, and now she had bangs that nearly covered her eyebrows. They made her expression hard to read.

"You're avoiding me," she said.

"Not true," you said, with even less conviction.

"Then why don't you come out of your room when I'm here? Also, we haven't gone to Perkins in weeks, and I'm going through bottomless-coffeepot withdrawal. Look at my hand. It's shaking."

She smiled and waved it in front of your face. You took a step backward toward your room, but she didn't seem to notice.

"We should go tonight," she said suddenly. "I can't take the smell in that room anymore. It smells like a candle store. Oh, and I have this hilarious new phrase to teach you! Baba let it slip when she was trying to get the cable box to work. Get your keys, dude!"

She was laughing now, but you couldn't seem to move. Your socks might as well have been Velcroed to the carpet.

"I think it's better," you said, "if we didn't . . . do that tonight."

It was amazing how fast her smile disappeared, like someone had spliced the movie of this moment and removed a few frames.

"Oh," she said finally. "Sure. I mean if you don't . . ."

Her whole posture changed, and that's when you came to a realization that made all of this so much more painful. Those nights at Perkins, just sitting in a peeling vinyl booth, talking about nothing and drinking bad coffee, were actually important to her too. You always assumed she could take them or leave them, and that when Sean finally woke up and decided to pay attention to her again, she would happily go back to spending most of her time with him. But here was Sean, awake and giving her his all, and here was Diana in the hallway again, asking you to leave with her.

You wanted to take it all back in that moment. You wanted

to tell her you were kidding, that of course you were going to get your keys, and you hoped your favorite booth was still open. But something had already shifted. She was looking at you with such disappointment. She was not playing it cool. She didn't understand what had changed, and you were powerless to tell her. So, of course, very quickly, your anxiety showed up at the party. You could feel the sweat prickle at the nape of your neck. Above your lip. You started to feel lightheaded.

"I have to go," you said, and your voice sounded like it was being played a click too fast.

"Just wait a second," she said.

Your mouth was so dry.

"What?" you said, and just stood there dumbly.

She pushed her bangs away from her eyes. Then she stuck a hand in her pocket and pulled out a small rock. She reached over and opened your hand and pushed the rock against your palm. You closed your fingers. Your breathing was speeding up, but the rock slowed it again. Just holding something tangible, something substantial, allowed you to take a full breath. You looked at the stone. It was diamond shaped and jet black. Almost like a piece of charcoal, but it left no residue on your fingers.

"What is this?" you said.

She looked at the ceiling, and you couldn't tell for a moment if she was going to answer you. Then she looked you in the eye.

"My uncle lives in Detroit," she said. "And a couple of years ago there was this flash in the sky at night. Like, super bright. People thought it was a bomb or a UFO or something. There were 911 calls. The whole city was freaking out. Then the next day, my uncle goes outside and he finds these weird rocks on his lawn."

"No . . . ," you said.

She nodded.

"A meteorite?"

"They think it was about five feet long when it came shooting in, but it, like, broke up into all these pieces when it hit the atmosphere. A couple of them landed in Uncle Novak's yard. He was shaking his head when he talked about it. Saying, 'This is from space! It could have killed me!' Then he handed one to me. It's always kind of creeped me out, to be honest. So now I'm giving it to you."

You didn't have time to say anything.

"Hey, babe!" came a shout from your brother's room, startling you. "C'mere. I want to read you something."

"Sweet Jesus," she said. "If he's writing poems again . . ."

Earlier, she might have looked at you for a conspiratorial laugh, but now there was nothing. She was just talking to herself. And you felt it then: the full impact of the heartbreak. Everything was changing between you and Diana. You knew it and she knew it, even if she didn't know why. You felt some anger, sure, but mostly just the ache.

You were heartbroken that your brother, who you loved and idolized, had just taken away your best friend so effortlessly. Because that's ultimately who she was. Even if she would never love you the way you loved her: She was the friend you liked best. You were heartbroken that he didn't understand something so simple—Diana meant something to you too and now you had to lie to her.

Suddenly, you felt pain that was outside your mind, and it wasn't until you unclenched your fist in the hallway that you saw what had happened. Your palm was bleeding. Right where the rough edge of the meteorite met your hand, it sliced open the skin. This rock had survived its white-hot passage through the earth's atmosphere only to smear your fingers with sticky blood. And when Diana closed the door to Sean's room behind her, without once looking back, you were faced with another one of the sayings that had been taped to the outside.

Love is the whole thing. We are only pieces, it read.

You weren't sure what it meant.

For a few seconds, you tried to understand. Maybe it was saying that love is bigger than any one person. That it is this incredible force and you and everyone else are just tiny fragments. Or maybe it meant that everyone is broken and you are united by your brokenness. You just didn't know. You only knew that your hand was bleeding, and so you walked into the bathroom to clean yourself up.

And when you grabbed the bandages, you found that you were still gripping the rock, holding it tight even through the pain. It felt, in that moment, so silly and humiliating. Your unfortunate crush. Your ridiculous hope. Your belief that Sean would do the right thing even though he usually didn't when it came to anyone else but you. And you knew then, as you switched on the hot water and watched it steam, that it was probably time to let go.

SIXTEEN

Everyone packs up in a hurry. It might be the charge in the air after the storm, or the surreal landscape of fallen trees leaning on one another, dark against an orange sky, but nobody lingers. You all work hard, loading up your packs to leave this broken place that almost killed you. When you're done, you stand with the rest of the group, everyone weighed down with gear, looking more like overdecorated Christmas trees than hikers. All dressed up with no place to go. That is, until Fran reveals that she actually knows how to use a compass.

"Wait, really?" says Diana. "You were listening?"

"Look," she says. "I have ADHD. But I think my anxiety about getting lost and dying in the woods was able to override it somehow."

"So, like: One disorder beat the other disorder's ass," says Will.

"Something like that."

"You can actually navigate?" says Troy.

"I mean, I wouldn't bet our survival on it . . . ," Fran says.

"But that's exactly what you *would* be doing!" says Troy, his face frozen with incredulity.

"What?" says Fran.

"You would *literally* be betting our survival on it! Like, whether or not we die. Here. In the woods. Now. Would depend on exactly that. So it's kind of important: Do you know or do you not know how to navigate?"

Fran is silent. She has her hood down this time, but you can see her itching to pull it back up. She shifts her massive pack to a more comfortable position and takes a breath.

"Just get me a map, and I'll see what I can do," she says.

At which point everyone sets off to search what's left of the campsite, looking for anything that might provide direction.

What you hope you'll find:

A waterproof trail map

A hand-drawn route on a sheet of notebook paper

Some kind of satellite GPS that Silas was keeping just in case

What you actually find:

Absolutely nothing

"I never saw him with one," says Troy eventually. "Did you guys ever see him take out a single freaking map?"

"Maybe he had the route memorized," says Diana. "He's probably been doing this awhile."

"Great," says Will. "So our map is stored in the brain of the sadistic bastard who left us."

"I thought he said something about a loop," says Fran. "Does anyone else remember that, or am I hallucinating?"

"A loop?" asks Troy. "What kind of loop?"

You get a brain zap then. The good kind. Not the kind that happens when you run out of medication, but a flash of a memory newly translated.

"The Devil's Loop," you say.

"The what?" says Fran.

She turns to look at you, the frustration slowly leaving her face.

"The Devil's Loop," you say again. "That's what he was saying to me! 'Are you ready for the Devil's Loop?' God, I was *so* confused. I thought he was going to kill me or something."

"I'm still confused," says Will. "Is that a place?"

"Sure," says Fran. "For outdoorsy satanists. I bet it's perfectly safe."

"Maybe the drop point is somewhere near there," says Diana. "If we can find it. Whatever it is."

"But how do we know which way to go?" asks Troy.

Another weighty silence descends. One so long, you can make out the sound of the distant rushing water your brain has filtered out over the past twenty-four hours. But then, Fran is fumbling frantically in the pocket of her nylon pants, and you all watch as she finally pulls out a small white compass, the size of a credit card.

"True north," she says.

She squints down at the compass.

"That's why he was teaching us the difference, remember? Because, at first, we were going to be traveling straight north. Not magnetic north. It wouldn't work because the declination would be off! But the loop. The Devil's Loop. That's got to be true north."

"You've already lost me," you say.

She shushes you, and then holds the compass steady and level with two hands. Slowly, she rotates it to align the *N* on the dial with the needle. What she's doing is probably the most basic thing any outdoors person learns to do, but in this moment, it seems holy, like a kind of summoning of forces from the other side to provide guidance.

"So this is magnetic north," she says softly. "But Silas told us the declination was about thirteen degrees west. Which would actually be . . . here."

She rotates the compass again until the needle is over a few notches to the left. Everyone gathers around and looks down at the small piece of plastic that is maybe going to determine whether you will all live or die. The needle wobbles a little, and your gaze follows it into the woods, where the thick pines keep you from seeing any more than twenty feet in front of you.

"There's not really a trail there," you say.

The sky has cleared and the sun is just starting to peek through the lifting fog, but deep in the woods, it still looks dark, and you instantly think of fairy tales and horror movies, and all the times someone could have easily avoided a horrible fate if they had just decided to stay out of the goddamn forest.

"It might be all we have to go on," says Fran.

You look at the empty campsite then, with only the scorched remains of the fire to alert anyone that you've been here. It isn't high season, and you haven't seen a single other paddler on the water. Nobody is likely to find your site and rescue you. But still, none of you moves.

There's a simple choice here: woods or the campsite. Stay put or risk action. Oddly enough, something inside you twitches. And for a reason you don't totally understand, you start walking. Breathing in through your nose and out through your mouth, you make your way down to the lake to pick up a canoe.

It's not a smooth operation. You have to struggle with it for at least a minute, trying to flip it just right so the "portage yoke" that Diana mentioned gets centered over your neck. You feel a bit like a malnourished ox, but you finally manage to do it. Then you stand up, and immediately the weight shifts and you topple like a felled tree. You fall to the side, and the boat goes crashing to the ground next to you.

No one speaks. They continue to watch.

You stand back up. You grab the boat again. You lift, and though your bony arms start to buckle, you manage to keep the boat still. And when it's steady, you hold it up until the yoke is over your neck and you gently set it on your back again. You take a step. The canoe wobbles like a teeter-totter. You steady it. Then you take another step. And another. Finally, using the slowest steps imaginable, you walk back across the campsite and line up behind Fran, your shoulders already screaming under the weight.

You don't expect anyone to follow you, especially after that performance, but gradually Fran steps forward too, her compass held out ahead of her like a metal detector. Then Will solemnly takes the other boat, the one stuck in the bushes, hefting it with ease. Diana works with him to carry it. And Troy steps behind you and holds up the back of yours. Three will have to go in one. Two in the other. For now, you just stand there, like a family of confused snails, pointed toward what you hope is north.

"Does anyone have an inspirational speech?" Troy says, his voice echoing around your boat. "I could really use an inspirational speech."

There's another silence then. No one so much as clears their throat until, finally, Diana pokes her head out from under her boat and looks at everyone.

"Okay, adventurers," she says in a counselor voice. "All we have to do today is not die!"

And then you all start walking.

SEVENTEEN

It's almost exhilarating at first: the thrill of marching into an uncertain future. But, after a while, when that future arrives and then just kind of keeps going, and all you're doing is trudging forward on a rocky path with aching shoulders and blistered feet, your enthusiasm starts to wear thin. For most of the morning, you and Troy are in the front of the line, shouldering a canoe, and trying to go fast enough so that Fran, Diana, and Will don't smash into the back of your boat.

"Pick up the pace, NARPs," Will says occasionally, and it's hard to tell if he's being sarcastic.

Midmorning, the trail turns marshy, soaked by the storm. Your boots cake with crusts of thick, fragrant mud, and your legs feel ten pounds heavier. Nobody speaks. Nobody knows if you're headed in the right direction. Or if this is all part of the great wilderness-therapy adventure you signed up for. And nobody knows if you'll ever see Silas with his backward hat and all your medication again.

Finally, by late afternoon, it's all over. You can't walk another step. A cold wind sweeps through the trees, and your boots are soaked through to your socks. Your arms feel like they're no longer a part of you. If you could be fully present in your body, you'd probably be starving. But, as it stands, you have no idea what other needs you might have beyond the urge to cease all movement.

You don't remember stopping, or heaving the crushing weight of the boat from your burning shoulders, but the next thing you know, you're sitting on what appears to be the shore of a lake. Coarse rocks jut out around you, lily pads dot the water, and the soil beneath you is the color of rust. After a while, someone shoves a bowl of what appears to be reconstituted hummus under your face, and you mechanically shovel it into your mouth with your fingers. Then you wipe your hands on your pants and close your eyes.

When you wake up, it's dusk, and you immediately hear a hollow clicking sound. It sounds like it's coming from inside your body, and it takes you a moment to realize it's your teeth chattering. The temperature has dropped. Precipitously. It must be 30 degrees cooler than it was when you first set out this morning. You lift a hand to wipe your eyes, and you notice that it's shaking too. You dig through your pack for a hoodie, and once it's on, you pull the hood up, tightening it around your head like a ninja mask. As you sit up, you hear the sounds of an argument going on.

"I told you that was the groundsheet!" says Will.

"The fly and the groundsheet are basically interchangeable," says Troy.

"Says the guy who has never been camping!"

"Just shut up and hand me a peg."

"I already—Ah god! I'm freezing!"

The two of them are violently rubbing their arms to stave off the cold, fumbling all the while with a large tarp that is either the groundsheet or the fly.

"I gave you the pegs a minute ago."

"I have zero pegs, Will!"

Nearby, Diana and Fran sit zipped inside their tent, which is already pitched. You can see them through the mesh. You slowly stand up, a little lightheaded, and start to zombie-shuffle over to them to ask how you got here. You're not warm yet, but your teeth have stilled for the moment. You stop walking about half-way there because as you get closer, you see that the two girls are locked in conversation, the kind you think maybe you shouldn't interrupt.

They're both sitting cross-legged on the floor of the tent, hold-ing water bottles. Diana is nodding, and Fran is talking quickly and softly gesticulating with intensity. You have no idea what they're talking about—you're just out of hearing range—but you know what it feels like to be with Diana like that. To be blocking out the rest of the world and just lost in a simple moment of connection.

It's what you miss the most.

There aren't many people you've been able to just be with in that way, where you're not hiding somehow or feeling self-conscious to the point of distraction. Sean was one. And the other is right in front of you. But she couldn't be less aware of your presence at the moment. You know you should turn around, go back and help Will and Troy with their shelter so all of you do not die of exposure, but you're too woozy to make it happen. So you just stand there, knees locked, staring through the slit in your hoodie.

"He lives!" says Fran finally. "He walks among us."

Diana looks at you and blinks, and you think of what she said after the storm: *I'll cut you loose.* You had never heard her so serious, and since that moment, you can already feel it happening. Less eye contact. Most comments made in passing. You want to say something about it now. Something that lets her know that you don't want to be cut loose, but instead you say:

"Where are we?"

Fran takes a swig from her water bottle.

"North," she says.

She closes her eyes to think.

"And . . . by a lake."

You take a cold breath and blow it out hot into your hands.

"We're north by a lake," she says. "Is that enough?"

You look down and see that her knee is touching Diana's. She watches you watching her, but doesn't move it.

"Fire," you say.

They both just look at you. You are, you remember, standing there like a ninja with bad posture. And you're speaking in one-word sentences.

"What was that, Frankenstein?" says Fran.

"We need to make a fire. For the cold."

Diana nods slowly.

"Or you guys could put up a tent," she says.

As if on cue, Will's voice erupts from behind you.

"HOW COULD YOU LOSE A PEG?! IT WAS IN YOUR POCKET!"

In other circumstances you might laugh at the absurdity. But now you wonder if you're going to survive the night.

"Somebody fed me," you say to Fran. "Was that you?"

"Not I, said the fly," she says. "That would be this one."

Diana looks away. You try to wait her out, but she's persistent.

"Thanks," you say.

The light is disappearing quickly, and you know you'll never start a fire when it gets dark. It will be hard enough in the remaining daylight, so you shuffle back in the direction of Troy and Will.

"IT FELL OUT! OKAY?"

"NO. NOT OKAY!"

"Guys," you say.

"I'M FEELING VERY UNCOMFORTABLE WITH YOUR PROXIMITY RIGHT NOW," says Troy.

"YOU'RE GOING TO FEEL MORE UNCOMFORTABLE WHEN I IMPALE YOU WITH THIS TENT POLE!"

"Guys," you say.

Troy kneels on the ground and starts exhaling loudly.

"I'm done," he says. "Just bury me now!"

"GUYS!" you scream. "WE NEED TO MAKE A FIRE! OR THIS COLD IS GOING TO FREEZE OUR DICKS OFF! DO EITHER OF YOU IDIOTS KNOW HOW TO USE THE FLINT?"

Will looks right at you, like he's seeing you for the first time.

He shakes his head.

"I think Silas took the flint, bro."

Troy blasts a breath from his nose.

"I haven't seen it," he says.

You look back toward the girls' tent.

"No flint in here!" says Fran.

You reach down and extend a hand to Troy, who looks at it a moment before accepting. You pull him up, then you warm your hands again.

"People made fire, like, two million years ago," you say. "I saw it on a National Geographic series."

You start to shiver again, so you hop in place.

"They had flat skulls and ran around in the woods butt naked! And they could function better than we can. What the hell happened to us? How did we go from making fire with our bare hands to having panic attacks in a closet a couple million years later? What went wrong, guys?"

You're on the verge of tears somehow. You're not sure why talking about early humans has brought this on, and not, say, being abandoned by your Adventure Therapy counselor, but your brain remains mysterious to you. And it's likely to stay that way. You put your face in your hands, so no one can see the brewing tears of evolutionary shame.

"Hey," says Troy, and walks over to you.

You slowly lift your head.

He's opening pockets on his camp shorts. It takes him a moment to locate what he wants, but when he does, his eyes seem to jump.

"Look, Case," he says. "Cavemen did a lot of badass stuff. No doubt. And it's true that they would probably stomp us in a fight. But those guys didn't have . . ."

He does a fake drumroll with his mouth. Then he brandishes something from his pocket.

"CAPITALISM!" he shouts.

With a flick of his thumb, a small flame shudders to life in his hand, emanating from a bright orange cigarette lighter. It's a miraculous sight, a vision of pure, glowing hope. The fire flickers in the breeze, and you all follow its every shiver, transfixed.

"Behold!" he says. "I am modern man, and I make fire with my thumb!"

EIGHTEEN

The fire is too small. And, as it turns out, small fires aren't that warm. Nonetheless, everyone huddles around the meager flames while you finish up "dinner," aka some undercooked oats made from the almost-boiling water in your single pan. The food is just a drop in the bucket of your empty stomach, and you know you're only going to get hungrier in the coming hours. With all the calories you burned today, you should be eating a ten-course meal. Instead, you've had the dinner of a medieval prisoner.

The recent dark has brought quiet. You thought the night here would be full of sounds. Strange birdcalls. The rustling of small creatures in the brush. But instead, it's near silent and the occasional sound makes you jump. Everyone is exhausted, but nobody wants to be the first to go into their tent alone. You notice the small circle of your group growing tighter around your poorly built fire. There's a long period of time when no one says anything. Nobody wants to be the first to say what you're all thinking.

There's been no sign of Silas so far.

Not even a footprint.

And it's been twelve hours since any of you have had access to the supplemental medication that is the only salve against severe panic attacks. If this is a test, you're barely past the beginning and it's likely to get much worse. But nobody puts a voice to all this.

Maybe because saying it will make it real. Instead, when someone finally speaks, it's for a reason that surprises you.

"You guys want to play Fear in a Hat?"

Even more surprising: It comes from Diana.

Predictably, Will scoffs.

"Oh my god. Why would we do that?"

"Yeah," says Fran. "No offense, but the guy who came up with that game didn't exactly have our best interests in mind."

You and Troy are silent. But your heart rate has already increased.

"That might be true," says Diana. "But it also might be true that we're not going to make it back to our old lives, and we don't really know anything about each other. Is that what you guys want? To die out here with complete strangers?"

The wind has picked up again, and all you can do is listen as it whistles in your ears and threatens to put out your hard-earned fire.

"We don't have a hat," you say.

"Or any more paper," says Fran.

"That doesn't matter," says Diana. "Just say what was on your sheet the first time. I know you remember. C'mon. Who wants to go?"

You've always been bad with awkward pauses. They make you deeply uncomfortable. So much so that you think about breaking the silence this time. It would be easy to do. You'd just say that your paper was blank and then talk about why. Then you'd say his name, speak that one syllable that matters. But before you can summon the courage, someone else speaks up from across the fire.

"The total annihilation of planet Earth."

It takes a minute for this to register.

It's Troy, and apparently, that's what he put on his paper.

"You mean the whole earth?" you say. "That's what you're afraid of?"

"Damn," says Fran. "I picked sushi."

"But what do you mean, exactly?" says Diana. "Like, nuclear war or something?"

Troy shakes his head.

"Climate anxiety," he says.

"So, like, you're afraid of the weather?" says Will.

Troy sighs.

"Well, yeah," he says. "Weather's a part of it. There's the heat waves, and storms, and droughts, and floods, and wildfires. But then there's the dying oceans, the millions of animals facing extinction, the refugee crisis. And how, if we don't do anything, it's all going to be irreversible in five years."

Will doesn't respond. Nobody says anything, in fact, for a few seconds. And this time the pause doesn't bother you so much, since you're still trying to add up all the things he just said.

"Sorry, I'm not supposed to do that," says Troy.

"Do what?" says Fran.

"Obsess about the doomsday stuff. That's what got me in trouble in the first place."

He reaches out a stick and pokes at the fire.

"What do you mean by *trouble*?" says Diana.

"I got expelled," he says. "I'm homeschooled now. It's also why I'm here with you guys, I guess."

The smoke blows toward him, and he turns to cough, rubbing at his left eye under his glasses.

"You got expelled?" says Fran. "That is *hard*core, my friend. Why?"

When he speaks next, it's a little on the quiet side and the wind kicks up at the same time so no one can quite hear him. But everyone inches nearer. Will puts a hand to his ear in the universal sign for louder. Troy clears his throat.

"I set a classroom on fire," he says.

"WHAT?" says Will.

Suddenly, the cold isn't bothering you so much. And the undersize fire is far from your mind. Everyone stares at Troy.

"It's kind of a complicated story," he says.

No one stops staring.

"We don't care," says Fran. "Please tell us how you set the school on fire!"

Troy pokes at the fire with a stick.

"Right," he says. "Okay. Well. I guess there was this biology teacher, Mr. Shiftler. That's probably the first thing you need to know. He's this old white dude with big bushy caterpillar eyebrows and a Colonel Sanders mustache. He wore the same polo shirt in five different colors, one for each day of the week, and he used the same worksheets every year, so people just copied them and handed them down to the next class.

"His class was, like, the most useless hour of my life. Usually, I just put an earbud in and listened to podcasts while I copied down the formula for photosynthesis, and it was all good. I had some other teachers who were all right, so one bad one wasn't the end of the world. And I think I would have just finished out the year like that, just zoning in sixth period, but then there was this cyclone that hit."

"What cyclone?" asks Diana.

"Idai. You probably didn't hear about it, because it was in southern Africa. I didn't even pay attention at first. But it hit Malawi and Mozambique and Zimbabwe. It destroyed people's homes and crops, and killed a thousand people right away."

"You set someone's class on fire because of a cyclone in Africa?" says Will.

"Let him finish!" says Fran.

Troy takes a breath.

"My dad is from Zimbabwe," Troy says. "Originally, I mean. He came here when he was nine, but he still has lots of family back there. So for weeks after the storm hit, we saw the landslides and all the devastation on the internet, and we didn't know where my dad's brother was. I started reading about it. And some articles were saying that this wasn't a place where tropical cyclones usually hit. And it was probably climate change that was responsible for how bad it was. The storms were getting lethal and their paths were changing. And it wasn't even the fault of Zimbabweans! They didn't release much carbon at all.

"But *we* did. We do. We're second on the list of the biggest carbon emitters. Us. And now my uncle was missing, and my dad's home country was all messed up. And after that, I sort of stopped sleeping."

The fire starts to flicker out, and Fran tosses a handful of broken sticks into it.

"I stayed up every night watching climate scientists on YouTube and reading about how there's more natural disasters these days, and millions of people are killed by them each year. I looked at pictures, and I read about all the inaction from our leaders. And then one day, I was in biology class and I was taking a quiz on vestigial structures that I had already taken the week before, and I wasn't sleeping at night, and I just took out my earbud and said:

"'Why aren't we learning about climate change in here, Mr. Shiftler?'

"At the time, Mr. Shiftler was going through some boxes. My guy was about to retire and he was doing his packing on our time. The day before, he had unboxed this hideous model of the solar system made of Styrofoam and pipe cleaners and hung it right over his desk like a trophy.

"'Finish your quiz, Troy,' he said in his usual bored voice.

"So I said: 'I'm not in the mood today.'

"And before I really knew what I was doing, I threw my paper on the ground, and I said, 'Vestigial. Having become functionless in the course of evolution.'

"He looked at me, like, kind of surprised I actually knew the material, even though I always did. So I added:

"'Like this class.'

"And then I stood up on my chair because I saw someone do it in a movie once and I said, 'Wake up, everybody! People are dying in Zimbabwe right now!'

"It wasn't a great line, really. Most of my classmates probably don't know where Zimbabwe is on a map. But it was all I could think to say.

"'Get down from there, Troy!' said Mr. Shiftler, and I saw him start to come out from behind his desk and walk toward mine.

"'There are brush fires in Australia!' I yelled. 'Our children are going to be scavengers in a barren landscape! This is serious!'

"He started tugging at my shirt.

"'Next Monday I'm holding a climate walkout,' I said. 'And we won't come back to science class until we get some climate-change education! Who's with me?!'

"Nobody stood up, guys. Most people were laughing at me. Maybe they thought I was being funny, like, just ragging on old Mr. Shiftler. Finally, he pulled me down from my chair and took me out into the hallway, where he told me that global warming was a liberal hoax and if I did my own research, I would figure that out. And then I got detention.

"I spent the next week making pamphlets and memes and setting up a booth in the cafeteria. I handed out stuff and told everyone about the walkout. But when Monday came, I marched at noon out to the football field where we had decided to meet, and realized I was all alone. There wasn't a single other person there. Just me. And I lay down on the field, and I looked up at the clouds and thought about everything I had been reading.

"About how we had this small window to make things right, and about this scientist I heard on a podcast who said that we don't have any wisdom as a species. That we're intelligent and we know how to make iPhones and stuff, but we're not wise enough to save ourselves. And whether or not we survived was going to depend on if people could get wiser.

"And then I felt so pissed off and lonely and frustrated because I wasn't that wise myself and it seemed like nobody was going to ever listen to me. And that it was probably going to take us too long to get wise. We'd all be dead first. So I marched back in the school, and into Mr. Shiftler's class, and I took out a lighter. This lighter, in fact, and I reached up and held the flame to the bottom of the Styrofoam planet Earth hanging from his model.

"Shiftler screamed at me, but I just kept it there, because I thought maybe if everyone saw the Earth literally on fire, they might finally get what I was saying. But maybe because of the old enamel paint, the thing burst into flames in, like, a second. Just like: *whoosh!* There was a lot of fire, and before Mr. Shiftler could get up on a chair to grab the thing, it burned through the pipe cleaner and spread to Mercury, which was even more flammable somehow.

"People were screaming at that point, and while they were running for the door, the whole solar system fell from the ceiling and landed on a pile of old boxes he'd been packing. Those went up too, and someone pulled the fire alarm, and I don't remember much of what happened next."

"Oh my god," says Diana.

"But it caused thirty thousand dollars of damage," Troy says. "Which came out of my college fund. And I was never allowed back in that school again."

"Oh my god," Will says.

"And to keep from facing charges and being sent to this school for troubled kids, I've been going to therapy ever since. It was my therapist who suggested this trip, actually. She said: 'Troy, you're always talking about protecting the environment—why don't you actually get out in nature and experience the beauty of what's still here?' So here I am. In nature. And I have to tell you guys, my therapist was right that it has helped in one way. Yesterday, I was worried about the total annihilation of the earth. But tonight, I'm kind of just worried about the annihilation of us."

The fire is dying, and there isn't any more wood. You didn't gather enough because of course you didn't.

"I just wish I could go back sometimes," he says.

"To school?" you say.

Troy shakes his head.

"No. To before all of this. I went years without knowing anything about the planet's temperature. I was oblivious. There's this day I can remember, before the cyclone and everything else, where I took Turbo to the dog park on a Saturday. It was the one he likes with the little dog pirate ship to play on. And I ran around with him for hours, chucking tennis balls with the launcher until he was so worn out, he slept on the floor in the car on the way home. Then I got fast food, fed him some french fries, and watched *Shark Week* in my room until midnight. And that was maybe it."

"Maybe what?" you ask.

But you already know what he's going to say, so you wait patiently while he stares into the fire, then looks up with a sad smile and says:

"The last good day."

NINETEEN

Those words haunt you when it's time to sleep. Not because of climate change—which, you'll admit, is a much bigger problem than yours—but because when Troy said them, you immediately thought of your own last good day. The funny thing is, though, that, looking back, it maybe wasn't the best day overall. But it started off good. The last *good-ish* day? And it was the last time you remember feeling happy with your brother.

It was after Sean's spiritual awakening. After he'd imprisoned himself in the house for weeks, reading self-help books and dipping his toes into the world's major religions. It was after he had unknowingly destroyed your friendship with Diana. You'd been wondering if he was maybe going to join a monastery when one morning he woke up and came into your room fresh from the shower.

"Get dressed, Case!" he said. "I have planned an *outing*."

He said the last word in an accent of some kind, and you immediately thought of something New Agey. So you were surprised when he told you to grab the cobweb-covered cooler from under the basement stairs. You went down and excavated it, and when you brought it up, he started loading it with sandwiches and sodas from the fridge.

He didn't tell you where you were going, or that Diana was coming. And when he picked her up, he didn't tell her anything either. He only said that it would be memorable. You got on the highway going north, and for maybe an hour or two, you lost track of time. You were in charge of changing the radio station when the song went bad, and you surfed the frequencies with precision, turning the knob whenever something felt like a mood killer. This job helped keep your mind off Diana, who sat quietly in the back seat, hiding behind an enormous pair of old-lady sunglasses she'd borrowed from her baba.

It had been two weeks since she asked you to go to Perkins and you turned her down. Two weeks since you'd had a normal conversation when you ran into each other in the kitchen, or outside Sean's room in the morning. Sean had started taking her out again, so they were gone more often. But now the three of you were back in the Corolla, pretending that everything was normal.

And for the drive, at least, it almost was. Sean told a story about the time a guy at the ice cream shop spilled a whole milkshake on himself right before a job interview, and his impression of the guy's face had Diana giggling in the back seat, in spite of herself. And then he reminded you of this game you used to play when you were young called "escape artist," where one of you would tie the other one up using anything you could find: toy handcuffs, scarves, ropes, a blindfold. Then the captured person would have to escape in a room with all the lights off.

You remembered this game as being genuinely scary, but the worst thing in the world was if you had to admit defeat and scream for your captor to come set you free. On the other hand, if you managed to escape, there was no better feeling. When you saw the light of the hallway and your brother's disappointed face, the victory filled your entire body.

"So, basically, you guys were into bondage," said Diana.

"Har har," said Sean, reaching over and slapping a palm on your neck. "Nice try, but you'll never understand our bro-lationship."

And for the first time in a while, the contact didn't feel weird.

Sean drove straight through to his destination, only stopping when he got to the parking lot of what appeared to be a nature preserve. There were lots of hiking trails and signs for different numbered quarries, which you didn't totally understand. He looked at them carefully and then chose number two. He walked ahead of you and Diana with the cooler. Once he was on the right path, a childlike excitement seemed to enter him. He turned back and smiled.

"C'mon," he said, and started to jog.

You and Diana quickened your pace, but it was hard to keep up with him, and because the sun was high and it was getting hot, neither of you wanted to run. So that left you alone, side by side. You hadn't spoken a direct word to each other all day. You felt the urge to apologize to her, but for what exactly? For turning down an offer to go to Perkins? Just for being weird? It seemed like if you got started on a proper apology, you would have to explain yourself, and to explain yourself would be to do the unthinkable. Still, you had trouble even looking at her, so you stared straight ahead when you spoke.

"Do you know what this place is?"

Diana looked surprised to hear your voice, and you thought, for a moment, that she wasn't going to respond. But then she sighed and said:

"Not really. Some kind of old mining place?"

Around you were rows of aspens, their thin white trunks

slicing the blue sky into narrow rectangles. The light filtering through the leaves made long shadows on the trail that moved up and over your body when you walked through them. It was so quiet you could hear the sound of the gravel crunching beneath the soles of your shoes. Your familiar anxious urge to fill the silence came back to you quickly.

"Did you know the Japanese have a word for light scattered through the trees?"

She looked at you, mildly curious.

"Komorebi," you said. "There isn't really a direct English translation. But it's basically . . . you know . . . this."

You waved your arms toward the light and stole a quick glance at your brother, who was even farther away now. He also appeared to be taking his shirt off, which was odd, but not entirely out of character. You looked back to Diana.

"Do they have a word for an awkward attempt at conversation?" she asked.

You couldn't see her eyes through her sunglasses, so it was hard to tell what her expression was.

"I don't know. I don't really speak Japanese," you said. "I just like untranslatable words. There is this one in German, Verschlimmbessern, which basically means the more you try to fix something, the worse it gets. Is that what you're thinking of?"

She stopped then and took off her sunglasses, her pupils retracting in the sunlight. Her face looked genuine for a moment, open. She said your name.

"Case."

And that's when you heard Sean's scream.

You both turned in time for him to take the last couple of

steps before jumping into the air over the edge of an enormous cliff. His scream faded as he dropped out of sight.

Your breath stopped.

There was barely a moment's pause before both of you were sprinting. Already, the adrenaline was pouring through you, and you couldn't remember the last time you had run so hard. Your head was buzzing, and your whole body was boiling. Halfway there, you heard the splash, and you felt a small relief. But you still didn't know how safe he was, or what was really down there. It wasn't until you and Diana reached the end of the path and looked down the sheer face of a granite cliff so high that it made you dizzy that you exhaled.

There he was, floating in the dark blue water.

He wasn't even looking at you. He was on his back, face to the sun, and with what looked to be a serene smile on his lips. In the shock of the moment, you couldn't even conjure a sentence. All you could do was watch him drift. Beyond his body, there were disparate groups of teenagers floating on inner tubes, splashing, and laughing with one another. If any of them had watched his leap from out of nowhere, they were over it now. The anger came to you then, as you took a single shaky step back from the cliff, and you wanted to yell down to him, strings of profanity from the core of your being. Instead, you just said a single sentence out loud to yourself.

"I thought you were gone."

Diana didn't seem to hear you. She was staring fixedly at the water below. Then, in a matter of seconds, she did something you never would have considered: She took off her shirt and jean shorts and jumped in after him. She landed feetfirst in the water with an incredible splash, and when she surfaced, she swam directly over to Sean and dunked him under the water.

For a moment, you thought she was actually going to kill him. They were under the water for a long time. But when they finally emerged, they were both laughing and Sean had her bra in his outstretched hand. You wanted her to punch him. You could almost feel what it would be like for her fist to connect with his jaw. But instead, she put her arms around him and bit him on the ear. He shrieked, but in a kind of delight, and then kissed her, while some nearby teens whooped at them.

"I thought you were gone," you said again, to yourself.

Of course, you couldn't bring yourself to jump. You were too scared. Plain and simple. But Sean climbed back to the top and executed a heart-stopping array of dives that almost gave you a vicarious panic attack. Each one brought him so close to the rock face of the cliff, you were sure he was going to scrape against it. Diana cheered him on below, fully converted to the strange turn this day had taken.

According to Sean, his diving career was over now—there was no point anymore if he couldn't go all the way—but you wouldn't have known it by how sharp and fluid his movements were as he spun and flipped through the air. You weren't sure if he was even supposed to be diving since his concussion, but by the end of the afternoon, he was putting on a one-man show for the whole quarry, soaking up the attention like his old self.

You eventually found a path down to the water and waded in from the rocky shore. The water was freezing, and when you dove under, it was surprisingly clear. You could see at least twenty feet below you, but the quarry must have been deep, because there was no sign of the bottom. You felt so many things at the same time, it was hard to separate them. Anger. Jealousy. Pride. Relief. So you weren't sure what to do when he swam over to you and dove under the water. When he rose again, it was under your legs so that you were sitting awkwardly on his shoulders, while he stood on a rocky outcropping near the shore, water up to his armpits.

It felt good to be up there, the wind blowing against the cold water on your skin, but the sun still heating you. You hammed it up for a moment, the way he expected, waving your arms and saying you were going to fall.

"I've got you," he said. "Don't forget that I'm amazingly strong."

"Oh right," you said. "How could I forget?"

A breeze kicked up and gave you goose bumps, so you folded your arms.

"Not feeling the diving today?" he asked.

"Or any day," you said.

He laughed.

"I'm sorry," he said. "I should have known this wouldn't really be your thing. But I just had to do it one more time. It feels like . . . it's hard to describe."

He wobbled a little before holding you tighter.

"It feels like I'm leaving my body. Like I'm no longer part of my own body, but pure energy or something."

"Sounds like a panic attack," you said.

"I think it's better than that. Like I momentarily disappear. But then I come back. And the coming back is the good part because I feel so clear-eyed. And I know what to do."

Diana had climbed up to a smaller cliff, and she stood there now, poised at the edge with her arms raised. Her curly hair lay flat down her back, and she apparently had no shame about being in her underwear in front of a crowd of local high schoolers. She pointed her hands into the sky and then dove sideways into the water like someone in a musical number from an old movie.

"People don't get married young anymore," said Sean. "But I'm thinking that's the right move for me. I think that's going to be the next trend. Early monogamy."

Diana popped up out of the water and kicked her way to the shore. She climbed up on a rock and lay back to sun herself like a lizard. You both stared like idiots. She was beautiful. That was obvious. But she was also just so wholly herself sometimes that you always felt steadier being around her. You knew that Sean did too.

"Sean," you said. "You have to tell her."

You could feel his shoulders tense under your legs. He stood absolutely still for a couple of seconds. You thought maybe he was going to drop you on the rocks. Or maybe just yell at you. But he didn't drop you. And he didn't say a word. He ducked down into the water, submerging himself slowly like a submarine.

For a moment, you were still attached. And you thought of the way he would always escape during your old games, no matter how tight you tied him up. He could always seem to wriggle free from the hardest knots or the trickiest toy handcuffs. Now, in the cold water of the quarry, you kept your legs clenched over his shoulders, trying to hang on to him. But he went deeper. Then deeper. And instead of pulling you down with him, he just kind of slipped your grasp.

And was free.

TWENTY

It's almost daybreak when you hear the scritching sound. There's a dim blue light in the tent that's not quite the full darkness of night, but not morning either. At some point, you actually fell asleep, but now you're awake and your anxiety is spiking. You've woken up in the middle of a panic attack before, and by comparison, this one isn't so bad. Still, you really wish you had a Xanax to clear out the spiders. Instead, as you strain to listen for whatever you first heard, it feels like an elephant is sitting on your chest, only making possible the smallest sips of air.

The sound disappears for a moment. You close your eyes and try for a long exhalation, and just when you manage a full breath, it comes back and sends another boost of adrenaline coursing through your blood. There are a few more noises in these woods as it gets closer to dawn—small moving and chirping things you can't begin to identify—but this one stands out because it's so close.

You shuffle out of your sleeping bag and sit up. You think about waking someone, but Will and Troy are still fast asleep, and they don't move a muscle even when you climb over them. Your only option at this point seems to be to peer out of the tent and see what has invaded your space. Ideally, it will be something benign and obvious and you can relax the old-fashioned way: by knowing you're out of danger.

Somehow you make it to the zipper without knocking the whole drooping tent down. But before you pull on the tab, you wait one last time, just in case all of this wants to go away. It's something you do at night, before another day has started and everything becomes painfully real: You pretend that your life has reset. Sean is across the hall, unharmed. Diana is in your doorway, talking about nothing. And, in this case, there are no woods. No disappeared counselor. None of this at all.

You stop.

You breathe.

Then you hear it again.

So, like the painful easing off of a Band-Aid, you slowly open the flap of the tent and wait for your eyes to adjust to the light. When they do, you see a large black shadow against the backdrop of the moonlit lake. This is not nothing. It's something. And it's nosing at the ground nearby. As your focus sharpens, you start to see various items scattered around the campsite, and the first thing you realize is that you're looking at food.

An animal has gotten into your food.

The food that you should have hung up in a tree.

The only food you have.

You can't help it then: You climb out of the tent. And when you do, a fuzzy head slowly emerges from a bag and stares directly at you. You know you should wake the others at this point, or at least make some kind of noise, but it's the size of the thing that keeps you quiet. Because, yes, there is definitely a bear ten feet away from you, but it's too small, you think, to be a full-grown one. It's a cub. And it looks more like an overgrown teddy bear.

An overgrown teddy bear who is eating all your food.

The cub has somehow nudged the cooler open, but there must still be food in it because it's trying to get at something with its snout. The cooler is not empty. Not yet. Along with a tidal wave of new anxiety, you feel a jolt of something foreign to you. Your competitive instinct.

On every bad team you ever played on (before you realized you were not destined to be an athlete), the coaches said the same thing: "Who wants it more? It all comes down to who wants it more!" You never understood this because you never wanted it more. You didn't care if the soccer ball went in the net or the ball went in the hoop. You always, *always* wanted it less.

Until now.

The problem is, you're still not an athlete and wanting is not the same as getting. You are not an athlete, but you know some-one who is.

"Will," you whisper-shout. "Will!"

You hear the shuffle of his sleeping bag, and after a few seconds, you feel his presence behind you.

"Case, man, I do not like being woken up . . . HOLY SH—"

You put a hand over his mouth.

The bear has returned to sniffing something in the cooler.

"Will," you whisper, just audible enough for him to hear. "What's your sport?"

"What?" he whispers.

"You're sporty," you say. "You've made that clear. We're NARPs, you're not. So what is it? What's your sport?!"

He takes a long breath.

"Tennis," he says.

"Oh," you say.

"What do you mean *Oh*? I was almost state champion last year; if it wasn't for this knob-head Eric Tulliver, I would have—"

"It doesn't matter," you say. "Can you get that cooler?"

Will stops talking and rubs his eyes. He studies the bear. Then the cooler. Then the bear again.

"Sure. It's a shuttle run," he says.

"A what?"

"Just a drill we run in practice. You sprint to the baseline to pick up a tennis ball. Then you sprint back to drop it. Over and over. Sounds simple, but it's torture. The worst. I can crush them, though. I am the freaking king of the shuttle run, bro."

He's lacing up his boots, and it's like he's suddenly in some kind of other mode of being.

"Tulliver had a killer backhand," says Will. "But I had better footwork, which gave me a chance. I took him to a tiebreak in the final set. And I think it was all the shuttle runs. If it wasn't for the . . ."

"Will," you say, and point. "*Cooler.*"

He looks at you, and he's about to say something when you hear another voice.

"Psssst. Here, little guy. Come over here."

You both look up, and in that blue light of the predawn, you now see Diana sitting on a tree stump, holding out a granola bar. Fran is beside her. The bear turns its head and looks at them instead of you and Will

"You don't want that cooler," whispers Fran. "You want this delicious nut-free granola bar with chia seeds in it. That's right. Chia seeds! Lots of antioxidants."

She's using the kind of singsong voice you'd use with a baby.

And when she gets to the last word, Diana motions to the cooler ever so slightly with her head. Will's whole body tenses. And what goes down next all seems to happen so fast, but it also feels like you can see every frame of it in slow motion.

Will takes off. And Will is indeed very fast. Faster than you ever could have imagined. He makes it to the cooler in seconds. So quickly, in fact, that the cub hardly notices him. Will scoops up the cooler with a single fluid movement. He has it in his grasp. It's his. But then two things happen in quick succession. The first is that the baby bear finally notices what's going on. It yowls and Diana jumps back, tripping over her own feet. Fran catches her. The second thing is that instead of running back, Will's body freezes entirely like he's been hit with a stun gun.

He doesn't move at all.

"Will," you say. "You got it! Get back here."

But there's no movement. You can't even tell if he can hear you.

In moments, you see something bursting out of the brush. And, somehow, you know what it is before you even see it. But still, seeing it is utterly terrifying. It is, of course, the mama bear come to get her child, and she smashes through, leaving a trail of trampled vegetation in her path. She is very large, and she is less than twenty feet away from Will. She does not appear to be stopping. And Will, you're certain, is going to die right now in front of all of you.

"Will," you say. "Get out of there! Now!"

Will turns toward you finally. But it's only for a moment. You're sure he's going to run now. As he has just proven, he is extremely fast. If he took off at a sprint, would the bear really follow him? Would he have a shot at outrunning her? You'll never know, because instead, he locks eyes with you, and his face looks desperate, like he's powerless to move. Before you can ask him what he's doing, he swings the cooler by the handle.

"No!" you say. "Don't . . ."

Then he lofts the whole thing in the air, right toward you.

You're completely shocked, but somehow you stumble into position to catch it. It comes winging in, spinning like an asteroid, and hits you hard in the chest. You almost drop to the ground, the wind knocked out of you. The handle pounds your chin, but you manage to clasp your arms around it and hold it tight. It's possible your jaw is broken, along with a couple of ribs, but Will's pass was right on the money.

And, of course, the movement startles the mama bear. She pauses for a moment. Then she keeps walking forward. And when she gets a few feet away from Will, she blows hard at the ground and swipes a paw at a nearby tree. Will doesn't move. The mama bear looks up at him and moans. Then she slams both of her paws into the ground. The next pause seems to last about three hours. Maybe it's five seconds in real time. You have no idea. But right when you think Will is going to have to fight a bear, and that you're going to have to help, the tent flap flies open and what appears to be a shirtless Troy emerges from its depths.

His hair is wild from a night of bad sleep, his glasses crooked. His eyes are wide open, and he is carrying a frying pan and some other object you can't quite make out. From the second he's out of the tent, he starts wailing on the pan like a drummer for a metal band and walking toward the bears. He has his eyes closed and he is singing a song at the top of his lungs that is so loud and off-key, it takes you a moment to realize what it is.

"COUNTRY ROADS! TAKE ME HOME!!"

Will turns around, and in that moment he seems to come back to himself. He's scared and angry, but he starts waving his hands.

"Troy, no!" he says. "Get back in the tent!"

But Troy does not get back in the tent. He keeps walking toward the bears. And the mama bear takes a good look at Troy. She takes in his pan and his horrendous singing. She clocks him coming closer, cocking her head slightly.

And she stops dead in her tracks.

"WEST VIRGINIA!" Troy screams atonally. "MOUNTAIN MAMA!"

And you wait, wondering at which moment both of your companions are going to be ripped apart in front of you. You also can't help wondering if you will be next. But the mama bear, who is probably 250 pounds to Troy's 115, does not charge for some reason. And she does not immediately attack, claws flying, the way you imagine.

Instead, she snorts once and slowly turns around. She does a complete 180. And she doesn't just walk; she *bounds* back into the woods with her cub behind her. She runs on all four bear legs and does not stop to take another gander at the fresh hell behind her. And Troy, who never stops banging, switches from John Denver to some kind of war cry and then to screaming:

"THAT'S RIGHT, BEAR! YOU BETTER RUN! DON'T COME BACK! DON'T MESS WITH US AGAIN, BEAR! DO NOT! DO NOT! AIIYEEEEEEEEEEEEEEEEEEE!"

Will actually has to put a hand on Troy's shoulder to get him to stop screaming. At which point everyone is watching. Diana is on the rock, clutching her granola bar. Fran is holding her. You're still hugging a cooler like your life depends on it (which it might). And Troy is in some kind of warrior pose, holding his weapon aloft, which you can see now, in the brighter light of daybreak, is actually your collapsible whisk.

TWENTY-ONE

"Gimme the whisk," says Will.

Troy holds tight.

"Give it to me, bro. You're going to whisk your eye out or something."

This has been going on for a few minutes, but Troy will not let go of the whisk. If anything, his grip has gotten tighter. So Will finally gives up. He drops his hands to his sides and just stands next to Troy. It's strange to see the two of them next to each other without fighting. But here they are. And when Will speaks, his voice is soft and calm.

"Do you want to sit down?" he asks.

Troy shakes his head.

"Look, I'm pretty sure you just saved my life," says Will. "Sit down. Rest."

Troy doesn't move. Finally, he puts his face in his hands and mumbles something no one can hear.

"What was that?" asks Will.

Troy raises his head.

"She was showing bluster," he says.

"What does that even mean?"

"It means I didn't save your life. Black bears don't really attack much. It's almost unheard of. Even if they think their cubs are in danger, they retreat. All that stuff the mama bear was doing was just out of fear. It was fake. You were going to be fine. I didn't save anything. I'm just having a breakdown."

Troy takes a few breaths and looks up at the sky.

"I don't know," says Fran. "She looked pretty pissed to me."

"Also, how do you know all that . . . about bears?" says Diana.

"Discovery Channel," he says. "I have insomnia."

Everyone takes this in. We all have different ways of dealing with the sleeplessness. This, apparently, is Troy's.

"So your anxiety saved us," Fran says.

Troy actually looks her in the eye this time.

"Ha," he says. "Right."

"I'm serious," she says. "If you didn't have anxiety, then you probably wouldn't have insomnia. And if you didn't have insomnia, you wouldn't've stayed up watching nature documentaries. And if you didn't watch the documentaries, you wouldn't have known how to scare off a blustering bear. So, Will, Troy's anxiety saved you. I think you should thank it."

Will is quiet. He doesn't thank Troy's anxiety. But he doesn't *not* thank it.

Troy just holds tight to the whisk, and everyone is silent as the sun finally makes its way over the horizon and sheds some salmon-colored light on the campsite. The lake is pink and orange, and it meets the sky at a point on the horizon. The clouds hover over it all, reflecting the light. You stare for at least a minute, as the night disappears around you. Once again, it would be beautiful in other circumstances. It would be beautiful if it wasn't for the revelation the light brings. Because even though it's faint, you can see everything around you now.

"Oh my god," says Diana.

Decimated.

That's the word that comes to mind.

What looks like every bit of your food has been shredded and half digested. Wrappers strewn all over. And when you open the lid to the cooler, you almost begin to cry. Because it's empty. At least, that's what you think at first glance. And you're almost right. At the very bottom is a small package of lemon drops. The one food Silas brought with zero nutritional value. He had them, he said, to dole out on the hardest hikes in order to boost morale. And now here they are, the lone survivors of a devastating attack, the last of your store-bought food.

"Is it that bad?" asks Troy in a matter-of-fact voice.

Instead of speaking, you tip the cooler upside down and let the package tumble out. It hits the grass with an anticlimactic *thwap.*

"Whoa. I risked my life for lemon drops?" says Will.

The package stays in the grass until Will finally gets off his seat and picks it up. He looks at it briefly, then he rips open the package. For a moment, you're afraid he's going to chuck it into the woods out of frustration. But, instead, he starts walking around. He walks, and he solemnly hands out some candy.

Nobody protests or tells him to save it. Everyone knows not to argue. You could all be eaten by a bear any minute. So you take the candy. You take what is offered, and you put the hard, tart lemon drop directly in your mouth. It could be the last sugar you ever have. So it is both amazing and deeply sad at the same time. Your taste buds are overwhelmed by the citrus and sweetness, almost burning, but there's no way you're going to spit it out.

"Hey," says Fran suddenly.

There's an odd expression on her face. Your body is so exhausted from the panic that you can't bring yourself to look up the way you normally would. This time it takes the words she says to bring back the tingle that had only moments ago receded.

"Is that Silas's hat?"

TWENTY-TWO

For a moment, it's hard to distinguish the voices. Everyone is talking at once, and all at the same frantic, high-pitched register. But Fran's the one who actually wanders out of the clearing and snatches the cap from the low-hanging branch of a pine. She brings it back and drops it in front of you on the ground.

At that, everyone goes silent. Because it's definitely the hat. His hat. Red with white mesh and a faint halo of sweat around the back and sides. In the front, just above the bill, it clearly reads ADVENTURE CLUB. You all stand in a circle around the cap like you're praying over it. And maybe a few of you are.

"Okay," says Will. "Now we're getting somewhere."

You look at him, surprised by the hopeful half smile you find on his lips.

"Go on . . . ," says Fran.

"Well, we know now, right? It's a test! He left us a clue. He's making us work for it."

Will is in his arrogant stance, the one where he crosses his arms to make his biceps look bigger.

"I mean . . . I guess it's a possibility," says Diana.

"Of course it's a possibility!" says Will. "We just have to man up and complete these challenges. Then we can go home. It's like *Survivor!*"

"Man up?" says Troy. "Is that still a thing?"

Diana looks around at the remnants of food scattered in your vicinity. No one has even gathered the scraps. You've barely had time to take in how quickly everything was devastated. How one mistake left you with nothing. Now this.

"But why a hat?" she says. "If he was going to leave a clue."

"Why not?" says Will.

"Well, he barely took that thing off. It was practically a part of his head. Why not a note or something if this is all just a game? Why not a note that said, *Watch out for bears?*"

In the humidity, Diana's dark curls are frizzing out, and without a hair tie she looks like she's always lived in these woods. Like she might have a little gnome cabin on the other side of the lake.

"Yeah," says Fran. "And what's he doing anyway? Just, like, staying one step ahead of us and watching from the woods while animals rampage through our campsite? Somebody could have been killed. What kind of game is that?"

"It's not a game," says Troy.

He says it softly, but everyone hears him. It's possible he commands more attention now that he scared off the bear. He's still shirtless, and he stares down at the hat, his fist still clenched around your whisk. He looks even skinnier than he did before, like a day or two without proper meals is enough to send him to the brink of starvation.

"Troy, dude. You're the one who brought it up in the first place. We're troubled teens. These things are messed up, right? This is all part of it."

Troy sighs. You wait for him to get in Will's face again. But instead, he just reaches down and pulls something out of his pocket.

It takes a second for you to realize what it is. It's clear and a dark orange color. And when you finally see that it's a pill bottle, you feel your mouth fall open. Before anyone can ask a question, he says:

"I found it yesterday when we set up camp."

He hands it to Fran, and when she turns it over, you can see her name there in tiny letters. FRANCES DEAL.

"Frances?" says Will.

"Up yours," says Fran.

She holds the bottle upside down.

"It was already empty," says Troy. "I promise."

"Another clue," says Will.

You let this sink in a moment.

"But then where are my pills?" says Fran. "It would really help to have them right now."

Will starts pacing.

"How should I know? He moved them to another container. He threw them out!" says Will. "He's trying to get you to go cold turkey."

Will's voice has gone up a full register, which is a little eerie, actually. And his face is turning pink. You close your eyes.

"One day. One hour. One minute," you say.

Everyone turns toward you.

"Is that supposed to mean something?" says Troy. "Because it doesn't mean something."

You reach into your pocket and remove the piece of paper, still where you left it.

"I found it near the fire at our old site. I think he wrote it."

"Jesus!" says Will. "Does anyone else have something to share? What's wrong with you guys?!"

"I wasn't sure it was his at first," you say.

Fran stuffs her hands in the kangaroo pocket of her hoodie.

"It means something to me," she says. "It means he's losing it. That's what it means. Look, I know we probably shouldn't use words like *crazy*, right? Like, I've been called crazy, mostly by ex-girlfriends, but still. We're all alone out here, and our therapist is writing abstract poetry in the middle of the night. What else am I supposed to do with that?"

"It's not poetry," says Diana. "It's a mantra."

She reaches down slowly and scoops up the hat. Then she looks at the pill bottle. A story is forming, but for the moment, she's the only one who knows it.

"What's a mantra?" says Will.

"It's just a sentence you repeat," says Diana. "For meditation mostly. But people use them for a lot of reasons."

She clears her throat.

"I know about them," she says, "because my mom used one when she tried to get sober."

Hearing the word *mom* come from Diana stops you cold. You've only heard her mention her parents a handful of times, and if you ever asked a follow-up, she usually pretended not to hear it. All you know is that she doesn't talk about them and she lives with her grandmother. And you're not supposed to ask. She pauses a second now, maybe to make sure she's actually willing to keep going.

"My parents were . . . addicts. Functional addicts for a while, and then not so much. My dad left. My mom tried to quit."

She stops for a breath.

"The point is, she was at this meeting once when someone

told her she should have a mantra. Something to repeat to keep her centered and focused and everything. She came home and had me help her choose one. I think, in the end, she picked 'I am healing,' but there were some others she read me. And that was one of them. The thing you said about the days and hours and minutes. Like just a minute of sobriety was supposed to be a victory. Mom didn't like it. Even a minute was too much pressure for her."

"So you think it's, like, a sobriety thing for him?" says Fran.

"Maybe," says Diana. "Probably."

Troy is already muttering to himself. And when Fran asks him to speak up, he says:

"It's not a game."

Will is noticeably silent now. The whole Boundary Waters seems to have stopped moving, just to give you all a moment to come face-to-face with this.

"No," says Diana. "It's not."

She throws the hat to the ground.

"He's not coming back?" you say.

Diana shakes her head.

"And he's using all our pills," says Fran. She squeezes her empty bottle like an amulet.

"He can't help it," says Diana. "That's the thing. I mean, it's okay to be pissed at him. But, like, it's not even him. My mom . . ."

Her eyes are red, but there are no tears. You wonder if she's cried them all already. Maybe there aren't any left for this.

"My mom loved me. She still loves me. But she couldn't beat it. Some of her relapses were . . ."

You all wait for the next word. But it doesn't come. Instead, she switches gears and says:

"He might be more scared than we are."

"I don't think that's possible," says Troy.

But you all have a hunch that it *is* possible. Because you know what it's like to be so deep in a spiral that even the worst decisions seem reasonable. And you know what it's like to want something so badly, you'd do almost anything to get it. How suddenly the most ridiculous thing can seem like a good idea. Getting out of town. Taking a medical leave from school. Signing up for something called "Adventure Therapy."

"We have to find him," says Troy. "There's only so many pills he can take at once. If we find him, we'll get something back, and we'll make him take us to the drop."

"Yeah," says Will. "And we'll beat his ass."

"Well," says Fran. "If this is any indication, he's headed north. So maybe that means we're on the right track."

Suddenly, the cut on the back of your head pulses with pain, and you look around with blurred vision. You're not sure what you're searching for. A sign of Silas, running through the trees, spying on you from a distant hill. But you don't see him. All you see is trash. Trash and an empty cooler that used to be filled with food. Not long ago you had some and now you don't. You close your eyes. Somebody's stomach growls.

It's a loud noise, but you all pretend not to hear it.

TWENTY-THREE

You ordered the two-egg combo at Perkins with an entire pot of black coffee. Four days had passed since the last good day at the quarry, though you didn't know to call it that yet. At this point, you assumed there would be more good days. That somehow things would get back on track with Sean and all would eventually be well. The problem was: You couldn't quite see the path back. And in the meantime, you didn't know what to do with yourself. Sean and Diana were the only people you liked to spend time with, and now it was painful to be around both of them.

So you sat alone in your favorite booth. You weren't sure what to expect going to Perkins by yourself, but it was as if someone had put the whole place on a dimmer. The lightness you'd once felt just sitting in this booth, the one that faced the car dealership across the street, was gone, and you noticed things that you previously hadn't. The ancient cigarette burns in the upholstery from when you could still smoke in restaurants. The cobwebs in the hanging light above the table. And the regulars, who once seemed like a lively cast of extras from an indie film, now revealed their true nature as lonesome insomniacs scowling over a cup of coffee.

Geoff came to take your order, and he paused when you were done, like maybe he wanted to ask about Diana. But he didn't. Instead, he just looked at the empty spot across from you and muttered your order to himself before disappearing to put in the ticket. In the lobby, a middle-aged man in sweatpants played the claw machine, and no matter how many times his three-fingered robot tried to abduct a unicorn, it came up empty-handed. Still, the guy fed it a seemingly endless supply of crisp dollar bills.

You tried not to read into this, but suddenly everything felt like a painfully obvious symbol for the human condition. When you're depressed, the whole world is a tragedy. Especially if you're in a Perkins alone.

"Sta radis, bre?"

Before you could even turn your head to look, she sat down in the seat across from you and opened a menu, hiding her face like a spy. You thought you smelled alcohol, but there was a base layer of perfume that made it hard to tell.

"Whoa," you said. "Where did you come from?"

Diana ignored you, lazily turning the pages of a menu she had long ago memorized. She was wearing the same jean jacket she'd had on the night you met on the garage roof. Only in the time since, she'd covered it in buttons she found at thrift stores with Sean. Your favorite was a small green one that just read DANG! Ordinarily, it would make you laugh just looking at it, but this time, you were too distracted.

"Now," she said, "should I get the Pot Roast Stroganoff or the Hibachi Fried Chicken Skillet? So many choices . . ."

She slurred her speech just a little when she spoke, and there wasn't a hint of a smile on her lips. Instead, she just stared at you glassy-eyed and dropped the menu. In the time you'd been coming here, Diana had never ordered anything other than pancakes. Not a single time.

"How did you know I was here?" you said.

She clicked her tongue.

"Then again," she said. "The Double Seafood Catch does sound enticing. Because when I think fresh seafood, I think Perkins. Don't you?"

Diana folded her hands over the menu, and Geoff appeared as if summoned by a bell. You could have sworn you saw the beginnings of a smile on his face as he set your eggs down and paused next to Diana with his pad at the ready. She cracked her knuckles and said:

"Geoffrey, I shall have the pancakes this evening."

"You got it, boss," he said.

Then he was gone and so was the menu. And Diana looked at you like she was really trying to figure you out. You glanced down at your food, knowing you no longer had an appetite for it. You picked up your fork anyway.

"What does it mean?" you asked.

"What?" she said.

You poked at an egg, breaking the yoke and watching it erupt.

"The Serbian. When you sat down."

She wrinkled her nose.

"Did you learn absolutely nothing from me?"

Another pot of coffee was set next to yours, and Diana poured a cup, dumping in her usual packets of sweetener and watching them dissolve. You managed a bite of hash browns, and it felt like you had to tell your body to chew each time.

"Sorry," you said. "I guess I just don't remember that one."

She shuffled out of her jean jacket and adjusted a strap on her tank top.

"Sta radis, bre?" she said again, a bit more slowly. "It means 'what the hell are you doing?'"

"Oh."

"And I said it in Serbian because I didn't think you would answer me. At least not truthfully, and so what does it matter if I say it in a language you don't understand? I could whisper it or write it in the sand."

She took something out of her pocket, an airline bottle of clear liquor—vodka maybe—and poured it in her coffee. Nobody around you seemed to notice. Or if they did, they didn't say anything. Then she drank half the cup in one long gulp, and grimaced.

"I'm going to tell you something, Case, because I'm not sure if we're ever going to have a real conversation again after tonight."

You were already starting to sweat, and you had a lump in your throat. You wondered if she remembered saying something similar the night you met, but you couldn't bring yourself to ask, so you just nodded and held on to your own coffee mug without drinking it.

"I haven't known a lot of good people."

She looked outside when she said this, as if the car dealership was full of all the awful ones.

"It's bad luck, some of it. I get that. My family life was pretty rough when I was little. My parents were a mess. They couldn't take care of me, so I had to live with a grandma I barely knew. My mom said it was temporary, but then she never came back. And, along the way, I also kind of chose friends and boyfriends who weren't the best. Sometimes I think it was on purpose. Like, I had a homing device for assholes. I wish I could explain it to you, but the only thing I can say is that I felt terrible and part of me didn't want to stop feeling terrible. It was mine, that feeling. And it was . . ."

She stopped to burp and push her coffee away.

"Familiar."

You connected to this with your anxiety, the way it was better sometimes just to sink into it than to fight it. But all you said was:

"Okay."

"I thought that was the case with Sean. I thought I was choosing another jerk. He had all the signs with his dive-team swagger. But it turned out he was kind of a decent person. And so I stuck around. It's nice to be at your house, where things are quiet and your parents basically love you and let you live your own lives. It's nice to be there with him in that place. And it's nice to be there with you."

Your face was in flames, but her eyes were so unfocused that you wondered if she could even see you clearly. You set your fork down again.

"I wasn't expecting to find a friend too."

The word *friend* kind of destroyed you. It was the first time she'd said it about you, and it was so powerful to know she'd thought it too.

"And maybe it's weird that my best friend is my boyfriend's brother. I get that. It's kind of strange. And maybe it was always going to cause some problems. But this . . ."

She motioned around, at you and in the air.

"It's killing me, Case."

She took a second to rub her eyes, smearing her mascara.

"I can do breakups. I've done so many. For a while, I wondered if I even felt real emotions about them. But it turns out I do feel things, because *friend* breakups are heartbreaking! It's not like I'm tired of making out with you. It's like: I'm tired of *really knowing* you. So I'm going to ask you one time. Right now. Can you please just tell me what's happening? I asked Sean, and he said you were fine. That you just get kind of emo sometimes, and to give you some space. But I'm not good at pretending. And I'm tired of pretending I don't care about this."

Right as she finished talking, Geoff arrived with her pancakes. They were topped with a neon butter pat, and you watched as it oozed down the side of the top pancake.

"Sean said what?"

She seemed surprised at your tone. She didn't touch her pancakes. She didn't move.

"He . . . he just said, you know, with your anxiety or whatever you just kind of get in these moods where you hide from everyone. And that I shouldn't read too much into it. He said you'd snap out of it eventually, and everything would be fine."

"That I'd snap out of it?"

Your throat felt hot. And you barely saw what was in front of you. Your therapist had always told you to take some time. Think before you speak. Don't let your emotions do the talking. That's how the anxiety wins. But you were not feeling anxiety in that moment. You were finally feeling anger. So much pent-up anger. And you were not used to it coming over you so fast and so intensely. But you managed to take a single breath.

"I'm sorry," you said. "But it's just hard."

"What's hard? Being around *me*?"

You sighed.

"Yeah," you said.

You watched as she paused for a second and then laughed.

"Okay, well, I'm glad we cleared that up."

She picked up the coffee cup again and took another drink.

"I don't mean it that way," you said.

And you felt for a moment like you might actually split in two. That's how intense the rift was inside you. But you swallowed it, and it hurt in your chest.

"I liked our time together," you said. "When it was just me and you. And it's a little weird having Sean back. He's going through something. He's changing. It's a good thing, I guess. But it's just . . ."

"Different," she said.

"Yes," you said. "That."

She seemed calmer for a moment. The butter continued to move down the pancakes, and you couldn't help but remember all the times she ate them in front of you, cutting up the stack like a tic-tac-toe board and eating three squares per bite, talking you through some astounding Serbian swear word. You could probably count on two hands the number of times you came here, but already they felt so precious.

"You know what I think?" she said.

Your throat was so tight now, you weren't even sure you'd be able to speak. But somehow you managed a word.

"What?"

"I think you're really uncomfortable right now."

Food, you thought then. *You have food in front of you.* You stabbed one of the eggs on your plate and cut a bite, but you didn't bring it to your mouth.

"I'm going to ask you something," she said. "And I want you to tell me the truth. Can you please do that?"

You had a clear thought then, and though you tried to keep it at bay, it wouldn't stay down.

This is the last time you will ever sit in this booth, it said.

Because when she asked you about your feelings, you would not be able to lie. It would just be impossible.

"Yes," you said.

You tried to remember a few last details. The smell of the cheap coffee. The row of cars across the street, stretching into the darkness of the car lot. The bad nineties song that was playing. *I want something else . . . to get me through this semi-charmed kind of life . . .*

"There are messages on Sean's phone," she said.

"What?"

She didn't even blink at your question.

"From some girl named Echo. I know I shouldn't be looking at his phone, but he just leaves it out all the time and he's been acting so weird."

Your mind scrambled to turn around. This was not about you and your feelings. It was about Sean. You started talking before you were ready and your voice wobbled.

"Sean texts with a lot of people. You wouldn't believe what some of those dudes on the diving team say. I feel like they're all—"

She grabbed her coffee cup and spilled a little on the table.

"Here's what I think, Case," she said. "I think that Sean told you something. Something that you don't want to tell me. And

I think I know what it is. But I can't know for sure. And so, I'm sorry, but I need to ask you just to make sure I'm not crazy."

"Diana," you said. "Please."

"Listen," she said. "I still think Sean's a good person, and it's possible we can get past this. But I just need to know. Does the reason you're not talking to me have something to do with him?"

You shut your eyes then. Eye contact felt impossible. You willed yourself to disappear from the booth, but it didn't happen. Disassociation never seemed to kick in when you wanted it to.

"Case," she said.

"Yes," you said.

"Yes as in it has something to do with Sean?"

"Yes," you said again.

"Okay. And does it have to do with a girl?"

You didn't answer. But at this point you didn't really have to because you felt a tear sliding down your cheek. Which was the worst because you cried a lot when you were a kid and it was Sean himself who said it was okay. You were playing baseball at the park with the older kids, and you got hit in the thigh with a hardball. For a moment, you thought your leg was broken. The pain was unimaginable. His friends laughed at you—they were in junior high and basically sociopaths—but he made sure you were okay, and he said you could cry if you wanted. "It gets the hurt out," he said. Why was he so nice to you? And why was he so not-nice to the person in front of you?

"Does it have to do with the girl on his phone?"

You didn't think.

"Maybe one named Echo?"

You didn't speak.

But you thought of all his lies to Diana.

And you nodded.

Then you waited for the inevitable tears. Or the drunken anger. You waited for her to lash out and shoot the messenger. But when you turned back, you saw a completely blank expression. She wasn't going to have a meltdown. She didn't even seem shocked. It was simply a confirmation of everything she already knew. She had been waiting for this, and now it was here. But maybe that was a bigger disappointment, to have the world confirmed in its predictable ugliness.

Geoff walked past, and she reached out and touched him on the shoulder.

"Geoffrey," she said. "I'm sorry, my man. But I'm gonna need this short stack to go."

"No problem," he said, and grabbed the plate to box it up.

There was silence then for a moment or two. But eventually, she stood up and put her jacket back on. Her little bottle of booze fell out of her pocket and clanked against the table as she fumbled with the snaps. She left it there. Then she looked around at the restaurant, like maybe she'd just fully realized where she was. She pulled something out of her pocket, and you saw it was a bus transfer. You'd never even thought about how she got here. But of course; you had the car. She'd taken the bus all the way here just to see you.

"Diana," you said. "Please don't go right now."

"I'm not really in the mood to talk anymore tonight," she said.

Her voice was so quiet, you could barely hear it. You took out your car keys and set them on the table.

"I can give you a ride . . ."

Geoff brought out the box and handed it to Diana. She pulled her wallet out and threw a twenty down on the table. Then she was gone, walking off through the restaurant, the eyes of all the regulars on her. Even the claw machine guy interrupted his twentieth try for a prize and watched her go, flinching when the glass door rattled in its frame.

Geoff came by and just stared at the twenty. For some reason, he didn't even pick it up. So it just sat there, and it was still there when you walked out of the place for the last time.

TWENTY-FOUR

"Does anyone have a secret stash?" Diana asks now.

It's the first time anyone's spoken in minutes. After a rush of excitement for tracking down Silas, no one seems to be moving much. It feels like to get up and start going would be to admit what you all now know: There is no game. This is not part of the therapy. It's not a zany series of obstacles to overcome on a reality show. There is only the five of you, the indifferent wilderness, and your brains.

"Food?" says Troy.

"Pills," she says.

Will gets up and starts pacing again.

"Are you kidding me?!" he says. "Pills? We need clean water. We need sustenance, bro. We need to find Silas. Or we're dead!"

"That's true," says Troy calmly. "But for some of us, without our meds, we might not be able to do those things."

"Yo!" says Fran. "My mom forgot to call in a refill once, and after forty-eight hours I was getting the brain zaps."

You can remember something similar from the times you tried to wean yourself off your main script. Those little tingling jolts that went off like firecrackers with no discernible pattern. You haven't gone through benzo withdrawal, but it's not supposed to be fun.

"So then . . . ," says Diana. "About that stash."

Of course.

That's the answer.

Of course some people have a pill or two. If you're the kind of person who needs sedatives to make it through the day, you're also the kind of person to hide them places. In your pocket. In your bag. The cuff of a pant leg or a Pez dispenser or a hollowed-out Bible. You yourself used to keep one inside a mechanical pencil for emergencies at school.

Everyone has suddenly found something incredibly interesting to look at around the campsite. Eventually, you glance up and find Diana staring right at you. And you know the look. It's the same pleading one she gave you that night in the hallway with the meteorite. And you don't have the strength to ignore it again.

"Oh dammit," you say.

Then, slowly, you untie your wet hiking boot and take off one of the merino wool hiking socks your mom got to regulate your foot temperature. Inside this expensive REI sock is a small sandwich bag with a single tiny pink pill inside. You hold up the bag for all to see, then toss it in front of you. Seeing it leave your hand makes your breath catch, but you don't pick it up again. You let it go.

There is quiet after this. Then, gradually, you see a few hands digging in pockets, going up sleeves, inside socks. People open hip packs and zippered wallets. And, little by little, a rainbow of pills come out. Orange Klonopin. Blue one-milligram Xanax. The white five-sided .5 that reminds you of D&D dice. Fran even has a green three-milligram terminator, able to calm even the peskiest neurotransmitters. In the end, there's five total and they all sit in a small pile on top of your plastic bag.

"We're not that different from him," says Diana.

You look up from the pills, along with the others.

"Seriously?!" says Fran.

"You guys are staring at these like they're the last pills on earth. Tell me you don't wish you had the whole stash to yourself."

"Yeah, but he was in charge of us!" says Troy.

"He was human," says Diana. "Humans are the worst."

You can tell Fran is getting angry at this. You can see her pupils dilating. But before she can say anything, Troy breaks in.

"Where are yours, Will?"

Will sits cross-legged, looking blankly at the pills.

"Everybody put something in, Troy. Relax," says Fran.

"Will didn't," says Troy. "I watched. And Will didn't add a thing."

Troy doesn't get up this time, but he looks Will in the eye.

"You can't pretend you're not part of this anymore," he says. "You can insult us. But it's not going to save you. You're not special. You're here just like us. And you need to pony up!"

"Relax, Troy," says Fran again. "We have an okay stash here."

"I'm not going to relax!" says Troy. "We're in deep shit right now. Why should he get a private supply when the rest of us are sharing?"

Will doesn't look angry for once. And there's no trace of that cocky smirk you've come to know.

"He's right," Will says after a few seconds. "I didn't put anything in the pile."

"See!" Troy says. "He admits it! I told you!"

"What the hell, Will?" says Fran.

He crosses his arms. When he speaks next, his voice is almost monotone.

"I didn't put anything in. That's true. But it's not because I'm hoarding."

"Then why?" asks Fran. "Why didn't you add anything?"

He moves a lock of black hair out of his face.

"Because I'm not on any medication."

"Liar!" says Troy. "You're a liar."

Will shakes his head.

"It's true," he says.

Troy just stares at him.

"Huh," says Fran. "Must be nice. Look at you out here, just mainlining reality."

"It's not nice," says Will.

And this quiets everyone for a second. There's an odd look on his face, one you haven't really seen from him yet. It's a kind of pained half smile that doesn't seem directed at any of you.

"I probably should be on something," he says finally. "Okay? But I'm not."

"Why?" says Troy.

Will chews his bottom lip.

"Too scared," he says.

More quiet. But it doesn't take long for curiosity to rear its head.

"Of what?" asks Diana. "Don't take this the wrong way, but you don't strike me as the scared type."

"Not usually," he says. "But this is different."

No one interrupts him, so he just keeps talking.

"I was scared to tell my dad. And my coach. Once I told

them, I knew they wouldn't see me the same way again. And it would be real. This defect."

"It's not a defect," says Troy.

"Oh really?" says Will. "Then what do you call collapsing on the court at State, and forfeiting the match I spent all year training for? What do you call crying in the fetal position for a week afterward with my whole body shaking? What part of that am I supposed to be okay with?"

Tears are running down his face, and you're not sure if you should look at him.

"I don't want to feel good about it! I don't want a goddamn therapy dog and a bag of pills. I don't want it. I just want to kick Eric Tulliver's ass and get a big trophy and a scholarship and free sneakers and a private plane to take me to tournaments. I don't want to be like you guys, and I don't want to die in the woods. I can deadlift three-hundred pounds!"

He gets up and grabs the empty cooler then and throws it at a tree, and when he sits down again, he's staring at the ground. The cooler is broken, the handle dislocated. It was a really hard throw. Will sobs into his palms. Time passes; you don't know how much. But finally he seems to calm.

"I need help," he says with a sniffle.

The sun is getting warmer, and it's tempering the chill in the air.

"And this was supposed to be the help. This trip!" he says. "Leave it to my dad to send me on a stupid-ass nature trip instead of just sending me to a doctor."

He starts laughing, or maybe laughing and crying at the same time. You haven't really seen him do either very much, so it's hard to tell.

"We'll make it," says Troy.

And at first you have to make sure you heard him correctly. But he gets up and walks over to sit next to Will. You almost gasp when he puts an arm around him. But Will doesn't shrug it off, and there it stays, around his broad shoulders.

"We'll find Silas. Or we'll find the drop point somehow. And when we're there, and we finally head home, you can get some real help. Who cares about your dad and your coach. You can do what you need to do and figure it out."

Will rubs his temples.

"I don't want a dog," he says. "I'm allergic."

"That's your loss," says Troy. "Because Turbo is fucking awe-some. But you don't need a dog to feel better."

Will sighs. Then, when it seems like maybe their interaction is over, Diana reaches down for the pills.

"This is actually perfect," she says.

And you watch as she scoops them up gingerly, like she's han-dling the delicate eggs of a rare animal. You watch as she takes them all in her hand and dumps them carefully into your sandwich bag. You watch as she makes sure that the bag is rolled up and fastened tightly.

"I'm not on anything either," she says.

Everyone stares at her, a few mouths hanging open.

"I'm kind of new to all this," she says. "And my family doesn't have a great history with pills, so . . ."

"Then where did all these come from?" asks Troy, looking at the bag.

Fran raises her hand. "Three of them are mine."

"My god, Fran!" says Troy. "Where were you hiding them?!"

"I'd rather not say," says Fran.

Diana gets up and walks over to Will, and you watch her hold the bag out in front of him.

"You're not on any meds, and you don't have a family history of addiction, right?" she asks.

Will gives the slightest nod.

"Perfect. You can be the pharmacy."

Will just blinks at the bag.

"If you need a pill, talk to Will," says Diana. "Emergencies only."

She claps him on the back.

Will looks baffled. But eventually, he takes the bag and puts it in his pocket, and each one of you, including Diana herself, watches it disappear, wondering if you'll ever see it again. Once it's gone, you're left back where you started, in a trashed campsite surrounded by woods and lakes with very few prospects for survival. You all look around at the wrappers glinting in the sun, the evidence that it all really happened.

"I don't want to be the one to ask," you say. "But you said we'd make it to the drop point, Troy. How exactly are we going to stay alive until we get there?"

Troy takes his arm off Will and stands up. He picks up your whisk and slices it through the air. Then he looks out into the woods, and in the same tone of voice he used to present the lighter, he says:

"I know about plants."

TWENTY-FIVE

Mushrooms. Berries. Burdock. Stinging nettle. Wild ramps. Troy rattles off names like an incantation. He sounds like a forager from simpler times. But, in reality, he only knows these because there's a guy on YouTube called the "Anarchist Vagabond" who makes videos about postapocalyptic survival. The videos, Troy says, are calming to him because after he watches them, he feels like he could live in the midst of climate disaster. And while most of them are about constructing water tanks or building a bunker, one component of the videos is foraging for edible plants.

"But have *you* ever actually identified these things in the wild?" Fran asks.

"That would be a no," Troy says. "But I've watched the Anarchist Vagabond do it, like, a hundred times. He's ridiculous at it!"

"Yeah, but the Anarchist Vagabond is not here," says Fran. "He's probably sipping kombucha in the comfort of his own home right now."

"The Anarchist Vagabond does not have a home," says Troy. "He is, in fact, a vagabond."

An hour later you're finally back on the water, paddling near the shore, looking for a trailhead that will keep you moving north, so you don't need to walk through the tall brush. Diana is in your boat this time, seated behind you. Fran and Troy and Will are piled together in the other boat to your left.

The plan is this: Go as far as you can on the water. Then stop to forage when you find a trail. Within minutes, however, everyone is dizzy with hunger, and your canoes are barely moving. Still, you make your muscles do what they need to do, working hard to slice a path through the frigid blue water.

Diana's paddle keeps getting stuck to the lily pads that cover this lake like a patchy carpet. When that happens, you get to stop for a moment and watch the spruce trees shimmer like a mirage in your lightheaded vision. If you look up, the sun sends spots dancing in your eyes, so you try to stare straight ahead. The pain in your head is back, but only intermittently, and it's hard to tell if it's from the cut or just hunger pangs.

In the boat next to you, Troy is defending his anarchist hero as both Fran and Will start lobbing skeptical attacks on his character. You turn and watch Diana peel a floating leaf off the blade of her paddle and chuck it across the lake like a Frisbee. You haven't had any one-on-one time since your moment in the tent after the rain, and you were surprised when she asked if she could paddle with you. But now that she's here, she's not saying much, and you get the feeling like maybe she's waiting on you to break this silence that's been growing between you.

The other boat is far enough away that you could probably have a real conversation, but everything you want to say is something you shouldn't. Eventually, it comes to you. Something you're surprised you haven't asked yet.

"Hey," you say. "Why did you come on this trip?"

She sinks the wooden blade back in the water and pulls it through with a small exhale.

"You know, I'm asking myself the same question right about now," she says with a glazed look in her eye. You watch her face for a moment, waiting for it to change, but she doesn't seem to be paying attention to you.

"I'm serious," you say. "Why did you sign up for this? How did you find out about it? You haven't told me."

You both paddle for a moment. Closer now, Troy is talking about composting worms in reverent tones, waxing poetic about something called a "red wiggler." This prompts a dirty joke from Will that you can't fully hear.

"I mean, when you think about it," you say, "it's pretty coincidental that we both ended up on the same trip. There have to be a few of these. I think my parents were looking at, like, four different options. And it's kind of a weird thing to do, right? I mean, it's not everyone's idea of therapy."

You can feel yourself talking too much. And you know if you don't stop soon, you're going to say something stupid. But Diana saves you from yourself by letting you know you already have.

"Case," she says. "Are you a total idiot?"

This is not what you were expecting, so it takes you a minute to reply.

"Um. Maybe?"

She stops paddling again, and you turn around, thinking you'll see her tangled in aquatic plants. But you don't. She's just looking at you. Her hair's up in a ponytail, so you can see her face clearly. Her eyes are narrowed, and there's the beginning of a sunburn on her nose and forehead.

"It wasn't a coincidence."

Your neck is straining, but you don't turn around again.

"When you weren't calling me back," she adds, "I talked to your mom one night to see how you were doing. She told me about this trip, and that you had agreed to go."

"You talked to my mom?" you say.

"I thought maybe she told you," says Diana.

Now it's your time to turn red, the heat rushing to your face.

"She didn't," you say.

There are blisters on your hands already, but you tighten your hold on the oar grip.

"So, that means . . ."

"I came because of you."

She says it quietly, but you almost drop your paddle in that moment. Because Diana is exactly right. You are an idiot. It never once occurred to you that this might be the reason. From up ahead, Fran is staring at the two of you. The sun is so bright, but when you close your eyes, Troy starts yelling about something. You open your eyes again, shielding them with your hand, and you see him standing up in the wobbly canoe and pointing.

"Trail! Trail!"

"You're tipping the boat!" says Fran. "Sit down, man!"

Troy turns back to you and motions with his paddle.

"That's a trail!" he screams.

"Troy!" shouts Will. "Down! Now! Or I will end you!"

He pulls Troy back down by his pants. You and Diana start paddling again, inching toward what seems to be a trailhead. It's a small rocky beach, with a worn path beneath some overhanging brush.

"Then all of this is my fault," you say.

No response. Just the sound of a submerging paddle.

"In a way, I guess," she says.

It's unclear how serious she is being. But hunger is scattering your thoughts, so all you can do is nod your pounding head.

"I'm serious," you say. "I think . . ."

"How do we stop this?" Diana says.

"Well, I mean if we can find Silas that would be key . . . ," you say.

"No," she says. "I mean, how do we stop the boat. We're right by the shore."

A rocky shore. In your lack of attention, you're drifting toward a rock. And though you stick a paddle deep in the lake, your canoe immediately slams into the blue-gray outcropping and you jerk to a halt.

At first glance, nothing seems to be broken, but you immediately hop out and soak your boots, examining the front of the canoe. Diana gets out more calmly. And you don't say anything to each other as you both clamber up some wet rocks to the shore. You're still lost in your thoughts as Troy volunteers you to go on the first foraging mission with him and Fran.

"We have two days to make it to the drop," says Will. "So you can't take too much time. Bring us some calories. Don't poison us. Is that possible?"

Troy salutes him.

Will and Diana are going to stay back and make a fire so you can cook whatever you find. You look at Diana once more.

"If I hadn't told you at Perkins that night," you say. "If I'd been a better brother . . ."

Diana looks at you intently.

"Not now," she says. "Go. Forage."

Moments later, you are tramping aimlessly out into the woods, and Troy is describing plants. "So ramps are gonna have two leaves and a stem with a reddish hue . . ."

But you can barely hear him.

You're thinking of Sean, and the way he used to tease you about all the things you were oblivious to. *How did you get this far in life?* That was his favorite refrain. *Case! Seriously. How did you get this far in life without seeing that Dad hates his job? How did you get this far in life without knowing Aunt Gretchen is an alcoholic? How did you get this far in life without noticing that your social studies teacher is so hot?*

How many other things have you failed to notice? How many people have you misread? And how much is the anxiety to blame, the way it cloisters you in your own brain, chanting the same daily refrains?

"I've never been this hungry," says Fran. "It hasn't even been a full day, but goddamn, dude, I would punch a baby lamb for some veal right now."

Troy wipes his nose with his arm.

"I don't think there are any lambs in the North Woods," he says.

He walks over and kicks a fallen branch with his boot, checking to see if there's anything growing under it. You remember what you're supposed to be doing and immediately point to a plant with small purple blooms.

"Can we eat those?" you ask.

"That's bittersweet nightshade," says Troy calmly. "It will legit kill you."

"Oh."

And so you plod on, taking up the back of the patrol. An hour passes somehow. The hunger is an actual ache in your body at this point, clenching your abdominals. Fran manages to find some dandelions, which are on the edible list. And Troy takes some cattail shoots that are supposed to taste like cucumbers when peeled. But all of it only fills a single shirt-basket. It's a pathetic harvest, and as you stagger back the way you came, you can already imagine the reaction from the hungry troops.

No one speaks when you return and dump it all in the single cooking pan you have. And since the pan has been over the fire, it all starts to sizzle, giving off an awful smoke and a smell you can only describe as burnt lawn. It cooks down to about a handful of food apiece, which is chewy and tasteless and dirty. And when it's gone, everyone looks a little like they're about to cry. Even Troy, who seemed so pro-anarchy-foraging in the canoe. Finally, after the shock wears off and Diana starts packing up the cooking utensils, Will stands and looks at all of you.

"Guys," he says. "We're going to have to kill something."

TWENTY-SIX

"Don't. Let. This. Die."

Even through two closed doors, those words made it to your ears.

Sean and Diana were fighting. It had been almost an hour. They were trying to keep their voices down, but every once in a while, a phrase or two would break through. You knew you shouldn't be listening, but you also didn't know where else to be. Your parents were downstairs in the only common space, watching a reality show called *Naked and Afraid*, which sounded too much like your life story to be enjoyable. And Sean needed the car to go to some kind of weekly bike rally he'd joined called Critical Mass.

From what you could tell, it was a group of activists who rode through city streets to lobby for cyclists' rights. And in the absence of diving, Sean had thrown himself into it with his usual zeal. Suddenly, he was bathing less and chastising your parents about how they imagined "public space."

"Do you know what he does there?" you'd asked your dad earlier.

He was eating a fried-egg sandwich, only half paying attention to you.

"Bikes around with the other socialists?" he said.

Your mom shook her head.

"I just think it's good he's making new friends," she said.

She reached out and gave your side a squeeze. Neither of them seemed aware of the argument currently going on in their house. Or maybe they were just giving Sean his space, confident he would figure things out the way he always did.

"You okay, sweetie?" asked your mom.

When you glanced back at her, she was staring at your face. You weren't sure what it looked like, but it couldn't have been good. Each word you heard from upstairs felt like a jab to the ribs. And the same phrase played in your head over and over.

Things weren't supposed to be like this.

For the few weeks after you spilled Sean's secret at Perkins, things had somehow not imploded. Sean and Diana were still talking. And they even went out a few times—to a movie and on a nighttime bike ride with Sean's new fixed gear, which he was constantly modifying in the garage—and when they came back to the house, they usually sat close on the couch, joking and occasionally even kissing, until Diana inevitably stayed the night and sneaked out the window in the morning like old times. All of this helped to quell the crushing guilt you'd been feeling, but you also noticed that they rarely made time for you, or noticed you much at all.

Until one night when your parents were out.

Sean and Diana decided to make pot brownies, and around nine o'clock, they came upstairs to offer you a half. You'd never liked drugs that much (at least the ones you weren't prescribed). They affected your anxiety in unpredictable ways, and once, after a few hits from a joint, you ate a raw bratwurst from the fridge and fell asleep in the downstairs shower. But, this time, you were so relieved that you hadn't ruined your brother's life after all that you choked down the little chocolate square against your best instincts.

"It's a super mellow strain," said Sean. "Great cannabinoid profile."

You didn't know what he was talking about. Some guys he'd met from his biking collective were connoisseurs to say the least, and you had a hunch they'd been educating him. But he was right about the mellow part. That small cube glued you to the couch for a few hours, where you alternately talked to a stuffed animal and sang old songs from summer camp until eventually you felt Diana sit down next to you. She had been in a buoyant mood all night, talking more than usual, and laughing hysterically at Sean's impression of a confused foal being born. But now she seemed subdued. Drained of something.

"Be honest," she whispered. "Do you think I'm weak?"

These words made it through the haze and swirled around in your brain. For how long, you didn't know.

"No," you said. "Of course not."

Your high was fading, but the words still vibrated in your chest. Diana reached out and grabbed the stuffed animal you were holding. It was a pink octopus you'd won at a fall carnival when you were six. It was frayed and dirty, but you still kept it in your room because it was the only thing you'd ever won. Sean had tried first to knock over the milk bottles, but he had failed. Then a lucky shot from your right hand had sent them scattering.

"I've been thinking," she said.

She hung the octopus upside down by its tentacles and spiraled it around.

"You can try all you want, you know? You can do everything in your power. You can talk to yourself about all the rational reasons . . ."

She seemed lost in her head for a moment. Then she blinked and turned directly to you.

"But you can't help who you love."

You couldn't look into her pink eyes when she said this, so instead you stared into the octopus's googly ones. You finally managed a glance and tried not to notice how pretty she looked.

"I agree," you said.

She touched your hand and smiled, and you felt that same charge that went through you on the garage so many months ago. She kept it there longer than you thought she would. Maybe it was the high. But then she seemed to notice and got up to get another brownie. While she was gone, Sean wandered over and sat down across from you on an overstuffed leather chair. His freckles were prominent from all the riding he was doing, and he wore a T-shirt that read CYCOPATH. He looked at you, holding on to your stuffed animal, and burst out laughing.

"What?" you said.

"That thing is ragged, dude," he said.

You looked down at it with fresh eyes and saw just how rough it really was. One of its legs was hanging by a knotted thread, and there was a small rip under its left eye that looked like a prison tattoo.

"You're hurting Ringo's feelings," you said.

"Ringo looks like he made some bad choices in life," said Sean.

You could hear Diana in the kitchen, clattering the silverware, looking for a knife to cut the brownies. A drawer squeaked open.

"Case, please tell me it wasn't you," he said.

Instantly, your whole body stiffened, and you found you couldn't even blink.

"What wasn't me?" you said with a mouth dry as an old sponge.

"Who told her."

His face was as serious as you'd ever seen it. His brow low, and his mouth a straight line. You couldn't remember if you had ever outright lied to Sean. About anything. Even the Pokémon card you ripped that he never would have known about—you even told him about that, crying out to him in the middle of the night, sick with guilt.

"I . . ."

Diana yanked opened the dishwasher, humming some imperceptible tune.

"Ugh!" Sean said, sucking in a breath. "Forget I said that! I just don't know how she . . ."

In the kitchen Diana dropped the knife and started laughing.

"I was so careful," he said.

You nodded.

"Guys!" said Diana. "You *have* to come see this!"

Without sharing a look, you both got up and padded over the carpet onto the cold tile floor of the kitchen. You couldn't look at Sean, so you stared at the scene before you: Diana laughing, her mouth stuffed full of brownie, pointing down. It took you a second to realize what was funny until you saw the knife. When she'd dropped it, it had fallen inches from her bare right foot, and stuck straight up out of the tile like something from a horror movie.

"Shit, Diana," said Sean, snapping out of his stoned trance. "You could have been really hurt."

He reached down and yanked the knife out of the tile like a sword from the stone. Diana's face changed then, the goofy smile disappearing. She looked at the knife in his hand.

"Since when do you care if I'm hurt?" she said.

Then she walked out of the room, and you heard her going up the stairs and shutting the door to Sean's room. This left Sean holding a butcher knife in the middle of the kitchen. Slowly, he turned to you. For a moment, you wanted him to stab you. Just in the arm. Nowhere fatal. But enough to make things even. Instead, he wandered over to the sink and let the knife clatter in the basin. Then he walked out, shouting her name.

Something seemed to change after that night. Diana still came over sometimes, but the mood was different. You wouldn't see her for days; then you'd find her sitting in the living room after everyone else had gone to bed, reading one of your mom's books from nursing school. When you entered the room, she might look up just to give you a fact or two. ("Did you know that every second you produce twenty-five million new cells? Like, who even are you right now, Case?") And if Sean came down to try to engage her, she often couldn't be bothered.

One night, desperate and guilty, and looking for any kind of lifeline, you asked if she wanted to go to Perkins. For a second, the suggestion seemed to throw some life in her eyes. But it wasn't long before they dimmed again, and she shook her head.

"I'm going to miss it here," she said. "It's so . . ."

"What?" you said.

"Even," she said, and smoothed a hand in front of her.

"Is that the only thing you're going to miss?" you asked.

She looked up at you then, and for a moment she seemed to

see you differently. She looked intently at your face, studying you. You thought about sitting down next to her on the couch, but you were sober this time, and the distance seemed untraversable. Like she was already gone.

She stood up and put a hand on your cheek. Then she smiled slightly and walked out of the room.

"Good night, Case," she said.

It was the very next night that she went upstairs and said something you couldn't hear, and Sean started crying. You were standing in the hallway when it started, so you heard a few other things beyond his plea not to let things die. He promised to be better. He said she was the only person he had ever loved. And he quoted something from Ram Dass, which caused Diana to start laughing. It got too painful to hear at that point, so you left to go sit with your parents. But when you came back up, you watched her storm out of the room. She walked past you without even acknowledging you. Then you turned and saw Sean standing in the doorway sobbing. He looked devastated, and the full depth of your betrayal made you nauseous.

Had Diana already known about the girl? Maybe. But the way you were acting around her after Sean told you might have been a part of how she figured it out. Could you have convinced her that Sean was innocent? Possibly. But was there also a part of you that wanted them to break up? If this was ever true, it's not what you wanted now.

As Diana disappeared from view, and you heard her foot-falls on the staircase, you watched Sean again. He held absolutely still for ten seconds or so, waiting perhaps to see if she would come back. And then, when it was clear that that wasn't going to happen, he turned around and looked at his bedroom door, covered in his mantras and quotes—all the instructions for his moral change. He choked on a sob and then started attacking them like an animal.

He tore them off his door, his face bright red. You watched as the scraps drifted to the ground like flurries, settling on the dusty wood floor. Then you watched him sit down among the shards of his former wisdom and slump to the ground. After a moment or two, he went back into his room and grabbed the keys to the Toyota and sprinted down the stairs.

You finally came back to yourself then.

You said his name. You yelled it.

But he was already gone.

TWENTY-SEVEN

"I'm not killing anything that's not actively trying to eat me," says Troy.

He's sitting on the ground right by you, and his breath smells like burnt dandelions. Diana takes a sip from her water bottle, but like most of yours, it's running low and you haven't tried boiling any water yet. At least you've gotten a little better at building fires. Will found some driftwood near the shore and combined it with a few downed branches from the storm to get something more consistent going for cooking. There's a cold wind blowing again, so it's good to have something bigger. Keeping warm almost makes up for the lack of nourishing food.

You've been staring up at the trees in a famished daze for what feels like a small eternity. The site you're on has the tallest pines you've ever seen in your life, and they all seem to bend around you like a cage that sways and creaks in the breeze. The canopy lets in some sky here and there, but it's only when you peer out over the lake that you can see just how vast the horizon is. Normally you'd find the sky imprinted on the lake as well, but the wind is rippling the water.

"Killing is kind of against my belief system," adds Troy.

You can't tell how much time has passed since he last spoke.

"And what's that?" says Fran.

"I believe in the Four Noble Truths," he says. "Specifically: ethical conduct. I also think killing animals is, like, super messed up."

"Have fun eating grass, bro," says Will, sharpening a stick on the side of a rock. "You ain't gonna find any tofu dogs out here."

Troy rolls his eyes.

"That's Buddhism, right?" says Fran. "What does the Buddha say about starving to death and dying in a canoe?"

"Leave him alone," says Diana, shutting the argument down.

She plucks some wild grass and tosses it into the fire. Then she motions to the churning water.

"The way I see it, we have two options for some protein here. The lake or the land. Only we don't have a fishing pole or a gun, so we're going to have to . . ."

"Eat someone," says Fran.

She picks a cattail shoot out of her teeth.

"That is actually against *my* belief system," says Will.

"Improvise," says Diana. "I was going to say improvise."

"Or that," Fran says.

"We can make some kind of fishing pole, right?" you say. "I mean, how hard can it be? It's just a stick, some string, and a hook."

"Yes, Case!" says Will. "Hell yes. That's what I'm talking about, man. You're finally growing a little backbone."

He gets up and cracks his knuckles. You're ashamed to admit that you're encouraged by his masculine accolade, excepting the word *little*. So you stand as well and start circumnavigating the site, looking for a thin branch to use, but again, your energy is so low you can barely pick up your feet without getting lightheaded.

"I mean, I might eat something if you guys catch it," says Troy. "I just don't personally kill things."

"You kill the mood," says Will. "Is that a Noble Truth?"

You reach down and pick up a long stick that looks perfect, but when you try to bend it, it snaps like chalk in your hands.

"We need to make progress toward the drop," says Diana. "We shouldn't spend much longer here without covering some miles. If you could put a rod together, we can try fishing from the boats. Then we can hunt at our next stop."

You start searching for sticks again and instead decide to snap a small branch off a nearby jack pine. Will clocks what you're doing and holds a finger in the air. Then he somehow finds the energy to sprint over to his pack. He digs around, eventually producing a single travel dispenser of cinnamon-flavored dental floss.

"Line," he says.

You point to him.

"We just need a hook," you say.

This activates Troy, who immediately gets up and hunts around. You watch him as he eventually finds what he's looking for: his weapon of choice. The collapsible whisk. He looks down at it and sighs. It's his Excalibur, and he's not quite prepared for what he's about to do.

"Troy, no," you say.

But he's already getting to work, yanking one of the curved tines out of its slot, until what he's holding is a thin metal wire, which he slowly curves into something approximating a fishhook. When he's done, he hands it over to you to complete the holy trinity of homemade fishing supplies, knotting it in the cinnamon floss.

"What you imagine, you create," he says. "Gautama Buddha."

"That was almost cool," says Will. "But you just ruined it with the quote."

Troy flips him off, and you're about to ask him what the Buddha thinks of lewd gestures when Fran materializes behind you and taps your shoulder.

"Hold on a second," she says. "What the hell is that?"

"It's a hook," says Troy. "I made it out of the whisk. Didn't you . . ."

"No," says Fran. "*That.*"

You whip around, expecting another bear. Maybe a moose this time. Your heart is already pulsing through your chest. But Fran is not looking into the woods. She's looking up.

"What?" says Will. "Where?"

He gazes up, and blinks into a pocket of sky. You do too. The pines block most of it, so it's hard to see anything at first. But, eventually, sections of blue come into focus through the branches until you can piece together a patchwork of what's above, and just barely visible coming up from somewhere in the distance is a ribbon of light gray smoke. The wind is carrying it toward you, and it zags under a whisper of cirrus clouds.

"Wildfire?" asks Diana.

"Not big enough, I don't think," says Troy.

He stands on a rock on his tiptoes and squints.

"Campfire?" you say.

You look at the smoke from your own fire. So does everyone else. It's the same color, more or less. And about the same amount.

"Maybe," says Diana.

"Which means . . . ," says Troy.

"Someone else is out here?" says Will.

He shields his eyes with his hand.

"And not too far away," you say.

"Silas," says Fran.

And then you all get quiet.

When you look back at Fran, she's no longer staring at the sky. She has her compass out, and she's pointing it toward the column of smoke.

"There's only one problem," she says.

Diana walks up and stands close to her, leaning in for a look.

"It's not true north," she says.

TWENTY-EIGHT

The argument is not a long one. Everyone is too tired and too hungry for a showdown. But the agreed-upon facts are these: Another human is likely nearby (there's a possibility, adds Troy, of a lightning strike, but it's a small one). And if it is indeed a person, it might well be your defector in chief. Then again, it might not be. Either way, you decide, it's going to help to be in contact with another person. They might have food. Or a way to contact help. Or . . . food.

But it's also, undeniably, a gamble. Because if you can't find this person, you lose time. And if it's someone who won't help you, you lose time. Also, and this quickly takes over the conversation, you don't quite know what you're going to do if it actually is Silas.

"I think pouring honey on his ass and leaving him on an ant hill would be fair," says Will.

"We don't have any honey," says Fran. "And if we did, I would not pour it on an ass. I would eat it in front of all of you."

"Maybe just the ants thing, then," says Will.

You can tell Diana has thoughts about Silas, but she doesn't respond.

Maybe it's because you are portaging on an empty stomach again, heading toward the smoke, with boats on your shoulders and pain in too many places to count. In your pack is the makeshift fishing rod, and you hope to whatever god Troy believes in that it works, because any nutrients you gained from that hellish foraged stir-fry have already been burned. You remember your dad eating leafy greens a few years ago to *lose* weight, which means there probably weren't a lot of calories in those bitter tendrils to begin with.

Another problem, and one you're hesitant to admit to the group, is that the pain from the back of your head, which was intermittent at first, has become more persistent. At first you thought it was psychological. You've had a side order of tension headaches with your anxiety for as long as you can remember. But usually that's around your temples and forehead. This pain is definitely close to the place where you got cut by that rock before the storm. And when you reach back to run your fingers over the affected area, the wound is tender to the touch.

The portage is slow with frequent stops and dramatic moans along the way, and when you finally make it to the next lake, it's so big, you can't see the other side of it. Also, in the time you've been walking, the day has slowly grown overcast, and the clouds feel lower to the water. The lingering smoke, which is a bit to the east, is all but gone. Only a wisp remains, which might mean its maker is on the move. When you all shrug off your boats, balancing them on the rocky shore, everyone sits down to gather themselves for a moment. Diana walks off into the bushes to pee. Fran lies down and splays herself across the rocks.

"I'm too hungry to move," she says. "Are there any lemon drops left?"

Will shakes his head.

"Nah," he says. "Just the bag, which might be lemon-flavored if you eat it."

"I'll consider it," she says.

There's a prolonged rustle from nearby.

"Hold on. I've got something!" says Diana.

Fran sits right up, craning her pink head in the direction of the voice. Her expectant smile quickly fades when she sees what her friend is holding. It's a large grasshopper, lime green with electric yellow legs and bulbous compound eyes. It has wings and the largest antennae you've ever seen. It is eerily still in Diana's pincer grip, but it appears to be looking at all of you at the same time.

"I saw someone eat one on a reality show," says Diana, eyeing it. "They said it was like a cross between a potato chip and a grape, texture-wise. Good source of protein, though. He's all yours if you want him."

Fran's face is a mask of horror.

"Him?"

"I'm assuming it's a dude 'cause I caught him resting on a shrub, doing nothing."

Fran's face remains a mask of horror.

"I've never let a man near my mouth," she says. "And I'm not about to start with him."

"I'll take it," you say.

You're not sure why you say this. Possibly it's the head wound. Or it could be the slowly dawning fact that you're holding a fishing rod made from a broken stick and you've barely ever fished in your life. It seems very possible, suddenly, that insects are your best bet at survival.

"I think you're supposed to cook them first," says Troy. "The Anarchist Vagabond . . ."

You take the grasshopper and stuff it in your mouth.

You bite. It wiggles for a moment, but then it crunches and squirts and you have to close your eyes and do everything in your power to keep from gagging. It tastes incredibly bland and terrible at the same time, like a sour blueberry filled with guts, and you almost have it down when a barbed leg gets stuck in your throat. It takes most of what's left of your water bottle to wash it down. By that point, the rest of the group is watching in silence.

"I was actually joking," says Diana. "I didn't think . . ."

"You ate a grasshopper," says Will, a rare hint of reverence in his voice. "You ate that thing *raw*."

If you thought about it at all, you could easily vomit right now, but you're not thinking about the little bits left in your mouth. You're thinking that this experience could have easily triggered a panic attack, but somehow it hasn't. And maybe, in its own small way, that's a triumph.

"That was a RAW GRASSHOPPER," says Will.

"I know," you cough.

"I don't know who you are anymore," says Fran.

"Are you guys ready?" you say. "That smoke is disappearing fast."

You manage to keep your voice steady even though this taste will likely never leave your mouth again. At the end of your sentence, you cough again, and then there's a wing back in your mouth. You spit it into your hand, iridescent and half chewed, and toss it aside.

Troy squints at it.

"Was that a . . ."

"Yeah," you say.

You pick up the boat and set it in the water, and then you scramble into the front position, which you think you heard Silas call the "fore" one time. You're trying, despite your contempt for the man, to remember more of what he told you. Will gets in behind you this time and picks up a paddle. He tips his head back and screams:

"COME ON, NARPS. IN YOUR BOATS! CASE JUST ATE A RAW GRASSHOPPER. LET'S GOOOOOO!"

Fran somehow manages to peel herself off the rocks, and Diana and Troy follow her into the other boat. They all look to you for the lead. Somehow, with that stupid impulsive act, you have become the de facto leader. At least momentarily. So you start paddling, heading toward the remaining tendril of smoke. For a while, Will asks questions about the grasshopper ("Could you taste its brain?" "Do you think it was pregnant?"), but with the ache of work, his patter eventually dies out.

And there isn't much conversation from the other boat. Just the splash and plunk of wooden blades in water. You're hoping the sun will start to cut its way through the clouds, but instead it burrows in and the clouds seem to descend even farther until there's a gauzy fog over the cobalt surface of the lake.

"Are we still headed in the right direction?" says Troy a few minutes later.

People look up in a daze, like the question hadn't even occurred to them. And you're one of them. Time has come unspooled again, and you were heedlessly rowing, muscle memory keeping your brain from fully functioning. But when you look up now, you can't see far in front of you. A wind is blowing, and small waves on the lake lap against the sides of the canoe.

"I'm pretty sure we were pointed this way," you say.

But now it's hard to tell if you've kept on the same trajectory. Or if the wind has blown you off course.

"Fran," says Will. "Compass?"

"I don't know," she says. "We're a little east, but that's all I can tell."

For a few moments, you float. And without any scenery around you, it feels like you could be lost at sea. You can still taste the grasshopper, and you hope it's not the last thing you ever put in your mouth.

"HEY!" yells Diana suddenly. "If someone's out there, WE NEED HELP! HELLLLP!"

"Diana," says Fran, "that's kind of in my ear."

But it's no use. Diana screams again:

"WE HAVE NO FOOD! OR SEDATIVES!"

"AND NO SUPPORT ANIMALS," yells Troy. "I REPEAT. WE HAVE NO SUPPORT ANIMALS!"

There's no response from the fog or whatever lies beyond it. Just the light slap of the waves. A birdcall or two. You assume Will is going to let Troy have it for his exclamation. He's certainly made it clear what he thinks of Troy's emotional support wiener dog. But instead, Will takes a deep breath.

"HEY. MY DAD IS AN ASSHOLE!" he screams. "AND I'VE NEVER LIKED TENNIS."

He's breathing heavily behind you. But you don't turn around. You leave him his moment. In the next boat, Diana and Fran are holding hands, paddles across their laps.

"I'M NOT A SNOWFLAKE," yells Fran. "THE WORLD IS JUST A SHIT SHOW. THERE'S A DIFFERENCE!"

Diana tips her head back.

"I JUST WANT TO ENJOY NORMAL THINGS!" she adds.

The waves are getting stronger, and you can feel them turning your boat like it's a spinner on a board game. And though you don't enjoy the sensation, the slightly seasick feeling is really familiar. It's essentially how you've felt every day since the funeral. Only, when you were in the world, you had no illusion of control. Not even a paddle. You just had to endure it.

"I MISS MY BROTHER!" you yell.

Your eyes are hot, but no one can see them in the fog. No one says anything. You've all decided, it seems, that you're not going to talk about any of this (what is said in the fog, stays in the fog?). You wait for someone else to scream their next lament into the ether, but either everyone is screamed out or they're stuck thinking about what you said. Up until now, you haven't so much as mentioned a brother. Finally, you decide to look over at Diana. She meets your eyes, and you think you see a nod before she turns away.

Then, a second or two later, you feel a scrape against the bottom of your boat.

"Yo, what was that?" says Will.

"Probably just a . . . ," Troy starts.

Then a similar scrape, like claws against the bottom of the other boat, steals the rest of the sentence.

"Jesus!" shouts Fran.

And she's rewarded with another scratch.

"Are there alligators in the Boundary Waters?" asks Diana.

"Why would you say that?!" asks Troy.

With a juddering crunch, your canoe slams into a rock and pinballs to the side. Then you are barely afloat. Whatever is underneath you is taking over, and when you finally think to put a paddle down, it only goes a foot or so before it hits bottom.

"We're on land!" you say. "Or near it."

"It can't be the shore," says Fran. "This lake was huge. And we were right in the middle."

Meanwhile, your boat has stopped. And when you hop out into the ankle-deep water, the fog is patchier. You look around, and the land seems to curve around you until it meets water on both sides.

"It's an island," you say.

"No way," says Will.

And he stumbles across the water, landing eventually on his butt in the sand. The other three are still in their boat, unmoving, all facing forward. You step back toward the water and heft your boat up the shore, cutting a furrow in the gray sand. You look inside, but it doesn't appear to be damaged.

"Do you guys smell that?" says Diana, climbing out of her boat.

You cock your head and take a deep inhalation. The carbon reaches your nose in an instant.

"Woodsmoke," you say.

You start running then, onto the island proper, through brush and over gnarled roots and leaves. You can hear the water so clearly from all sides. The island can't be too big. The smell of the campfire is getting closer, and you can hear the sounds of your fellow travelers' boots pounding behind you. Diana races ahead, but not for long. Soon enough, she comes to a stop.

"Hey, Case," she says. "Come over here. I need to show you something."

Her phrasing sounds familiar, and you can't pinpoint it at first. But the thought scatters when you see the embers, glowing through the mist like magma. The coals are red, blinking when the breeze kicks up. And after you see them, you immediately see what's next to them. And so does everyone else who has finally caught up.

It's a tent that looks remarkably like Silas's.

TWENTY-NINE

You should be screaming. Or rushing the tent. But instead, you're standing there, lost in your thoughts. And that's because you finally remember why those words sounded so familiar. They're almost exactly the same ones she sent you in a text after she and Sean broke up. You hadn't seen her for a week after that. Not at school, where she left every day for lunch and often failed to make it back for the afternoon. And not at Perkins, where you circled the parking lot like the world's most obvious detective, peering in windows and scanning your old corner booth. Then one evening, you got a text from a number you didn't recognize.

Come over. I need to tell u something.

At first you thought it was a wrong number, and you were about to ignore it when something clicked and you fired off a response.

When did you get a new phone?

There was a substantial pause, the three dots flashing so long that you were expecting a novel when you got the next message. Instead you saw:

When I mastered enough Serbian vocab.

It was late, almost eleven on a Saturday, and Sean had been gone most of the day. He was, you figured, either out riding or hanging out at the bike co-op with his new crew of pierced waifs.

He spent a lot of time there lately, and most nights, he was out bombing through the city, finding new ways to hurl his body through space. Since the breakup, it felt like he was always in motion. Unable to sit down. He'd leave in the afternoon and come back near dawn, drenched in sweat, barely able to move or speak.

On the night you got the text from Diana, Sean had left at four o'clock that afternoon and still wasn't back. Unlike some of his new bike shop pals, he did have lights and reflective gear, but you were planning on waiting until he returned before you went to bed, just to make sure he was safe. Now you weren't sure what to do.

Part of you felt like it was your responsibility to help him through this time, since you had played a part in the end of his relationship, but he didn't seem to want your help. He'd rejected your offer to go back to the quarry a few days ago—and you knew it was probably time just to tell him what had happened. But then there was Diana. Until this message, you weren't sure if you'd ever see her again. Now you had a chance to say an actual goodbye.

In the end, you grabbed your keys and told yourself you'd be back soon.

Your mom was out working a night shift, but your dad had fallen asleep waiting for Sean, so you were extra quiet leaving the house. And you tried to go slow backing the Corolla out of the driveway to keep your bad muffler to a light wheeze. You looked down the street in both directions before you left, hoping you might see the blinking strobe of Sean's LED coming down the road, but there was nothing but darkness in either direction. So you tapped Diana's address into your phone and took off into the night.

You'd never actually been in her house before. And you were pretty sure Sean hadn't either. The place, she always said, was in a gentrifying neighborhood that was gentrifying very slowly on account of the snakes. The urban legend was that a pet escaped its terrarium in the eighties, but it was probably the proximity to the river. Once, when Diana was young, she watched her baba casually grab a garter snake from the washing machine and toss it into the open mouth of her dog (who gagged and spit it out).

The drive took ten minutes or so, but eventually you pulled up to her light blue rambler with overstuffed gutters and an attached garage. Though you had dropped her off here a few nights after Perkins, you'd only ever seen the place from afar, so it still felt unfamiliar, like the house of a distant relative. Tonight, the driveway was blocked by an enormous Buick, so you parked on the street. And when you made it to the front steps, a motion detector popped on and you froze in place like a thief. In the light, you noticed all the bird feeders, hanging around you like a floating city. You had to duck to get under one, and when you made it to the door, there was a single Post-it note on the screen that said ENTER.

You opened it up and stepped into a living room with wall-to-wall green carpeting and immaculate, dated furniture. Through a narrow hallway, you could see Diana unloading a small dishwasher and carefully stacking glasses in a cabinet. You walked down the hall, lined with formal pictures of Diana and her grandmother posing in cheesy photo studios over the years. From the pictures, it seemed like Baba wasn't a big smiler, and her glasses were the biggest you'd ever seen.

"Stop right there!"

You turned to find the woman herself only inches away, holding tightly to a Louisville Slugger. She was much shorter in person—barely over five feet if you had to guess—and she had sneaked up on you like a ninja and taken aim at your head. You stuck your hands straight up and took a step backward. She grimaced at you, and her upturned lip revealed a single gold tooth.

"Why you are in this house right now so late? Eh?!"

She gripped the bat tighter, and now that you had a chance to get a better look, she appeared to be wearing a kimono and some compression socks, and little else.

A flurry of Serbian came from the kitchen, presumably from Diana, and Baba's body went slack. She looked you over again, slowly lowering the bat in the process. Then she muttered something guttural and walked into the kitchen, where she started taking food out of the fridge like nothing had just happened. Your heart was still thumping in your throat as you entered the eat-in kitchen with peeling seventies linoleum and a two-burner stove.

"He doesn't need to eat, Baba," said Diana. "It's almost midnight."

"Men are always hungry," she said, dumping things out of yogurt containers onto a plate. "Always."

Diana, wearing a ripped tank top and a pair of overlarge sweatpants, just shrugged. Baba stuck a plate in the microwave, and before she closed the door, she pointed to things on the plate.

"Sarmas. Gibanica. Pljeskavica and ćevapi. You like it?"

"Sure," you said. "And it's, um . . . really nice to meet you. Sorry for the intrusion."

She nodded once and then walked out of the room, still clutching her bat. She shot one last comment at Diana, who fired back a barb of her own. Then it was just you and Diana, and the smell of gradually heating food in a cramped kitchen.

"What did you say to her?" you asked. "About me?"

"I said you had no sense of decency and always show up unannounced. But that you are a fragile man and you need our help."

"Cool. Appreciate it."

"No problem," she said, drying a cup still wet from the washer.

You weren't sure where your body should be, so you just hovered behind her for a moment before finally sitting in a ladderback chair.

"Why don't you ever have people over?" you said.

She grabbed a handful of silverware and shoved it in an open drawer.

"Perhaps you didn't notice that my grandmother just considered murdering you with a bat."

As if on cue, the microwave dinged and Diana brought the plate over to you and slapped it down.

"It's no Perkins," she said. "But Baba does make everything from scratch."

It smelled like cabbage and pepper and paprika, and ordinarily it would have been fun to try new foods, but you couldn't even pick up the fork.

"Despite being a man," you said, "I'm not really hungry. Do you need any help?"

She shrugged again and pointed at the top row of the dishwasher where all the mugs were, then opened a cabinet. The mugs were mismatched and coffee stained like the ones at your house, and you were careful not to chip them as you pulled each one out and wiped it dry.

"Can I ask why I'm here?" you said.

You put a diner-style mug face down on a floral shelf liner. Diana took a few bowls and nested them inside one another.

"It wasn't right," she said. "I just wanted to tell you that."

She stopped unloading the dishes for a moment, but she didn't turn to you either. She just looked out the small window over the sink that had a view of the dark backyard.

"What exactly . . ."

"The way I made you tell me about Sean," she said. "I shouldn't have done that to you, Case. It was . . . manipulative. And it's not something a friend would do."

You took out another mug and held it up. It read I'M NOT LOUD. I'M SERBIAN. You set it next to the last one.

"Okay," you said. "But would a friend have kept it from you in the first place?"

You grabbed another mug, but instead of putting it away, you just held it at your side.

"You're not my friend," she said.

You almost dropped the cup, but you managed, somehow, to hang on. And before you could say anything, or ask a shaky-voiced question, she added:

"You're in love with me."

There weren't any words then. Not one. Usually, there were a few in your head at least, even if they didn't always make it to your mouth. But this time, there was nothing. Just some dizziness and an inability to breathe. You found yourself wanting Baba to return and hit you with the baseball bat just so your outsides could match your insides.

"Diana," you said.

"I understand," she said. "It's not something you chose."

She reached over and opened the window, and a cold breeze came pouring into the humid kitchen. You couldn't help wondering how long she'd known. Was everything you did completely obvious to everyone? The evening was turning cool, and the wind through the screen gave you goose bumps. But you managed to walk back to the table and sit down. Neither of you spoke. So eventually, you cut into what she called a "sarma" with a fork and tried a bite. It was better than it smelled. Some kind of spiced meat on the inside. So you had another bite, and before you knew it, you were halfway through the dish.

"This is actually really good," you said.

"She might have anger problems," said Diana. "And strange ideas about birth control. But that lady can cook."

She joined you at the table, shoving a half-finished sudoku out of the way, and looking up at the ceiling. Then before you could get another nervous bite into your mouth, Diana suddenly leaned over the space between you and kissed you on the mouth.

You didn't move, and unlike every movie you've seen, your eyes weren't closed. You weren't sure if you kissed her back, but you didn't *not* kiss her back. And you saw the pained look on her face when your lips detached. She reached out and put a hand on your cheek, and her palm was still wet from the dishes. Then she pulled back and looked you in the eye.

"You taste like cabbage," she said.

And you noticed she was crying.

You set your fork down and sat back in your chair. You reached out and put a hand on her back. Everything had happened so fast, you weren't sure what to feel yet. This wasn't exactly how you imagined your first kiss going. Somehow, it never occurred to you that there might be tears.

You stood up then.

"Okay," you said. "I'm going to guess, based on that reaction, that things are maybe kind of confusing. And that I should go . . ."

Diana didn't make eye contact.

"Please give Baba my best," you said, "and tell her the sarmas were . . ."

"Don't go," she said.

So you stopped.

"I'm worried about Sean," she said.

You weren't sure if she meant in general, or what exactly, but you just decided to be honest.

"Me too," you said.

"He's got more going on than you think," she said. "He needs to talk to someone, and I don't think it can be me."

You nodded. And immediately the guilt came roaring back. What were you doing here? Diana stood up and faced you.

"Look. I have some complicated feelings for you, Case. I always have. Obviously, I need to think more about that. But I just don't want to lose you in my life. Do you understand that?"

"Yeah," you said.

"So can we just forget that happened?"

"I'm probably not going to forget that happened until the day I die," you said. "But I can pretend."

"Okay," she said.

"Zbogom," you said then, which you were pretty sure was goodbye in Serbian.

"Zbogom," she said.

You stumbled over the chair and made your way back across the green carpet and out the front door. A bird feeder slammed into your head as you ran down the stairs, but you barely felt it. You searched the driveway for snakes, but there weren't any in sight. They were all hiding out there somewhere in the dark.

Then you were driving, hitting turn signals by rote and merging without really looking. Your thoughts were racing along with the car. And about halfway home, it hit you so hard that you nearly stopped breathing: If you wanted a meaningful relationship with your brother, there was no way anything else could happen with Diana.

The two were mutually exclusive.

Even if it hurt, you had to choose the person you'd known your whole life, the one who had always been there for you, even if he made mistakes. Maybe, if you talked things through with Sean, you could still be Diana's friend. You could tell him that she was important to you, a close friend you didn't want to lose. Maybe he would understand.

There weren't many night owls in your neighborhood, so no one was out when you pulled back in the driveway around one A.M. You looked for Sean's bike but didn't see it. And when you stepped inside, the house was so quiet, you wondered if anyone was home.

"Where have you been?"

Sean's voice cut through the dark, and made you jump back, banging your hip on the doorknob. He was sitting on the stairs, sweat dripping down his face.

"Sean," you said. "When did you get back? I was worried."

"Were you at her house, Case?" he asked.

You were about to answer him. Honestly, you'd like to think. But before you could say anything, he flung a notebook across the room at you like a Frisbee. It hit you in the chest, and you caught it off the ricochet. For a second, you were so startled you didn't know what it was or why he'd launched it at you in the dark. Then you opened it and looked down, and even in the dim light, you saw your own handwriting staring back at you. You knew then exactly what it was, and you felt a stab of nausea.

It was the letter you wrote to Diana over Christmas break. The one that explained your feelings. The one you thought about giving her, but ultimately kept in this worn-out notebook when you clearly should have thrown it away.

The one your brother must have found.

THIRTY

"Silas," says Will. "Get your ass out here, bro!"

You're all standing around his tent now, which is zipped closed and looks hastily pitched. It shows none of the care and expertise you saw at the beginning of this trip, when there was an educational purpose to his every gesture. There's no sound from inside, and you all eyeball one another, daring somebody to make a move. Finally, Fran steps forward and slowly unzips the flap.

It ripples in the breeze for a second, then she yanks it open and you all peer inside at a wadded-up sleeping bag and a few food wrappers. Fran searches for something uneaten but comes up empty-handed. She does, however, find another empty pill bottle.

"Case," she says, and tosses it to you. "This one's you, dude."

You catch it and look inside to find a small residue of orange pill dust that you're thinking seriously about licking right then and there. Surprisingly, seeing your full name and the name of your pharmacy on the bottle makes your whole body ache with homesickness. You wouldn't have thought a pill bottle of all things would do this, but the way your mom would pick up your script after a shift and set it on your dresser without judgment or fanfare made you gradually lose the shame you felt at using it.

"The island can't be that big," says Troy. "He's here some-where, right?"

"Unless he took the boat . . . ," says Will.

"Boat's right over there!" yells Fran, who has wandered a bit.

And sure enough, nestled in some brush, not far from the tent, is the third canoe. You walk over and check it for gear, but it's empty save for a pool of dirty water in the bottom.

"We'll split into groups," says Diana. "If we each head one way around the island, we've got to find him."

You nod. Fran reaches out a hand to Diana, but this time, Diana, ever unpredictable, walks toward you. Will and Troy join Fran instead, and she pretends to be okay with that, staring at you all the while.

"Meet back here either way," says Will.

"Okay," says Diana.

"Good luck," says Troy.

"Good luck," you say.

Then you take off in opposite directions, following the coast of the small rocky island. The gradually dissipating fog cloaks the treetops and makes them seem a hundred feet tall. You and Diana walk side by side, seeking out patches of sand amid the chunks of blue-gray slate and snared driftwood. The roots that twist through your path are as thick as pythons.

"I miss him too," she says after a few minutes of silence. "I hope you know that. I just wasn't ready to shout it from a boat."

The water pools around the rocks, and you step in a shallow puddle, feeling the cold soak your dirty socks. You take in what Diana says, but you also scan in a cursory way for Silas, hoping to catch sight of his clothing, even just a blur in the woods. You don't know what you'll do if you see him, but you know your chances of survival increase if he shows. Even if you can talk to him, things will feel possible. Diana watches your face all the while; you can feel it.

"Do you blame me, Case?"

You instinctively look down at your feet.

"Can we please just look for Silas?" you say.

She shakes her head.

"No. I need to understand where you're at right now. It's been too awkward for too long."

Whether you blame Diana is a question you try not to think about, and one you wish you could say you've never considered.

"No," you finally say. "Maybe at first, but not anymore. That's the truth."

She looks you over and seems satisfied with your answer.

"So then you were serious earlier?" she says.

"About what?"

"You think it's *your* fault."

You're not sure why you're so quiet now. You were willing to list all the reasons this was true before, but now to say them out loud seems impossible. You peer through an opening in the forest, and a hint of movement quickens your pulse, but it only proves to be a bird.

"Why haven't we seen any loons?" you ask. "Have you thought about that? I thought this was supposed to be loon central. I thought you couldn't spit without hitting a loon up here."

Diana stops to tie one of her yellow boot laces. And you wait patiently while she does. When she's finished, she walks directly in front of you and blocks your path. She looks you in the eye.

"Case," she says. "I'm serious. Do you blame yourself for Sean's death? Yes or no?"

"Loons are, like, the only thing I looked up before I came here," you say. "I thought maybe I'd see one. Did you know they can fly seventy miles per hour? That seems oddly fast to me. They're actually really beautiful."

Diana picks up a stick. She's not even looking in the woods anymore. She's looking out toward the lake.

"The thing is, you don't even know the whole story," she says.

You turn toward her, and you feel your face going hot with anger.

"I know that I betrayed him," you say. "I know he never did anything to me, at least not on purpose, and I betrayed him. I made everything fall apart. I tipped the first domino."

"It's not that simple," she says.

She throws her stick and watches it rotate in the air and land on the water, where it floats on the choppy surface.

"What do you mean?" you say.

You both peer into the woods again, but see only the gnarly limbs of a few island trees. No counselor. No savior. No one to get you out of this conversation.

"He wasn't who he pretended to be," she says.

"Oh. You knew him better than me. Is that it?"

You've had enough therapy to know that you're probably not angry about this specific thing. But being aware of that doesn't help you stop it. You kick at a nearby stump, and it feels good to connect with something, to feel the jolt of pain in your toes.

"Calm down," she says. "I'm not claiming that. But maybe just in this one way. He knew you looked up to him, so he didn't always show you everything."

A small memory then: the sound of Sean crying after a diving meet his freshman year where he was disqualified for taking too much time. His door was open a crack, and when you tried to go in to comfort him, he slammed it in your face. Then later at dinner, he smiled like nothing had happened. When you brought it up, he seemed befuddled, like he had excised it completely from his memory.

"Okay," you say. "So . . . what didn't he show me?"

"There were two people," she says. "There was Sean, and then there was Sean the destroyer."

You can't help it: You laugh a little bit.

"Sean the destroyer?"

"That's what I called him. That version of him."

"Okay . . ."

"Things would be fine," she says. "He'd be totally good. For months sometimes. Confident. Charming. Then some other part of him would come out. Some compulsion to tear everything down. He'd do risky, dangerous things. Mess up his life. You didn't really know this part of him, I don't think."

You traipse forward. The island isn't huge, and you wonder how far you are from meeting up with the other half of your group, and what you'll do if there's no sign of Silas. You try to look through the trees, but they've gotten too thick to see through now. You think of Sean ripping down all his mantras and quotes.

"That's why it's not your fault, Case," she says.

You don't respond. But she is not done talking.

"It's mine."

You stop walking.

"I knew what he was capable of," she says. "I knew he needed help. But I didn't do anything. I was too angry. And because I couldn't get over my anger, he . . ."

The scream doesn't come right away.

It feels like it does, but there's probably a five-second pause, give or take, where you're waiting for Diana to finish her thought. To hear why she blames herself. But then, suddenly, there's the sound of Fran shrieking, and before you and Diana can even look at each other, you're running again. Straight through the woods. You're bone tired. Your head hurts. But you find enough adrenaline to race toward your screaming friend.

The woods are thicker in the middle of the island. There isn't much space, but there's also no real path. Just dense vegetation, all of it up to your thighs. The group is somewhere toward the other coast, at a different point of entry. And when you find them, they're huddled close to one another. Troy is holding Fran. Will is leaning against a tree. They're all looking down, and you know what you're going to see before you see it. But you have to look anyway, just to confirm that it has happened.

Blue lips. Open eyes. Foam around his mouth. Vomit on his shirt.

His T-shirt is ripped, and his legs tangled in a strange way.

There are bugs flying around him.

You look away.

"We found these," says Fran through sobs, handing a bag to Diana.

It's filled with thick white pills that don't look like any benzo you've ever seen. They're clearly something different. Something stronger. Diana takes one look and hands them back.

"Opioids," she says. "Probably fentanyl."

She doesn't break her stare down at Silas's body.

"They're really dangerous, let alone if you combine them with sedatives," she says.

She finally looks away. She walks slowly over and hugs Fran. You're not sure what to do, but you know enough to know that people who have just seen a dead body are probably not okay. You reach out and put a hand on Troy's shoulder. Then, gradually, Will heads over and puts an arm around both of you. You stand like this for thirty seconds. Maybe a full minute. And when you start to cry, you're not fully sure what you're crying about.

Some of it is for Silas, to be sure.

He put you in grave danger. He did something unforgivable. But there was something about finding that mantra he dropped that altered your thinking. He was trying to get sober. He wanted a better life. He just couldn't get there. Of course, he shouldn't have been leading you, but you are also no stranger to self-delusion. How many days of constant panic attacks did you tell yourself you were fine so you wouldn't have to get on medication and confront the fact that you had a disorder? Silas made a terrible mistake, and his timing might get you killed, but he didn't deserve this. No one does.

Also: You are so tired and so hungry and so confused. Your head feels like it's caught in a vise. And the last time you saw a dead body was the absolute worst day of your life. You sit down, and a few others join you. And there's no worry about judgment anymore. You let yourself cry, and you wipe your snotty nose with your dirty T-shirt. Then, after a while, you stand up and you pull off Silas's shirt. It isn't easy to get it over his stiff limbs. But you pull it off and drape it over his face so you don't have to look into his vacant eyes. If anybody was in denial, they aren't anymore.

You are completely alone.

THIRTY-ONE

Evening comes somehow, and Will hands out the last of the sedatives like a priest offering communion. He doesn't place them on your tongues, but he puts them in your palms with a solemn sense of duty. When he's done, you wash them down with musty, boiled lake water and immediately start thinking about food again. You're all mired in shock and grief, but your hunger cannot be ignored even in these circumstances. Before you figure out what to do next, you need something—anything—in your stomachs.

You meet up just long enough to assign tasks, everyone nodding silently with tearstained cheeks. Will wants to hunt with a homemade spear. Maybe some small game or birds. Troy and the girls will try to forage again. This leaves you with the most sophisticated piece of technology on offer: a long stick with a line and a hook. Until this moment, you've been fishing exactly once in your entire life, a single afternoon with your uncle at a stocked pond in rural Iowa, but here you are: the group's greatest hope for protein.

You manage to dig up a few spasming worms from a moist bit of dirt near the tree line. And it occurs to you for a second that maybe your best bet is to cut out the middleman and just eat the bait. But after the lingering memories of the grasshopper incident, you decide to roll the dice and spear a fat one on the tine of your whisk-turned-hook. Then you take off your boots, roll up your pant legs, and wade out ankle deep in the murky lake, waiting for your final moment of pill-induced calm to kick in. It's sunset and the lake casts back the light, swallowing your feet in gold.

A half hour or so goes by in the repetition of movements, casting and waiting, casting and waiting, and eventually you can't help it: Your mind starts to wander back to Silas. What were his final thoughts before he died out here alone on the island forest floor? Did he think even once about you guys? Or was he lost in his own story? Was there any kind of final reckoning with the choices he made?

There's movement on the surface of the lake, and you pull the line in, only to find the second of your four worms devoured whole. Your strategy of tossing out the line only to sit and see if it moves is not working. You know there are fish in this lake, because they are eating the bait. They are so tantalizingly close, but they might as well be in the Arctic Ocean for all the good they're doing you.

You step a little deeper into the water and stab another writhing victim on the business end of the whisk.

"C'mon," you say.

You remember a neighborhood kid slicing a worm into five pieces when you were a child and saying they were all going to turn into new worms. Later that night, when your mom told you this wasn't true, you cried and prayed for each segmented soul. Now you say a prayer for this worm, who's giving its pale body for a chance at stopping the gnawing hunger you can feel in every part of you. You make sure he's stuck fast, and even though you have never done this in your life, you make the sign of the cross over its squirming little form, and then you launch the poor bastard into the fray.

The worm arcs through the air and lands in the small waves, and this time you decide to try something different. Instead of just letting it dangle there, you start inching it back toward you before a fish even bites. You don't know why exactly. It just seems like something you've seen before. Old fishing guys perched on old bridges in town, slowly reeling in their line over and over again. Maybe they were onto something.

The first couple of times you try this, you get nothing but the same beleaguered worm coming back to you, a little more swollen and lifeless than before. But on your third go-round, you feel a small shift in momentum, a tug from an underwater force. You pull as hard as you can, and for two miraculous seconds, you see something that looks like a bass come flipping out of the water, bending in the air like a wakeboarder doing a trick. In a moment of delirium, you drop the pole entirely and reach out your hands to catch it. But this Hail Mary isn't going the distance, and it lands with a belly flop about five feet away from you.

You sprint toward the fish, hoping foolishly that you can snatch it from the water, but within a step it's already gone, blurring through the shallows. Of course, the worm is gone too. Another lamb to the slaughter. You stand in the glowing lake for a moment, trying to calm your breathing. You can feel the Xanax working at the edges of your mood now, and it's been a long time since you've had any help in the fight against your brain's worse impulses. Medication can't do everything, but it can clear a path.

So you blink away your defeat and reach down for your last

worm, popping the whisk tine through his guts without any invocation. Then you close your eyes and bat away the image of Silas gasping for his final breaths like a fish. You whip back the line and cast it out into the liquid sunset.

You guide it back toward the shore with a little more finesse this time, and within seconds, there's another bite. When you feel the pull, you grab the homemade fishing pole with all your remaining strength. Two hands like you're gripping a bat, your knuckles aligned the way they taught you in Little League. And when you feel another tug, you pull on that line with everything you have left.

This time when you see the fish, you swear you look it right in its yellow eye as it soars past you—already much farther than the last one—and skids onto the beach behind you, turning angry flips on the rocks and sand.

"OH MY GOD!" you scream in a heavy-metal voice you didn't even know you had.

The adrenaline that surges through you makes your whole body feel lighter.

"YESSSSSSSSSSSSSSSS!"

You run toward the shore, tripping over your own feet, and just barely staying on them. This fish is bigger; you can tell that already. It's sleek and long with a broad, flat snout. And before you even get close enough to pick it up, you can see its rows of sharp teeth. Its body shimmers with green oblong spots. And when you pick it up with two hands, it goes slack in your arms. You've never been good at measuring things with your eyes, but you're thinking it's at least a foot and a half, maybe longer.

And when you carry it back to the campsite, dangling it

from the hook, everyone who's there—Will, covered in dirt and empty-handed, and the foragers with only a few paltry mounds of greens—forgets about their dire situation and their fear if only for a moment. For the handful of seconds it takes to walk it toward the fire, no one is thinking about the body in the woods, or how much longer you have to make it to the drop.

"Holy shit," says Troy. "That's a northern pike!"

"Jesus, Case," says Fran. "Did you have to chum the waters for that thing?"

Will, looking humbled and wrecked by his hunting expedition, just bursts into spontaneous applause. And Diana gives you a cautious smile. You wonder if this is what it was like to be an early human bringing back fresh kill for your family after days without food. You don't have any idea how to cook and prepare this slimy vertebrate, but you know that whatever you do, it's going to allow you to hang on a little longer.

Hours later, you find yourself shoving chunks of hot oily whitefish into your mouth with your hands, moaning with pleasure. Troy and Diana had enough common sense to gut the thing (poorly) and impale it with a stick. While it roasted over the dying coals of your fire, you went back to the lake and caught two more small fish. A real fisherman would probably have thrown them back, but they add to the total portion of meat. There isn't an abundance per se, but everybody gets something, and as they gorge on their helping of charred skin and flaky flesh, a temporary calm settles over your island.

For now, you've eaten, and you're medicated. And it's only when the final bites are swallowed that your thoughts return to the elephant in the woods. You can't avoid thinking about him for long because he's not far away. A hundred feet or so. Someone who was alive only recently and now is not. Someone who died doing exactly what you're doing now.

"What do we do with the body?" says Troy, peering back toward the east side of the island, where, you've since found out, he was the lucky one who stumbled over the outstretched legs of your former guide.

"We can't take it with us," says Will. "It will slow us down too much, and we've already lost time."

Nobody disagrees.

"Can we bury him, at least?" says Fran. "I mean, if we leave him out, won't animals . . ."

"Eat his face off?" says Troy.

"Yeah," says Fran. "That."

"We don't have time," says Diana. "It would take us all night to dig a grave with no tools, and we'd all be too exhausted to make up ground in the morning."

You wait for someone to insist in spite of the effort, but again, nobody does.

"Well, should we at least say something?" says Fran.

"Time is running out, guys," says Will. "There's no one who can help us now if we don't make that drop. What happens when the lighter runs out? Or your meds! If we were smart, we would be moving right now. Silas never cared about us."

As he says this, the sun proves his point by disappearing behind the water. You have a day and a half, give or take, to make it. And you all know the stakes.

"Nobody is leaving this island in the dark tonight," says Troy.

"We need sleep too, and this is a good place to get it. We have pills and there are no bears here. And look, I know Silas is the reason we're in this situation, but he tried. I mean he was trying before everything went horribly wrong. And he's . . ."

Troy closes his eyes.

"He's what, Troy?" says Will. "Your best friend?"

"One of us."

The fire is nearly dead now, and the last of the coals pop. Fran takes a stick and gives them a stir.

"How do you mean?" she says quietly.

"He went on this trip, remember? This same trip! And he had anxiety just like us. What he did was super messed up and dangerous, but he's not the first of us to self-medicate. I use a vape at home 'cause it keeps me calm. My friend Lenny from group therapy has his weed gummies. Diana, you brought vodka on a hiking trip! We're all looking for some way to quiet our brains. Silas made a stupid choice, but he was trying to battle like the rest of us."

The last line is the one that gets you.

And when you look over at Diana, you know she's thinking the same thing you are: You both know someone else who made choices he could never take back. Choices that ruined other people's lives along with his own. You stand up, and your body is woozy with exhaustion. The back of your head throbs. Diana stands up too and starts walking into the woods.

"C'mon, guys," she says. "It's time to say goodbye."

THIRTY-TWO

Sean let you stand there for a moment by yourself.

In the living room. In the dark. Rereading the words that mortified you. But in spite of the pain, you read every last sentence in that letter, all over again. *I understand nothing can happen—I get that—but I just need you to know about this feeling.* And: *I'm not sleeping. I barely eat. If it wasn't for Perkins, I might be dead.* Part of you knew you were never going to give this to her, so you wrote exactly what you felt. *I've never been in love before, so even if this ruins everything, I want to thank you just for giving me that.* Your hands were sweating, smudging the blue ink on the page. Sean sat on the stairs all the while, letting you marinate in your own shame.

And, finally, when you were done reading the words you thought you'd never read again, you closed the notebook and set it on a nearby table. You scrambled for something to say. You wanted to explain everything, including the realization you'd come to on the way home. You wanted to take him through the whole thing, starting from that first spark in the corner booth at Perkins and how you came to realize it could never happen. But he stood up on the stairs and looked at you from over the railing, and you felt yourself getting weak.

"I'm sorry," you said. "I just need to sit down for a minute."

Which you did, on the floor. Sean kept watching. He didn't move from his spot. He was not the type to break eye contact, or shy away from a tough moment. That had never been his style.

"It must be so easy for you," he said finally.

You weren't sure what he meant, but you found yourself unable to ask.

"To be the one everybody worries about."

He was looking right at you, but you couldn't return his gaze. He gripped the railing, and you watched his fingers tighten.

"I know you didn't ask for your anxiety, Case. And I know you don't want it. But you have to admit it's pretty convenient sometimes. You get to stumble through everything, and when it's all too much for you or you make a mistake, you can get in bed and take a mental-health day. And everyone loves you and babies you and nobody expects anything from you."

"Sean," you tried.

"But I expected things," he said.

He either hadn't heard you or didn't care. His hair was tousled from his bike helmet, and he ran a hand through it, combing it into a cresting wave above his angry face.

"And I expected that you wouldn't take advantage of this situation."

"What situation?" you said. "What are you talking about?"

He pinched his brow and took a deep breath.

"How oblivious are you, man? The fact that Diana should be with you."

If it hadn't seemed so inappropriate, you might have laughed. But the idea felt so absurd to you, even then.

"What are you talking about?" you said again.

Tracks of sweat cut through the dirt on Sean's face. It occurred to you that all this bike riding might not just be about chasing a new thrill. In that moment, seeing how tired he was, the whole thing seemed like a punishment.

"I can't open up to people the way you do," he said. "Okay? I don't really know how. You're a genuine person, Case. And I didn't let her in. I acted like I usually do. I didn't deserve her. But I just wanted . . . a chance to fix it."

You stood up again, unable to sit still anymore.

"Sean, listen! I haven't taken advantage of anything," you said.

You picked up the notebook and held it out.

"I never gave this to her! I knew it was wrong. I didn't act on anything!"

Sean was quiet a moment, and you wondered if he was actually hearing you this time. But then he shook his head and smiled.

"And next you'll tell me you weren't just at her house," he said.

He held your gaze for a moment, giving you a chance to deny it. But on a loop in your head was the kiss, Diana leaning across the table and the feeling of her lips against yours. Why didn't you stop it? Why didn't it even occur to you to stop it? You knew the answer, and it hurt your chest to think of it.

"You just assume everyone is going to forgive you," he said. "That you get a free pass for life because you're the breakable one. The one we all need to tread lightly around. But it doesn't always work like that. Some things . . ."

"Sean," you said. "Can you just let me talk for a minute?"

But he was already up the last steps and disappearing from sight. You waited a minute to see if he would come back down and scream in your face or shove you to the ground. In that moment, you wanted him to do it. To do something that would be painful enough to settle the score. But Sean had never hurt you, even when you were little, and you knew he never would.

What he did instead was worse. From that day on, he didn't treat you cruelly. He didn't scream at you or put you down. He didn't even look at you with spite or derision.

He just cut you out of his life.

THIRTY-THREE

You gather around Silas's body with nothing but moonlight and a makeshift torch for light. Will holds the flame out in front of him, and the gentle flicker sends long shadows rippling across the forest floor. Everyone looks down at the body, where you can still make out the outline of Silas's face under the shirt you used to cover him. There are bugs crawling on him, but Diana brushes a few of them off. The only sound is a cold wind through the leaves. Troy steps forward, and you all form a half circle around the body, waiting for him to speak.

You're expecting something Buddhist now that you know Troy better. Maybe something about emptiness or impermanence. You don't know that much about Buddhism, but Sean read you the Heart Sutra once, and there was a lot of stuff in there about how nothing exists. Nothing is born. Nothing dies. That kind of thing. But *this*, you know, is real. There is a corpse here that was once a person.

Troy shuffles in place. Since he was the one who spoke up for Silas, everyone just kind of assumes he's going to be the one to talk now, and he seems okay with that. He gets a little closer to the body, then he clears his throat.

"Almost heaven," he says.

He pauses a moment.

"West Virginia."

He has his eyes closed and his head down like he's delivering a eulogy, so he doesn't notice the confused squints on the faces of his fellow mourners.

"Blue Ridge Mountains," he adds.

"Um, Troy?" says Fran. "What is this?"

Troy doesn't look at Fran. But when he speaks again, his voice is louder.

"Shenandoah River," he continues.

You look around, but everyone else is staring down at the body. Troy's poem sounds incredibly familiar, but you're still not sure what he's reciting. It's possible others catch on sooner, but your confusion doesn't fade until Troy speaks the chorus.

"Country roads, take me home . . ."

No one joins him, so his voice is all alone. Unsupported in the woods. But still he goes on, just saying the words.

"Take me home, country roads."

When he's done with the last phrase, his voice tapers off and leaves only the sound of the lake water lapping on all sides of the island. And you're pretty sure this is it for his speech, so a couple of you start to turn away. But then Troy looks at all of you, his smudged glasses gleaming in the firelight.

"Guys," he says. "Do you remember how embarrassed you were when he first sang that on the bus?"

He gives you a moment to call it back: the song blaring through the bus's bad speakers, Silas marching down the aisle making unnecessary eye contact.

"I wanted to die," says Diana.

"Me too," says Troy. "And I still don't know why he picked

that song. Was he from West Virginia? Was it just the most embarrassing thing he could think of? Is it because we're in the country? I've got no idea."

He looks down at Silas.

"I didn't know him well enough to be sure if we should celebrate him right now. But he told us we had to give up our embarrassment and be vulnerable if we wanted to make any progress, remember? And that part at least seems true. Doing that with you guys is the only thing that's made me feel better."

"So what are you saying?" asks Will.

"I think you know what I'm saying," he says.

A cool breeze blows and the torch sheds a few sparks.

"I don't get it," says Fran. "Somebody tell me what's going on."

You look over at her. She's back in her hoodie, huddled inside.

"You don't have to sing it," says Troy.

Diana scoffs, but Troy is already beginning to speak the words of the chorus again.

"No," says Fran. "No way. I refuse."

Then another voice joins in the recitation, and you're surprised to see that it's Will. He's not much louder than a whisper, but he's speaking.

"Will!" yells Diana. "How dare you!"

But it's too late now. This is quickly becoming a true chorus, and you're next. And you don't just speak; you start to sing the chorus, atonally. And the lyrics, which you've always found pretty cheesy, suddenly have some inexplicable new power over you. In fact, in this moment, they kind of make you want to cry. It's just those three words, you think:

228

Take me home.

In this small forest, on an island in a lake you may never return from, it sounds like a prayer, one everybody can identify with. If you could make it work like a spell, you would. *Take me home. Take me home. Take me home.* And then you're gone, back to a hard life that suddenly doesn't seem quite as hard.

Fran is the next to break. She pulls her hood down over her eyes and starts to sing too, just a few decibels over a whisper.

Then, it seems, Diana has no choice. She's the last to join, but join she does. Nobody knows the rest of the verses—not even Troy—so you just sing the chorus over and over again. You try to make it as loud as it was your first day on the bus. You're not sure how long it should go on. Maybe all night. Maybe you'll never stop singing. But then, after ten or so choruses, you all seem to understand intuitively that you don't have any more in you. So you belt it out, hitting that last "take me home" with raspy throats.

When you're done, you all take one final look at the body beneath you. In spite of everything, it still seems sad to leave him like this with no burial, no shroud, no Viking funeral. Just your off-key voices. But if you want to keep from ending up like him, you know you need to move forward toward your only chance at survival. Will waves the torch above his head and starts walking. You all follow him back to the campsite, which now consists of three tents instead of two. At least he gifted you another shelter and boat before he died.

Everyone knows it's time to go to bed. But no one goes into their tent just yet. Instead, you all sit by the fire, staring into the coals, which are still breathing red in the wind. It's a chilly night again—they're definitely getting colder—and you all put on your extra clothes until you're bundled up like arctic explorers. In the morning, you will start the final part of your trek. The most important part. The only part that matters.

"I've never seen a dead body before," says Will finally. "That was my first time."

He rests his chin on a palm, watching the embers blink out.

"Do they all look like that? Like, so freaking sad and empty?"

Nobody says anything for a moment. You feel so drained suddenly. The surge of energy you got from eating real food has faded. Just as importantly: so has the Xanax. You know this comedown well, the moment when your anxiety senses a drop in defenses and starts lurking in your chest. Soon, before you even know it, it will move to your head and everything will be charged with a foreboding edge. You really want to say something to make Will feel better, but you find that you can only tell him the truth.

"Yeah," you say. "They do."

Everyone looks at you.

"When I saw my brother for the last time, I didn't feel anything because I knew it wasn't him. Not anymore. It was just this sad husk."

You don't know how much people remember about what you were shouting in the fog yesterday, but everyone keeps quiet now. Even Diana can't look at you for long. Will is the only one who maintains eye contact.

"How did he die?" he asks.

It sounds like a simple question, but there are actually a thousand answers. You've constructed so many different timelines and explanations. There are, of course, basic facts to rely on, but they don't tell the whole story. The facts never do. Still, saying all this to the group is too much, so you dig into the pocket of your pants and pull out a blank piece of paper. It's the paper from the very first game of Fear in a Hat—the paper where you should have written Sean's name—and you set it on the ground in front of you.

"It's complicated," you say.

And then, because you don't know what else to do, you start to tell the story.

THIRTY-FOUR

You start with the day after your fight, the first day you can remember that your brother ignored you. You don't tell them why; just that he'd gotten angry and now he wouldn't engage with you in any meaningful way. He avoided you in the hallway in the morning, and when you spoke, he listened with dull eyes. Or he just walked past you, down the stairs, and outside to the garage where his bike hung upside down like a vampire.

You tell them about the biking. And how Sean had always launched himself into things with an all-consuming passion. How most of his obsessions were at least a little risky or adrenaline fueled. Diving, for example. And before that, when he was in junior high, half-pipe skating. And before that: jumping off the garage to practice "being a stuntman." By comparison, riding for miles on a fixed-gear bike seemed positively benign. Like a hobby for old people after their knees were blown out.

At first, he mostly rode at night, but then he started adding mornings too. Every day before the sun came up, you heard the vibrating drone of the garage door, and if you made it to your window quickly enough, you'd see Sean take off down the street, head down, legs cranking away at an inhuman speed. And for a while, you told yourself this could be a good thing. Maybe it wasn't just a penance he'd given himself. Maybe it was a way to quiet his mind, and once he achieved some peace, everything would eventually go back to normal.

But that's not what happened. Instead, it all seemed to intensify. You were so desperate for contact with him that you walked into his room sometimes when he wasn't there, just to feel near him. And that's how you found the flyers for the bike races. They weren't anything official. These were street contests for bike messengers and crust punks. No real rules. From what you could tell, the racers followed a series of checkpoints to a mystery finish line, downing beers along the way.

You'd found the latest poster on top of the dryer when you were doing your laundry. The biggest race of the year. An all-day event that promised hundreds of riders. You decided to do a little research. And after falling down a rabbit hole of racing forums and YouTube videos of people evading the cops and racing each other drunkenly through the streets, you knew you had an important choice to make:

Leave it alone or tell your parents.

You were pretty sure they wouldn't want him doing this, and that they would probably do what was necessary to stop him.

There was just one problem. If you went to your parents, you would be ratting him out again. The *again* part you didn't share with your friends. They didn't need to know about your first betrayal. They just needed to know this would be a stab in the back, and if you ever wanted Sean to forgive you, it wasn't the way to go. So, in the end, you didn't mention it to your parents.

You didn't tell anyone, in fact. What you did was wait for the day of the race to arrive. And when you saw him getting ready in the days ahead, making his own practice maps, and even chugging one of your dad's Coors before heading out for a workout, you made plans to follow him.

If he was going to do this, then the least you could do was show up and see how it went. In other words, you could be there for him. And maybe if he saw your support, he would begin to thaw a bit. You don't say much about how badly you wanted his forgiveness. How desperately you wanted him to talk to you again. Instead, you just tell them about your brother. About how he was the person who knew you best. The person you went to when you pissed your pants in day care and needed help getting rid of the evidence. And how before you knew what a panic attack was, you told him you weren't feeling right one day at the pool, and he sat you on a bench by the concession stand, bought you some Johnny Apple Treats, and made jokes about the lifeguards until your heart rate slowed. Sean was the parent you loved the best. Only he wasn't a parent. He was an eighteen-year-old who was subject to mercurial moods, and he didn't always make the best decisions in the best of conditions. So you decided to keep an eye on him.

It was cold and rainy on the day of the race. You waited until you heard him open the garage before you got in the Corolla and followed him to an alley behind an abandoned Kmart in Minneapolis. You weren't sure what you were expecting, but the people gathered there were not elite athletes. They were like his bike-shop friends, tattooed and wiry, many holding cans of cheap beer and cigarettes at eight o'clock in the morning. They were largely unprotected against the freezing drizzle.

Sean rolled up on his bike, which looked a little too new

compared to the well-worn frames of the other contestants. He paid his entry fee. He received a T-shirt with an hourglass full of beer that read CLOCK'S TICKIN' and a map to the first checkpoint. He stood around for a while, mostly keeping to himself, jumping in place to stay warm. It seemed like he was debating whether to stay.

You kept out of sight on a side street with a clear view of the alley. And as the hour edged toward nine, you saw someone handing out beers. Sean accepted one and looked at it closely, maybe wondering if he was really going to do this. Then somebody blew a whistle and everyone began chugging. At the sound of this shrill signal, something seemed to flip and Sean cracked his beer and tipped it skyward, Adam's apple bobbing, until he had polished it off.

He was already a little behind at this point—his momentary indecision had cost him a few seconds—but as soon as he got his bike going, he was quick to make up ground, weaving between some of the slow starters. You followed by car and tried not to get close enough for him to see you. It helped that you could always pick out his shiny new bike among the other racers' scraped-up models.

But mostly, you could barely stand to watch.

The race was mayhem. The rain picked up early on, and at each checkpoint there was another beer to shotgun. And after each checkpoint, there were more wrecks. People got less inhibited and skidded across the soaked asphalt. Which seemed like it was all part of the fun. Occasionally, another rider would stop to help a downed cyclist, but mostly people laughed even when competitors wiped out in the middle of a busy street. You even saw one rider kick at another on a tight curve.

Yet, in spite of all this, Sean stayed upright. He too laughed at the antics of his fellow racers, and the beer seemed to loosen him up a little bit. He had a similar look on his face to the one he wore that day at the quarry, a kind of manic joy, grinning as he leaped, without warning, from a thirty-foot cliff.

As the race went along, he stayed close to a pack of five or so seasoned riders, who increasingly whooped at his efforts. By this point, no one was trying to knock the others down. It wasn't a grudge match anymore. It was an endurance race. Who among this final crew could down another beer and make it another mile? At the second-to-last checkpoint, the group of other riders buddied up to Sean. They slapped his back and seemed to be welcoming him to the fold. But something had shifted in Sean. He smiled at them, but you recognized the look in his eyes from his diving days. This was how he'd been at meets: stone-faced until it was over. And there was just one more stop to go.

He stood alone, and when the whistle blew for the last time, he downed his beer in what looked like one epic swallow. The final checkpoint was near the university, and there was traffic from a football game that was about to start. You were trying to follow, but you got stuck behind carful after carful of raucous frat boys, howling into the rain, while Sean and the others soared around the traffic, dipping in and out of bike lanes, medians, and sidewalks.

Finally, your visibility was so bad that you pulled your car over and hopped out, running on the sidewalk, trying to make it to the next intersection. It was one of the biggest in town, the convergence of five streets, bars on all the corners. A game-day hub, with partyers out on cold patios in ponchos, braving the rain to tailgate. And from the moment you started moving, you had a nervous feeling about it. Sean was leaning against a stoplight, still on his bike, one hand keeping him balanced.

The noise was deafening. Tables full of drinkers chanted fight songs. Cars honked their horns and launched muddy waves from puddles. And there was even a crew of drummers, pounding on white buckets in perfect synchronicity. There wasn't much farther to go. And maybe it was because he just wanted to get it over with. Or maybe, and this is the part that still keeps you up at night, part of him wanted what would happen next. But before the light turned green, Sean ran the red light and shot out into the intersection.

He was going fast. Faster than you had seen him go all day. His head was down. His hands gripped tight to the handlebars.

You yelled his name.

You screamed so loud, your throat would hurt for days after. But he either couldn't hear you or he didn't care. He was nearly past the intersection when the SUV rounded the corner. Sean was low, and going so fast that he might have been a blur in the periphery. A flash in the side mirror before he was suddenly right in front of the bumper.

There was no time for the SUV to stop.

There was a terrible noise.

You didn't see the impact clearly; you only heard the awful thump and saw where Sean's body ended up, which seemed an improbable distance from the crash. And when you ran to him, his eyes were already glazed over, and there was blood coming out of his nose, mixing with speckles of rain. He was unconscious.

You said his name so many times.

You screamed for an ambulance.

It took so long for one to arrive, and you held his hand the entire time, saying only the word "sorry," over and over again.

When the paramedics showed, you were still saying it, and they thought you were the driver who hit him. They told you to talk to the police, but you pleaded to ride with him. They waved you away and loaded him on a stretcher and put him in an ambulance. They took him to the hospital.

You don't know what to tell your friends now, because what happened next is not even a story. Just a series of fragmented moments. Crying on a sidewalk. Calling your parents and making no sense on the phone. Lying in the back seat of the Corolla. Replaying all the memories of the moment. Wondering if you were hallucinating. Vomiting outside an e-cigarette shop. Sitting in the waiting room of the hospital with your parents and already knowing what the words were going to be when the young doctor came out with the look on her face that said everything was about to be more horrible than you could possibly imagine.

You don't know how to say this part, so instead you say:

"I know he was hit by a car. So I guess I know *how* he died. If that's really what you were asking. And for a long time, I even thought I knew why. I had a lot of ideas about why, and they mostly involved me. But now . . ."

You finally manage to look at Diana.

"Now I'm not so sure."

THIRTY-FIVE

Finally, it's time to sleep.

No one else wants to be in Silas's tent that night, so eventually you volunteer. Partly, it's for the extra space. But mostly it's for the privacy. A half hour ago, when you finished talking about Sean, everybody seemed to look at you differently. There were pats on the back, and I'm-sorrys, and I-can't-imagines, and the kind of looks that most people save for puppies at a shelter. And while it felt good to let these people know who you really are, it also felt a bit like you were stripping down to your underwear in front of them. So it's oddly calming now to zip yourself into the tent of your dead counselor and be alone until morning.

Only it isn't morning that interrupts your shallow sleep. When your tent flap unfastens in the middle of the night, every part of you tenses, ready to fistfight a vengeful bear if necessary. But this time it isn't a predator; it's a person who looks remarkably like Diana. She enters the tent quietly, and once inside she fumbles with the zipper again, struggling to get it closed. The wind has picked up, and before she can get the flap closed again, a biting gust makes its way through the mesh.

"Damn," she whispers. "It's getting cold out there."

Then, while you watch through barely open eyes, she does

the unthinkable: She gets into Silas's abandoned sleeping bag and lies down next to you.

"What are you doing here?" you ask.

She's quiet for a few seconds, which gives you time to wonder if *she* even knows what she's doing here.

"He told me about the race," she whispers.

Your eyes open wider, a spike of cortisol flushing away your sleepiness.

"When?" you ask.

"A couple of days before," she says. "He called me in the middle of the night on Baba's landline and told me he was done with all the self-help and religion. That it wasn't working. And he just needed to get out of his head for a while. He said he needed to get back to the surface."

"Surface?"

"I don't know what it means exactly. But he said he was having these intrusive thoughts. He didn't know to call them that, but that's what they were. Like: violent things he wanted to say and do. Basically, the destroyer was back, but this time, wholly focused on himself."

Your eyes are adjusting to the dark. Clouds must have moved in, because the moonlight is dim, but still, Diana is only inches away from you so you can see that she's just looking at the ceiling of the tent. She blows a tangle of hair off her lips.

"What did you say to him?" you ask.

You hear a slow exhalation in the dark.

"I told him . . . I didn't care what he did," she says.

She wipes at her eyes.

"A few days before that, that girl from the ice cream shop got my number somehow. She called and screamed at Baba on the phone. I don't know what it was about, but I was embarrassed and jealous and when I told him about it, he barely acknowledged it. He just kept talking about this bike race. I still loved him as a person, Case, but I couldn't be the one to help him this time. I was done."

She was really crying now.

"I knew how bad things were and I didn't do anything."

"You were upset."

She manages a full breath.

"So many people I've loved have disappointed me. It's happened again and again. I knew he needed someone, but I couldn't risk getting pulled back in."

She seemed to get herself under control, if only for a moment.

"I didn't know that you guys had a fight," she says. "I didn't know he didn't have you. I left him with nobody."

You sit up entirely now, and even though you're cold outside your sleeping bag, you don't want to feel trapped by it anymore. You put a hand on Diana's shoulder.

"The last thing he said to me was so weird," she says.

"What was it?"

"He said, 'I am not an Atlantean.' Do you know what that means?"

"I don't," you say. "I have no idea."

She's not crying anymore, but sometimes it's worse when your body can't purge it, and you're just living with the clamp of guilt. You sit in silence for a while, listening to the night wind, until finally a single thought occurs to you. And you say it out loud before you even know for certain what you mean.

"We can't both be right."

She turns to you.

"What are you talking about?" she says.

"We both think what happened to Sean is our fault, right? We both think we caused it. But we can't both be right. It's not possible. At least one of us is wrong."

It takes a moment for her to respond. You assume she's thinking it through, but you don't know for sure. You don't know until she speaks again.

"Or both of us," she says.

You nod.

"Or both of us."

It's unclear if either of you really believes this. But even making room for a version of things where you're not the sole cause of what happened to Sean feels lighter. Saying it out loud feels important. But if you're not to blame—and it's not clear if this is true just yet—then why did it happen? Why did he take such a risk? And why did he start pedaling in that moment where the whole world seemed to be screaming around him? Why did he propel himself into the eye of the storm?

You think back to the night he was so angry on the stairs, after he found your letter, and what he said. "It must be so easy for you." It was a hurtful thing for him to assume, that your anxiety gave you some kind of free pass in life. But given what Diana has told you, maybe it wasn't so much anger as it was longing. What was it like for him to have to be the "normal one"? Did he refuse to get help for problems of his own because he thought there wasn't any more room in the family? Because you were filling the quota? You wish you could go back and tell him that if things were hard, there was space for him too.

"You were there," says Diana, tucking her head against you. "Do you think he did it on purpose?"

It's hard for you to picture clearly now. And you're not sure if the view you had of the crash is even accurate, obscured as it was by passing traffic and the rain. It seemed, in that moment, like he was just taking off to get a jump on the competition, but he knew the light was red. He must have.

"I don't think I'll ever know," you say.

She moves closer to you, and then both of you sit there for what feels like hours—but is probably minutes—in the semidark tent. Outside, the cold wind finds little openings to get in, but your combined breath warms the small space.

"Did you actually come here because of me?" you say. "Was that true, what you said?"

Diana is quiet for a second or two.

"Partly," she says.

"But does that mean you're just, like, here as a spy? Or did you actually need help?"

When she uncrosses her arms, her hand brushes against yours.

"I wanted the help too," she says.

For just a second you're disappointed it wasn't all for you, one giant ploy to be close to you. But that's quickly overridden by real concern.

"It started after he died," she says. "I've been depressed before, but this was different. Not just the numbness and lack of energy; suddenly I was on edge all the time, hearing noises in the night.

And drinking was the only thing that helped, but I didn't want to do that all the time. I wasn't sure how to handle it. It's part of the reason I called you all those times. I thought you might know what to do."

The unanswered calls bring back a current of shame, but you manage to set it aside. Diana stays in the sleeping bag next to yours, a softly breathing caterpillar. And for a moment, it feels like anything could happen. You've never been further away from your lives than right now. But the wind howling outside reminds you that you've also never been closer to losing them. Diana starts to move.

"I should go," she says.

She pulls her legs out of the opening, but when she's removing her feet, something leaves the sleeping bag with her. It rustles in the dim light. You catch a glimpse and it looks like some papers, wadded into a ziplock bag.

"Whoa," you say. "What is that?"

Diana opens the tent flap to a window, letting in more moonlight. She gathers up the ziplock and turns it around in her hands.

"I don't know," she says, opening the bag. "I can't believe we never checked his sleeping bag."

She takes out the contents and unfolds them, turning them in the soft blue light. There's enough visibility now to see her expression, which is one of quiet awe.

"I could be wrong," she says softly. "But it looks like a map."

THIRTY-SIX

It just sits there overnight, sealed in its plastic wrapper. You wake up frequently from anxiety dreams. But every time you check, you find the map right on top of the sleeping bag where Diana left it. And when daybreak finally illuminates your tent like a lantern, and the island comes alive with birdsong, you take it out of the bag and carry it to the middle of your campsite. Fran and Will are already up, organizing their packs and nibbling on handfuls of bitter, foraged plants.

"What's that?" asks Will.

You set the map on a sizable rock and motion for them to come closer.

"I think it's what we've been looking for," you say.

Fran's jaw drops when she sees it. You didn't know people's faces actually did that, short of severe injury. Will leans in closer, gnawing on a bunch of greens. The map is the color of raw honey, spattered with cobalt lakes that nearly glow in the morning light. It's been heavily worn, but the colors are still vibrant, and near the top of the map is a single red dot, made from a Sharpie who knows how long ago. Fran reaches down and sets the tip of her pointer finger there.

"How did I miss this?!" she says. "Was it in his tent the whole time?"

"Yeah," you say. "It was tucked away. But Diana found it last night."

Fran gives you a strange look for a second, her brows nearly forming a triangle. Then her eyes go back to the map, taking in the mottled surface and scanning a finger across the lakes. Within seconds, she has found your island in a body of water called Long Gull Lake. Then she leaves to grab her compass and a small twig dipped in mud. When she returns, she's lining up the base plate of her compass on the map and drawing a line to your potential destination with the mud.

Troy and Diana wander out of their tents as Fran works, yawning and hunting for something to eat. They notice her and gather around, watching her position the compass. She uses the ruler on the side to measure the distance to the dot in centimeters. Then she finds the map's legend and converts the centimeters to miles. How she knows this basic map skill, you have no idea. From there, she zeros out the compass and adjusts it for declination. Then she lifts it from the map and aims it in the right direction like a magic wand.

No one has spoken for what feels like minutes, and you could probably wait hours if you had to. Fran is the only one with answers here. But she doesn't keep you in suspense for long. Soon enough, she turns to all of you and holds up the map.

"Okay, party people," she says in a monotone. "Here is the situation as I see it."

Will immediately falls to the ground and starts doing push-ups.

"Will, what in the actual hell?" she says.

"This helps me focus!" he says. "Go on!"

Fran looks away from his rapid movements and puts her finger back on the red dot.

"Assuming this dot is the drop," she says. "Which I hope to God it is. We have about eighteen miles to travel today. And that's if we don't take the trail but just go in a straight line, bushwhacking."

"Bushwhacking?!" says Diana. "Who are you?"

Fran does not stop for this interruption.

"I doubt we've ever made it more than ten miles in a day, but I'm not sure I know where we started, so it's all just a guess. Anyway, there's also some water involved in this trip and paddling is faster than walking, so that helps a little."

Will's movements are getting quicker, and his face is bright red.

"Just tell us if we're going to make it," he says, panting. "Is there even a chance?"

Fran scrunches her nose.

"A slim one," she says.

Will pops up next to you, breathing hard and cracking his knuckles.

"Okay, then. So what are we waiting for?"

"Well," says Fran, drawing you in closer. "There's just one more thing."

You all huddle in a tight circle around the map.

"If the drop is actually here," she says, landing on the red spot again, "and we take the water as far as we can, then we have to contend with *this*."

You lean in and squint at where she's pointing. Most of the map is made up of lakes, a long chain of them that lets you hop from one to the next with the help of small portages. But near the red dot, there appears to be a river cutting through the path, and not just a river, but one that bends in an odd way. It's almost a full circle that leads directly to your destination.

"What do you think it is?" says Troy.

You feel a shooting pain from the back of your head. You wince, and the answer arrives in the midst of the ache.

"That's it," you say. "It has to be."

"Don't say it," says Troy.

"The Devil's Loop," says Diana.

"It's not labeled on here," says Fran. "But I mean . . ."

Everyone looks at the little squiggly blue line. It's almost like a question mark punctuating the end of your route. Each of you is probably picturing some unique horror. Something that terrifies only you. For you, of course, it's heights. A cliff to jump. A mountain to climb. You close your eyes and see the view from the top of the highest cliff at the quarry—the way the water below looked so far away, it seemed like an optical illusion. You feel your heartbeat starting to pound.

"We could just take land," you say. "Skip it entirely."

"We could," says Fran. "But it might be one in the morning by the time we get there. How long are these people going to wait at the site?"

"We don't know that either way," says Troy. "They might just drop the supplies and go. So why take the risk? It's called the Devil's Loop, people! The word *devil* is in it!"

"It's true. They might be gone," says Fran. "But . . ."

"But what?" Troy says.

"But that's probably your anxiety talking."

Everyone is quiet at that. You think about your last comment, and how you're still hoping everyone will side with you and decide to go by land. You're hoping that you can take the long way, by trail, maybe crossing a couple of calm lakes, and find Silas's colleagues waiting for you, making sure you're okay. But even as you imagine it, you know it cuts your odds in half.

"Fran's right," you say. "At least about me. I'm . . . afraid."

Will is still next to you, breathing heavily from his push-ups. He watches you.

"Me too," says Troy.

Will puts his head down.

"But . . . ," you say, "the whole point of coming on this god-forsaken trip in the first place was to try to quiet that voice that tells us we can't do anything, right? I mean, I get panic attacks in movie theaters because of the dark and the noise. I don't feel good in crowds, even small ones. And after my brother died, I couldn't even ride a bike anymore without hyperventilating. I mean, how much more am I going to lose? What else am I going to give up if I don't start to fight back a little?"

"I hear that," says Troy. "I've had panic attacks watching kids' shows with my baby cousin. Like, the situations this talking dog was in were too intense for me."

"Crossing a crosswalk," says Fran. "Full-on attack. Couldn't make it to the other side."

"I fainted in a grocery store," says Diana, "because the lighting felt weird."

Will takes a breath, still looking at the ground.

"I had to lie down in the middle of a tennis match at State. I felt so scared, I just had to curl up on the court while everyone was watching. My dad was screaming at me to get up, but I couldn't. They had to carry me off."

He looks up at the sky and lets out a long breath.

"That shit was so embarrassing," he says.

"Look," you say. "Can we be honest for a minute? None of us are leaving here cured."

Silence.

"Trees and fishing can't cure anxiety disorder," you say. "They just can't."

Now everyone is hanging their heads.

"It sucks," you say. "I was pretty much willing to believe anything when I signed up for this. I thought I'd leave it all out here in the woods. But I think I knew all along I was stuck with this for life."

"So what are you saying?" asks Diana.

"I don't know. Maybe I've been thinking about it wrong. Maybe we don't need to be cured."

"Did you not hear that list of pathetic situations?" asks Troy. "We're broken toys. All of us."

Everybody looks at you. You're not sure how to refute that. But you take a moment to regroup.

"Okay, look," you say. "Just think of it this way: The world outside these woods is totally screwed up. Can we agree on that? It's burning, for one thing."

Troy nods.

"People are getting shot by the police. There are wars. And pandemics. And so many people in charge of things are super racist and homophobic and awful. We work really hard in school just so we can have a boring life someday where we work even more just to get stuff we don't really want. At my school, we have to do active-shooter drills once a month. I don't understand how all these so-called normal people can go through all of this every day, feeling okay. Like: What's wrong with them?! Maybe we're the ones having a normal reaction to messed-up shit! Have you guys ever thought of that?"

Your head is starting to pound again, the pain flaring up. But you take a breath.

"Say we have this forever, and there's nothing we can do about that; can we just push ourselves a little more? We were stuck out here with nothing, and we figured out shelter, water, and food. We scared away a bear and dealt with a dead body."

"I pooped in the woods," says Fran

"We all pooped in the woods!" Diana shouts.

"And we did all that while fighting our own brains," you say. "I think maybe that makes us strong. So maybe we can do one last strong thing."

Troy holds his hand up, and you take a step forward to high-five him. And that's when it hits you again. Another wave of pain, this time with a hint of nausea thrown in. Before you know it, you're down on one knee. Will immediately crouches and tries to steady you, but you're a little on the wobbly side.

"Bro," he says. "Are you okay?"

You feel clammy, and as you stand again, a deep chill runs through your body. Your breaths come quickly. You're sure, at first, that you're just having a panic attack, which is a little funny given your big speech, but then you notice the throb coming from the back of your head, a pain that's been slowly growing for days.

"Hey," you say, sucking in a breath. "Can somebody check my head? I think maybe . . ."

When you put your fingers to it, the pain is so sharp that your words vanish before you can speak them. You close your eyes, and when you open them again, someone has hands to your head and is pushing your hair out of the way.

"Oh my god, Case," says Diana.

"What?" you say.

"This cut does not look good."

You ask her to describe it, and for a moment, she's at a complete loss for words. Then she's not, and the words that follow are not ones that you want to hear about a wound. They include "red," "swollen," "all messed up," "ooze," and "spreading," not necessarily in that order.

"It's probably infected," says Fran. "That happened to my aunt once. She cut her leg on a rusty fence gate, and a week later she was babbling about chemtrails. We had to take her to the hospital."

"Not sure that's helpful, Fran," says Diana.

"I feel like I've been stabbed with an ice pick," you say.

"Look," says Will. "Just sit for a minute. I'll pack your stuff. We're in the water first, so we'll throw you in a boat."

Everyone watches while you take a couple of deep breaths.

"It's okay," you say. "It's okay. I think we're just at a decision point."

Concerned stares all around.

"A what?" says Troy.

"You know. From Choose Your Own Adventure books!" you say. "Didn't you guys ever read those?"

"See!" says Fran. "He's already hallucinating."

"Case," comes Diana's voice. "Relax, okay? Just close your eyes and we'll take care of the rest."

"No," you say. "I'm not closing my eyes. I'll be fine!"

And then, of course, you close your eyes.

THIRTY-SEVEN

You're not asleep.

But you're not necessarily awake.

You're in some kind of head-wound fever dream. And in that state, a memory of Sean returns and you let it. It's from a few summers ago during a late-July heat wave. Each day, you and Sean did nothing but sit next to an old window air conditioner, trying to think of anything to pass the time until the sun went down. There were board games, card games, and epic rounds of "would you rather?" But one day, despite the heat, you were conscripted to help your dad clear the storage space over the garage. And that's when you found the books.

When you opened the box in the sweltering garage and saw the words *Choose Your Own Adventure*, you immediately knew it was something from your father's childhood in the eighties. You could tell by the mildewed smell of the brittle, yellowed pages. Your dad wasn't the most revealing guy, and finding artifacts from his youth always felt like unearthing a chunk of his personality you'd never get to know otherwise. There was something almost thrilling about it.

The first thing you noticed about the books were the titles. Because they were amazing. *The Cave of Time. Vampire Express.*

Tattoo of Death. The covers were just as good. Pulpy scenes of kids outrunning spaceships, rafting through the Amazon, and karate-kicking cyborgs off cliffs. You and Sean spent an entire week of summer vacation devouring them all in order.

You loved them.

Both of you.

The interactive nature. The high-octane plots, and the second-person narration that put you right in the story as an active participant. You read every single one of them to your dad's bewilderment, but only Sean became obsessed with figuring out how they worked.

When he was done reading, he spent entire afternoons mapping out all the options in each book and trying to find a key that would allow him to cheat death. There was one book called *Journey Under the Sea* that particularly vexed him because he kept dying no matter what decisions he made.

"Dammit!" he'd shout from your carpeted floor. "Not again!"

Each read-through brought a new torture. In one he'd be eaten by a shark. Then killed by pressure in his submarine. Drowned in a sea cave. Eventually he mapped out every single ending, and then came the moment you're remembering now, a night when you were about to get in bed and Sean burst in with a stricken look on his face, gripping the book.

"I've done the whole thing!" he said. "Every page. Every option. Twice! And over seventy-five percent of these choices end in disaster! Can you believe that? What kind of sadist writes these things?! It's an outrage!"

"Sean . . . ," you said. "I think it might be time to put the books back in the garage."

You expected a laugh, but he didn't seem to hear you. He just produced a piece of notebook paper with some wild diagram he had drawn.

"Forty-two endings, and thirty-two of them leave you completely screwed!"

He stood in the doorway, simmering. Then his rage kind of faded, morphing into something quieter.

"What's the point even?"

You wanted to make fun of him, how upset he was getting about this one hokey book about deep-sea exploration from 1988, but in the face of his very real disappointment, it was suddenly hard to joke around. He seemed personally offended, like this book was an affront to his most deeply held beliefs.

"Maybe they're just trying to make them challenging," you said.

He opened the paperback and flipped through it idly. Then he tossed it on the bed.

"Maybe," he said.

He walked over and sat down next to you. The air conditioner was chugging away in the window, and the manufactured breeze tousled his hair.

"But what if it's true?"

"What do you mean?"

"Like, what if you really make a couple of bad decisions, things that seem so small and insignificant at the time, and then there you are . . . in the sea cave forever? Do you ever worry about that?"

You didn't know what to tell him but the truth.

"I guess not . . . ," you said.

At the time, he was still diving, and his life seemed so perfect to you. He had made varsity as a freshman. He had a string of teammates and pretty, sporty girls with ponytails dropping by the house just to joke around with him. And your parents seemed to let him come and go as he pleased. You couldn't imagine what kind of decision he might be talking about. But still, he seemed genuinely worried.

He looked down at the cover of the book. A submarine propelling itself through the dark water, and in the background, lurking, a menacing shark. In one part of the drawing, the main character was safe in his submersible. In another, he was spinning around in some kind of whirlpool, the shark bearing down on him.

"They don't all end in failure, right?" you said. "There's still that twenty-five percent."

You took the book and tossed it across the room. His eyes followed it, clearly unnerved by its absence. And you wonder now, if you hadn't tried to cheer him up that night, if, instead, you'd been willing to listen, would he have told you more? Would he have told you about what was really going on with him? But, at the time, after you'd thrown the book, you watched something shift in his expression, a sudden desire to let you know everything was okay. Even if it wasn't.

"Yeah," he said. "You're right."

And then he rolled over on his back and let the cold air blow across his face. You can still see him there so clearly, even now in your head. His face tensed for a moment before finally relaxing and going slack. And you wish now that you had lain down next to him. Maybe fallen asleep the way you did when you were kids when a bad storm would send you running to the same bed, even after you were too old to be bunking together. Back then, just knowing the other was there beside you was enough.

It would still be enough.

THIRTY-EIGHT

You hear the water before you open your eyes again. The now-familiar plunge and suction of the paddle and the soft trickle of water dripping from the blade. When your eyes open, the sun blurs your vision and turns everything a fiery orange. A small moan escapes your lips, and it takes everything in your power not to touch the tender spot on the back of your head. When you can see again, you find Will at the front of your boat, shoulders rotating, dragging the paddle through the dark blue lake and muttering to himself.

"How did you get me in here?" you ask.

Will turns around and smiles through gritted teeth.

"Dragged you, bro," he says. "You're heavier than you look. Need to cut back on those grasshoppers."

As you become more aware of your body, it feels like you were dropped in the canoe from a great height. Your limbs are sprawled everywhere, with a foot hanging over the gunwale to your right.

"I think I need medical attention," you say.

"No shit," says Will. "You're messed up."

You manage to gather yourself and sit up. The boat wobbles, then steadies again when you're upright. You look around. Behind you, the island is just a dot. This first lake, you remember from the map, is a long and spindly one. It's so quiet, it takes you a minute to realize that nobody else is around you.

"Where's the rest of the crew?" you ask.

Will stops and points ahead of you.

"They were hauling, man. We're meeting them at the shore. I've got dead weight to carry. No offense."

"None taken," you say.

You find if you just concentrate on the things around you—the lake, the sounds of the water, the cool breeze—you can kind of ignore the pain. It's never gone exactly, but it fades into the background like distant music.

"We're not too far off," says Will. "That's the good news. The bad news is that then you'll have to walk 'cause I'm not about to piggyback you."

You nod even though you know he can't see you. It's hard to imagine hiking through the woods without a trail, backpack straps digging into your shoulders, but you know if you want to survive, you're going to have to find a way. For now, you're grateful there's at least one athlete on this trip to transport you. You lie back, and the sky is so bright you can't look directly at it, so you peer through heavy lids.

"Hey," says Will. "Sorry if I was asking too many questions about your brother last night."

He hasn't turned around, so you don't see his face. You're trying to remember if he was overly aggressive in his questioning, but you only remember one or two.

"That's okay . . ."

He keeps propelling you through the water, but you can tell

he wants to say something else. And after a few powerful strokes, he speaks again.

"It's just that, I'm pretty sure that was going to be me."

He rests his arms for a moment, wincing as he moves them in slow circles. There's a sunburn turning his thick neck pink.

"How do you mean?" you ask.

"Well, things were bad, and I wasn't telling anyone. I'd go through my days like nothing was wrong, but then, in private, I was having these epic breakdowns. Crying in my car or in a bathroom stall in the locker room. It's just me and my dad at home, and he's not the world's most open person. We talk about sports, and my grades, but not much else. He was raised by immigrants, and there wasn't a lot of focus on, um . . . well-being. They were too busy grinding."

He starts rowing again, breathing hard after each pull through the water.

"I didn't want help. That's not what I was taught. So I was gonna power through it, you know?"

"Then what happened?" you ask.

He pauses and holds his paddle still.

"I couldn't power through it."

You can see the shore in the distance now if you squint.

"I hid some pills in my dresser. I didn't have a plan, but they were there and my dad found them. He told me he wasn't going to do anything, then he tricked me into coming here. I guess the joke's on him because I might die anyway."

He doesn't laugh.

"I'm glad you didn't die," you say.

He turns around and looks at you.

"There'd be nobody to paddle me."

A half smile. Then he starts in again.

"If we ever get out of this," he says, "I'll get some real help. Maybe some medication if I need it. I know I haven't been easy to deal with out here, but you guys have helped me. Just knowing I'm not alone. It got me thinking about some things."

As the shore grows closer, he paddles faster, his whole body straining. You can just make out some figures, and as the boat inches closer you see Diana, Fran, and Troy waiting for you. When the canoe hits sand, they all come running to help you out of the boat.

"He's awake!" you hear from Troy, along with a few other murmurs.

Diana reaches for your hand, and Fran grabs the other. Will leaves the boat and stands in the shallow water, waiting for you to climb out. Before you try a step, you look at their dirty, malnourished faces. Your therapist told you once that friendships formed in trauma aren't real friendships. They often don't outlast the traumatic experience itself. If you manage to escape those circumstances, the thing that bonded you is gone and everything dissolves. But as you step out of the teetering canoe and your group of exhausted survivors steadies you with their calloused hands, it's suddenly hard to imagine a life without them.

One of them especially. But you're surprised to feel a similar tie to the others as well. You're not sure when this happened; you only know, as they help you to the shore, that you all have to make it out of this somehow so you can see one another in better times. You feel a pull in you to keep moving. It wars against the very real fatigue and pain, but you manage to stay on your feet, which clomp through the cold shallows by the shore.

When you get to the land, everyone watches you. You realize after a few seconds that they're waiting to see if you can walk. What would they do if you couldn't? They would have to leave you behind, and if they wouldn't, you would make them. For now, however, you're vertical, and when you move one of your feet forward, it goes where you want. You don't know how far you can go, or how fast, but for now, you can move yourself in a chosen direction. You look up and face your friends.

"Which way, Fran?" you say.

And everyone sighs in relief.

You're about to start moving when you suddenly hear a sound coming from across the lake. You all look up, and at first, all you see is a sky full of tiny pinpricks. Scattering dots like floaters in your vision. They morph as they grow closer, until you can finally see that they're birds. Whole flocks converging and flying over you. Some with drab feathers and small bodies. Others with sharp wings and hooked beaks. Birds of prey. Songbirds. Waterfowl.

They're making all the possible bird sounds—gurgles, chirps, and screams—that merge together like an out-of-tune orchestra. Each of you cranes your neck to watch them pass over a thicket of baby birch trees. It feels like they're never-ending until finally a few last stragglers disappear into the woods, and the sky is empty once again.

"Migration?" says Fran, staring out in the direction they came.

Troy has a puzzled look on his face.

"Maybe," he says. "But there were so many different kinds. I guess that happens sometimes . . ."

"Everybody's getting out of here but us," says Diana.

A few of you laugh, but Will still stares intently at the sky.

"It looked super urgent, though," he says. "Like they were trying to get away from something."

"Probably just the cold, right?" says Diana, hugging her shoulders.

Everything is quiet again in their absence. You all wait a moment, wondering what might come tearing through next. A moose? A herd of deer? But there's nothing. And because you have to keep moving if you want to live, you let it go. You chalk it up to yet another thing you don't understand about nature. But as you help Fran lift a canoe over the top of the two of you, your weakened body straining under the weight, you can't quite get that cacophony of screeches out of your head. What, you wonder, were they trying to say?

THIRTY-NINE

Bushwhacking, as Fran calls it, is not easy. And it's even harder with canoes. It's one thing to go off the trail and wade through waist-high brush, bugs crawling all over your legs, but it's even harder to haul a canoe with low-hanging branches scraping over the roof and pushing it down on your already beleaguered shoulders. You're still with Fran, who can more than carry her share of the weight, but the combination of your injury and the trees blown down by the storm makes the first long portage a hellish trek. Your hot, feverish breath fills your section of the canoe, and you blink the cold sweat from your eyes as you walk.

You're stumbling more than before, barely picking up your feet, trying to keep pace with Fran. From behind you come the groans and swears of the rest of your companions. No one is speaking in sentences, just grunting and moving as fast as their bone-tired bodies will take them. You're all going to need food again soon, but there isn't time to stop and fish, or to form another hunting party. Getting to the drop as early as possible is the only goal, even if you collapse the moment you make it. All you can do in the meantime is just pray that you get to the small river that's next on the map before your legs give out.

For a while, you seem to get in a rhythm, plodding forward without even thinking about your pain, trying to match your steps to Fran's, but then the wind starts to pick up again and suddenly the boat on your shoulders is swiveling and attempting to take flight. You hold on as tight as you can. A haze has moved in with the wind, and even though Troy and Diana are about fifty feet behind you, it's getting hard to see them. You hear them, though, when they crash into a tree.

"We're okay!" yells Troy a few seconds later. "Sort of!"

You brace yourself against another gust and stumble sideways a step before regaining your footing. The haze is thicker than the usual morning fog, and you find yourself coughing for a spell before clearing your throat.

"Hey, Fran," you say, muffling one last cough. "Listen. This is kind of weird, but I know I said Diana was in my tent the other night . . ."

Fran sighs.

"Seriously, you want to talk about this *now*?" she says.

She readjusts her grip on the canoe.

"I get it. Not the best timing. I just want you to know that nothing happened."

Another gale comes howling through the trees, and this time, both you and Fran have to lean against a nearby rock to keep from flipping over. Aside from the wind, there's a kind of deeper thrumming sound that you're hearing, but you can't quite put a finger on it.

"Can we please talk about this another time?" she says.

Her hair is in a ponytail, and when she stops for a second, it brushes across your forehead.

"Sure, of course," you say, trying not to get hair up your

nostrils. "I just don't want you to think . . . I mean, I don't want you to hate me."

Forward you go for another half mile or so, fighting the wind and the wild grasses that are now up to your chest. From above, it must look like your capsized boat is adrift on a green sea. But from below, it just looks like darkness and plants. There are burrs coating your socks like carpet. You hope there isn't any poison ivy, but you can't distinguish the leaves enough to tell.

"I don't hate you, Case," Fran says eventually. "You are a lot of things, but hateable isn't really one of them."

The ground beneath you is starting to get a little spongy, and you hear the soft squelch of your boots digging into the mud. Now it's Fran's turn to cough. But when she speaks again, it's clear as a bell.

"Diana is not into me."

She looks behind her to see how close she and Troy are to both of you. But they're still a ways back.

"And that's okay as it turns out," she says. "Even though there would be something kind of hot about a survival hookup, I think we're destined to be pals."

Fran does her best to shrug with a canoe on her back.

"It's nice to have friends too," she adds. "I haven't had that many."

Sweat rolls off your brow and down your nose. Your heart is beating in your ears. Fran steps over a jagged rock mired in a puddle. You both brace for more wind.

"I don't want to betray her trust, Case, but watching you guys do this awkward dance is starting to bring me down."

You didn't think what was happening was so obvious, but you suppose there isn't much privacy when you travel as a pack.

"All I'll say," says Fran, "is that she's told me a lot about you, and I think it was you from the beginning."

"What do you mean?" you say. "The beginning of the trip?"

She shakes her head.

"I mean the *beginning*, beginning. Your brother, I think, was the safe choice. I know he's gone, so I don't want to say anything that's hurtful. But from what she's told me he was just, like, a charming sporto when she first met him. She knew what that was, but I don't think she knew what to do with you."

"What *to do* with me?"

"Your connection. I think she just assumed it wasn't romantic since she actually liked you. That was a new thing for her."

Even through your fever and your sluggishness, Fran's words send your whole head buzzing. Below you, the mud is getting thicker and your boots are getting wetter.

"I think we're almost to the river," says Fran. "So I'm just going to say one last thing. I'm sorry about your brother, Case. It is tragic, and it is unbelievably hard to lose someone you loved so much. There's not really a timeline for feeling better. But *your* life is not over. Do you get that? At least . . . not yet."

And with that, Fran hefts the canoe over her head again. You follow her lead, and the two of you strain to get it back down to the ground, where there's more of a creek than a river cutting between the tall grass in front of you. You look at the thin body of water as it slips around the bog like a snake. The haze is even stronger now. The others set their boats down behind you.

"You guys clocking this fog?" says Troy. "It's weird."

"Where's Will?" asks Diana.

You try not to look at her differently, wondering how much of what Fran said is true. Did she really care about you from the very beginning?

"Who?" you say.

Diana frowns.

"Berries!" comes a sudden cry from the woods.

"That's him!" says Troy.

As a herd, you all stand and lumber toward the voice, walking again over the soggy earth, and the tan rocks and thick grasses. When you find Will, he is pulling down the thickest branch of a large bush, plucking red globes off it and stuffing them in his open mouth.

"They're terrible, guys!" he says, laughing. "The worst!"

You wait while Troy walks up to the bush and takes a long look at the berries. Even Will stops for a second to watch his face. Troy looks at a bloom and then examines the leaves, which look almost like maples.

"Am I going to die?" asks Will, squinting at the bitterness of the fruit.

"No . . . ," says Troy. "Highbush cranberries, I think."

He grabs a couple and chews them to a pulp. He spits out a red seed.

"Not poisonous. Just really bad."

At that, everyone dives on the bush, which is flush with the tart berries. Shockingly, you don't have much of an appetite, but you know you need calories if you're going to continue walking. So you manage to choke down a couple of handfuls of the astonishingly sour berries, while your friends look like they're in a game of Hungry Hungry Hippos. As this is happening, the sky behind you grows even darker.

But somehow you've developed enough instinct to notice that it doesn't really feel like rain. It's not humid at all. And the air doesn't have that ozone smell that comes before a thunderstorm. Still, the sun has disappeared and you notice something that you haven't witnessed before: an acrid scent that is blowing through along with the haze. Slowly, each one of you stops eating the berries. Diana is the first to walk into the clearing nearby and look up.

The sky is not just dark now. It's orange.

And the smell only grows more pungent when you gaze upward and notice what appears to be a giant mushroom cloud hovering above you. There are at least ten possible scenarios battling for supremacy in your head. Nuclear test. Alien invasion. Tornado. In the moment, anything seems possible. There's a humming sound too, and you're pretty sure it's not coming from inside your head this time. It's louder than before. Then the wind blows again and carries with it the unmistakable smell of burn and char.

"Fire," says Diana. "There's a wildfire."

FORTY

An hour later, the sky is bloodred, and the blowing wind carries visible particles of ash. The smoke-filtered light makes the heart of the afternoon feel like dusk. Most alarming, though, is the sound, which has gone from a distant hum to a slowly encroaching growl. You've been paddling the creek for an hour with Diana in your boat, but every half mile or so the water level dips too low, and you have to get out and lift the canoe over a hill of sand or past one of a seemingly infinite number of abandoned beaver dams. Everyone is coughing. Everyone is on the verge of tears. But out of all of you, Troy is taking it the worst.

Ever since the first glimpse of that smoke, he has been rattling off climate change facts nonstop for an hour.

"... and wildfires are burning seven million acres a year, which is up almost fifty percent since the 1990s. Can you even believe that? Fifty percent more of our country is burning each year! I mean, what the literal hell!"

At this point, you are all trying to tune him out, but nobody has the heart to stop him. It's possible this monologue coming direct from his anxiety brain is the only thing keeping him from a complete meltdown.

"... and because the fires are way bigger, it's tougher for these forests to regenerate, which contributes even more to climate change because they can't store carbon . . ."

When you turn around, he's not looking at any of you. He's just kind of blinking into the murky bog surrounding you. You look past him this time and try to figure out where exactly the smoke is coming from. Fran thinks it's the southwest, which is good because you're headed north, but you swear sometimes that it's coming from another direction entirely.

Before Troy started in on his lecture, he told you that depending on weather conditions, these things can change direction and burn fast ("fourteen frickin' miles an hour in an open space, guys!"). The uncertainty is making everything even more terrifying. Without any information, all you can do is try to move in the right direction as fast as possible.

"You okay back there?" asks Diana. "Still conscious?"

"Mm-hmm," you say, which is the most you've said in a while.

You were surprised when Diana asked to be in your boat, but ever since she saw your infected cut, she's been watching you closely, visible concern on her face. You wonder if it's because she thinks you're just going to drop dead in front of her. No matter where things stand with the two of you right now, she probably doesn't want to lose anyone else. You're glad she's close, though. Even if the two of you have been mostly silent since you started paddling.

You want to talk to her. You want to ask about all the things Fran told you, to see if they're true, but now that you're two feet away from her, you can't quite bring yourself to speak. It seems ridiculous, somehow, that you're likely being chased down by a fire and you still want to know what really happened between you. Will that itchy feeling ever go away? Is it with you for life?

Another problem: The smoke is burning your throat. Hers too. You can tell by the pained sound of her cough. She's running low on water, but eventually she just dips her bottle in the river and drinks. There's no time to stop and boil water at the pace you're going, so she gulps it down. Then she dips it again and passes it back to you. You look at the river around you. There's not a lot of algae or mud in the water, so when she presses the wet bottle into your hand, you drink deeply, and the water is so cold and clean tasting that it hurts your teeth.

And with this one drink comes a rare moment of calm. For an instant, you're able to stop thinking about your past mistakes and the uncertainty of the future. You just close your eyes and you can almost feel your cells absorbing the water. Even your headache feels better for a second or two. And with this calm, everything suddenly seems so simple:

The world is on fire. Offer water when you can.

You hand the bottle back to Diana.

"Thank you," you say.

Your red eyes are watering, and you're pretty sure it's from the smoke. But you're also thinking about how long it's been since you experienced uninterrupted tranquility. You've spent so much of the past year, and a good portion of your life before that, terrified and ashamed. But there are times, even in the midst of chaos, where you catch a glimpse of how simple it can be to exist in a moment.

"And God help our sorry asses," shouts Troy, "if the arctic permafrost starts to melt! Just stick a fork in the planet if that happens! There was a fire there, like, fifteen years ago that let off two million metric tons of carbon!"

And just like that, the moment is gone. At Troy's last word, the hull of the boat scrapes bottom again, and you stand on uncertain legs to heft it. There aren't any low-hanging trees this time, but the air quality is so bad that you can't see too far in front of you. Big rocks pop up out of the blue, along with trees knocked down by the wind. Will trips and scrapes his shin on an uprooted pine. Instead of swearing, he just releases a primal scream.

Troy doesn't even stop his lecture at the noise. He's still going on about the Paris Climate Accord, and you wait for Will to full-on throttle him. Will is not the most patient among you as it is, and listening to a live audiobook of the apocalypse while his shin is throbbing has got to be past his threshold. But he doesn't tackle Troy. Instead, he leaves the canoe with Fran for a moment and calmly walks back to him.

When he gets to Troy, he grabs Troy's canoe and helps him scrabble up some rocks and down to the deeper water of the creek again. Troy is still saying something you can't quite hear about average surface temperature when Will puts his hands on Troy's shoulders. Surprisingly, Troy goes quiet, like a radio that's been switched off.

"Troy, my guy," says Will. "Can I ask you a question?"

Troy says nothing. But he doesn't say no.

"Do you want to see Turbo again?"

Troy blinks and coughs into his hands. Life seems to return, however temporarily, to his eyes.

"Yes," he says, his voice shaky.

"Tell me. What's it going to be like when you see him?"

Troy doesn't hesitate at all.

"Beautiful," he says. "It's going to be beautiful."

A tear runs down his ash-stained cheek.

"Right," says Will. "Okay. Good. So here's the deal, bro. Nobody thinks you're wrong about all this climate stuff. We know how messed up it is. But also: That's the world, right?"

"What do you mean?" asks Fran.

Will keeps looking at Troy.

"It's full of terrible stuff. But it's also full of beautiful stuff. Like you and the pure love you have for that wiener dog. It's the same world, you know? Fires and wiener dogs. But that's a super hard thing to hold in your head, I think. That it can be both."

Troy is crying. He nods.

"Look, all I'm saying is if you want to see Turbo again, and take him to the dog park and watch him run on his pathetic, tiny wiener legs, then we have to keep going. And we have to stay positive. Just for now. When we get home, we can solve climate change. Right now, we need to live."

Troy is coughing while crying, and Will stares at him without speaking. Then, apropos of nothing, Troy just takes his shirt off. Everyone watches, unsure what he's doing. But then he doesn't toss it in his boat; he dunks it in the creek. Then he wrings it out.

"I saw this in a movie about firefighters once," he says.

Before anyone can ask a follow-up question, Troy starts wrapping the shirt around his face so that he's breathing through the wet fabric.

"Any better?" Diana asks.

Troy nods, takes a deep breath.

"A little, I think."

Everyone, including you, opens their packs and finds an old T-shirt. You soak the fabric in the river and, one by one, you too wrap shirts around your faces. The cold water against your skin feels better already, and when you pull in a breath, the moisture helps with the smoke. Who knows how long it will last, but for the first few breaths, it makes a noticeable difference.

You're almost past the shallow spot, so you all move your boats back into the creek. Fran takes a moment to look at the map. Then she looks behind you. Aside from the growing sound of the fire itself, the air is eerily silent. And you realize it's because there's no birdsong. All those birds you saw, and so many others, have left. They're gone. And if you could fly, you would be gone too.

"Six miles to the Loop," Fran says. "Give or take."

Another powerful gust of smoky wind blows, and you're all thinking the same thing: Whether or not you make it there is going to have more to do with the weather than you. You have been trying to work with nature since Silas left you. Trying to learn its rules. How to find food, and navigate, and work in harmony with it. You've been trying to meet nature halfway. But now you know the truth: There's no reasoning with it. It's either going to eat you or it isn't.

"What if no one's there?" asks Diana. "What if we get there and everyone's evacuated because of the fire?"

"Possible," Fran says. "But what's our alternative? Go back the way we came?"

She points back toward the mushroom cloud. It looks like a nuclear-testing site. And the coming fire, which isn't yet visible, sounds like a million hungry cicadas.

"Forward!" shouts Will. "There's no other way. When you're down a break, you can't give up, guys! You gotta break back!"

"I don't know what the hell he's talking about," says Troy.

"Tennis, Troy!" says Will. "I'm talking about tennis. But I'm also using metaphors, bro. Now why don't you take the lead position this time."

"Me?" he says, his shirt-wrap muffling his speech.

"Yeah," he says. "You! You helped us with that shirt thing. Now paddle like you want to see your dog again. We'll follow."

Troy takes a hesitant step forward. Then he quickens his pace and gets in Will's canoe in front of Fran. He's quiet and there's something like resolve in his eyes. Will takes Troy's canoe.

And with that, you and Diana are back in your boat. The water looks deeper ahead of you, at least as far as you can see, and that's a good thing. Less canoe lifting. The creek is surrounded by grass and topped by a sky so orange it looks like you're paddling through Mars. You close your eyes, and for a second, you're not sure if they're going to open again. But they do, somehow. And what you see when they open is Diana looking directly at you.

"Hey, Case," she says. "Are you with me?"

"I think so," you say.

"Good. Because there's just one more thing I have to know."

"Okay . . . ," you say.

Your head is spinning, but you grab your paddle and get your hands in position.

"Was it guilt?" asks Diana.

She doesn't break eye contact.

"Was what guilt?"

"Is that why you never picked up the phone?"

"You mean . . ."

"When I called. All those times after the funeral? Was it just guilt, or did you really never want to speak to me again?"

In your head, you're answering her. But you're aware that in life, nothing is actually coming out of your mouth. Not even a breath.

"Case?" she says. "Are you there?"

And then, of course, you are.

FORTY-ONE

It was the second worst day of your life.

The first is obvious. But, even now, when you think about it, you can't help reminding yourself that at least you got *to have* a worst day. At least you got to sit there feeling terrible in an ill-fitting suit your dad ordered from Costco. You got the gift of feeling nauseous and sweaty as you sat in the hard pew in a church that neither Sean nor anyone else in your family had ever attended. Sean did not get another day. Instead, he was being spoken about by a reverend who never knew him.

You could barely hear the religious man's words because in your head, all you could think was that it should be you in that box. That's the thought that was on repeat. *It should be me. It should be me. It should be me.* You were the expendable one. The one who never quite figured out how to thrive. The sound of these thoughts drowned out the quiet gasps of your mom crying and the baby across the aisle cooing and stuffing the corner of a hymnal in her mouth. It even drowned out the loud scratch of the microphone when it brushed the reverend's collar and snapped all the mourners to attention.

It was not a bad service, from what you caught of it. The religious people who ran it must have at least gotten the hint that you were a clan of agnostics verging on atheists. They didn't speak much about heaven or hell or other things you'd heard at your Catholic grandmother's funeral five years ago. They had done their research about the deceased, and when the reverend told stories he'd been fed about Sean's lively personality, they sounded heartfelt.

But somehow this made things worse. It would have been easier to wallow if the eulogy had been incompetent, too holy, or sanctimonious. Instead, it was well done, but you still knew that barely anyone in the room understood the real Sean, much less the complicated circumstances of his death.

The exception, of course, was the girl at the back of the room, sitting next to her Serbian grandmother. You tried not to look back there too much, but you couldn't help it, and whenever you did, she was staring straight ahead like she had blinders on. Your parents couldn't stop crying. On top of everything else, they had been fielding calls from reporters all week, people who were trying to sensationalize Sean's death and make it part of an exposé about the dangers of illegal bike races. Your dad had been angrier than you'd ever seen him yesterday, screaming into the phone at some poor fact-checker from the local paper.

But now that he was in the room with everyone else, he just looked defeated. Your mom had thrown herself into every detail of the funeral, all the while wearing the same face she did after a night shift at the hospital: determined and resigned at the same time. Neither one of them asked you how you knew about the bike race or whether Sean had told you. They knew about his risk-taking past, and even though they were completely gutted by his death, they also had this look about them like maybe they'd known this was a possibility.

You only spoke to Diana once at the funeral. In the middle of a diving coach's speech about Sean's team spirit, you left to go to the bathroom. You couldn't listen to a man who knew nothing about anything talk about Sean's leadership in the locker room and how devastated he was when Sean had to quit. It was all too much, so you whispered to your parents that you needed water and ducked out into the hallway, where you could breathe.

In the hall, you could sigh and swear to yourself as much as you wanted. And when you went into the bathroom, just to run some cold water over your hands, you let yourself release some childish sounds of anguish. A long whimper that wasn't quite a cry and that echoed around the cavernous church bathroom. You sat down on the tile floor and listened to the buzzing fluorescent lights. Then you stood back up and walked out to the hall to find Diana waiting for you.

Her hair was cut short and dyed blond, but it was still curly, and escaping the confines of some bobby pins. If you didn't know any better, you'd think she cut it herself with some kitchen shears. She looked older, and the black dress she'd borrowed from her baba only added to the effect. Despite being just a year older than you, she'd always seemed more mature, like she'd had twice as many life experiences, which was probably true.

"I think we should leave," she said to you in the hallway.

You were the only two people there, and you could hear the echoing murmur of the diving coach still nattering on inside.

"I don't know . . . ," you started.

"We don't have to talk or anything," she said. "We can just drive."

At that, you acquiesced and pulled out the keys to the Corolla.

"You can drive this time," you said, and tossed them to her.

Leaving the church felt right the second you did it, abandoning the sad brick building and just getting on the freeway, where the weekend traffic was sparse and lazy. Midafternoon light came in through the dirty windshield, refracted and faded. Diana drove outside the bounds of the city, and then kept on going past the first-ring suburbs. You realized you had actually never seen her drive a car before, but she seemed perfectly natural behind the wheel. She turned the radio on and found a jazz station on the A.M. dial that was playing something from decades ago. A man improvising on a saxophone from a time before your parents were kids.

Diana was true to her word; you didn't speak as you made it out past the suburban sprawl to the first farms. You saw cows, lowing by the side of fenced-in lots, and goats stomping around in their proprietary way. There were even a few alpacas, twisting their long furry necks to watch you go by. You wanted to ask Diana how far she was going to drive, but she'd said no talking, so you didn't risk it.

You were aware of her, though. She smelled like cigarettes, and she looked like she hadn't slept in weeks. A couple of times she blinked, and you worried she wouldn't get her lids back open. Eventually, you looked out the window again, and there wasn't much around at all. Just some hills, birch trees, and a few clouds. She seemed relaxed, but then you saw her hands, white-knuckled on the wheel.

You only realized where she was going when you saw the familiar wooden sign for the quarry. You were coming around a corner on a tight two-lane road, and you caught sight of it along with the gravel parking lot, totally empty on a cool day. You looked at Diana, but she didn't look back. You didn't know if she had been planning to come here all along or if the car had somehow found its way here like a salmon returning to its natal stream.

She turned off the car. Then she got out and started walking. You weren't sure you wanted to follow, but the thought of just sitting alone in a car for the next hour seemed like the only thing worse, so you opened the door and stepped out. The feeling of the stones against your shoes felt both familiar and strange, and when you looked down at the rocks, you noticed a pink hue mixed in with the cream.

You had read a little bit about the quarry online since your day there with Sean and Diana. It was a former granite mine from the 1920s. They used the stone for foundations, streetcar routes, and monuments. It was hard to imagine it now that the mines were filled with water, but they used to be full of quarriers lifting stones with a giant crane, then using them to build statues of dead heroes.

As you walked the path to the cliffs, you wondered which famous men were immortalized with this stone. What had they done to be remembered forever? And why was everyone else buried out of sight where no one would ever think of them?

"Case. Stop!"

You might have walked right off the cliff if Diana hadn't held out her hand. Somehow, while you were thinking about statues, you'd reached the edge. Oddly enough, your adrenaline didn't spike; you just stopped and looked down. You weren't sure what you were expecting, but there was no one down in the water this time. No teenagers cracking beers and splashing. And no Sean in his serene back float. Just an upside-down sky, painted across the clear surface of the water.

The emptiness was unnerving. It was like no one else could come now that Sean was gone, and the thought occurred to you that maybe all the other kids had just been extras in Sean's movie. Now that the lead wasn't there anymore, doing flips from improbable heights, the extras weren't there either.

Diana took something out of her pocket then. A piece of paper. It wasn't until you saw the photo of Sean that you recognized it as the funeral program. Your parents hadn't chosen a bad picture necessarily, just a safe one. It was one of his senior photos, the one for the school yearbook where he wore a gray T-shirt under a navy V-neck sweater and looked a little like somebody's helpful grandson. There was none of that mischief in his eyes. No challenge in his smile. And you didn't have long to look at it before Diana began to fold it.

Her technique was precise. A fold lengthwise. Then the corners, so they met the center crease. Then she folded again until diagonal lines shot out from the middle. Finally, she tucked the whole thing in on itself and brought the wings down. She offered it to you then, a perfect dart, crisp from the heavy paper stock. But you couldn't take it. You could still see his eyes in the fold of the plane, and you didn't want to touch it.

Diana just shrugged. Then she cocked her arm back and let it go. She let it fly at a 45-degree angle. And for a moment it just seemed to hang in the air, like it might soar over the entire quarry and light on the top of a birch tree on the distant shore. But the wind seemed to take it then, and it nose-dived toward the water, speeding toward its target like a missile. Finally, it made contact with the surface, rippling the sky, and then just floating there, swelling with water.

It wasn't a stone monument.

But it was something. Temporary evidence he'd been there. And though you knew it would eventually dissolve, for a moment it felt like he was there with you. You're not sure how long you watched it. But it still hadn't sunk when you wiped your nose on the sleeve of your uncomfortable blazer and turned away. Diana pretended not to notice your tears. She followed you this time, and when you got back to the car, she handed you the keys.

You drove on the way back, and you didn't feel like music this time so you just listened to the road.

When you got back to the church, you thought this might be the last time you saw Diana. When it came down to it, you were both a reminder of the other's pain, and your last moments together had been filled with shame and confusion. You walked back down the hallway. Everyone was in a meeting room, eating cold cuts. Family, coaches, teammates. You peered in the window and saw your parents nodding at something the reverend was saying.

Get away.

That's the thought that came next.

As soon as you can.

It was too early for college, but you needed to find a way out of your current life. Away from the painful conversations with your family that were coming, and all the reminders of Sean that would greet you everywhere you went. Nothing was going to change if you stayed here, except maybe your dosage of medication. Somehow, you were going to have to find a way out.

About a month later, when you'd hit a dead end in therapy, and nothing seemed to be getting better, your parents would sit you down one afternoon with a plan. They'd tell you it was time to try something new. That they couldn't risk losing another child. Your dad would hand you his phone, open to a website. *Find your potential through experiential therapy in nature*, it would say, over a picture of a glittering lake.

"Sean would have liked it," he'd say.

And he would be right. But he wouldn't have to sell you. By that point, you would be ready to go anywhere that wasn't the same home and school where everyone knew you as Sean's brother. Anywhere that wasn't a museum of his life cut short. Even the middle of the woods.

Back in the church, before you knew about any of this, you were already saying goodbye. You were saying goodbye to this day and to this awful funeral. And in your head, you were already saying goodbye to the only other person you loved. The one you'd just spent the afternoon with.

"I don't think I can do this sad snack buffet," she said. "I'm gonna go."

"I understand," you said.

Which meant it was time to part. She stepped in to hug you, but you were pretty much already gone by then, so you instinctually backed away. She stopped and just looked at you for a moment, not quite sure why you couldn't even hug someone who was grieving beside you. You were positive, in that moment, that you would never hear from her again. But later that night, you got a phone call, and you just watched her name appear on your phone until it disappeared. She called again the next night, and the next. You let them all go to voicemail.

They're still there, the messages. In your phone. Un-listened to. You've carried them around as you sleepwalked through life for the past half year. And you carry them still, in a bag, in the woods, like a penance.

FORTY-TWO

"Case!" she yells.

A flash of pain and you're back in the canoe.

Diana looks terrified, and you know you were spacing out again. Your paddle is wet, so you must have been helping for a while. But you weren't present for much of it, and as usual you're not sure how much time has passed. All you know is that you're not yet on fire and you still haven't answered Diana's question about why you never called her. But she doesn't seem as concerned about that now. She grabs you by the collar and slaps your face. Hard.

"You can't go to sleep!" she says. "Do you understand that?"

"Ow," you say.

"I need to hear a yes," she says.

"Okay! No sleep. Got it."

She wipes a tear from her face.

"Nothing good happens if you go to sleep."

The smoke is even thicker than before, and you pull your damp shirt up over your mouth again. The temperature, too, feels like it's gone up a few degrees, but then again you might just have a fever.

"Is it . . . ," you say.

"Hotter?" says Diana. "Yes."

"How far are we?"

"I don't know," she says. "Fran's been quiet for a while."

Diana cups her hands around her mouth.

"Fran!" she says. "Where are we, girl?!"

Fran turns around, soot-colored sweat running down her forehead. She's about to speak when, instead, she looks over your heads and up toward the sky behind you. Her eyes widen, and she inches noticeably backward in her seat. Diana turns around next, and when you hear her gasp, you have to look too.

And there it is, just visible over a stand of spruce: a fire higher than the trees.

It's bright orange with tendrils reaching like spectral fingers toward the dark clouds above it. An enormous plume of ink-black smoke pours off the top of the fire, making the dusky sky even darker.

"Oh my god," says Troy, nearly falling out of his canoe. "That has to be a hundred feet high."

Will doesn't make a sound. But he starts paddling faster. Within seconds, he's passing your boat in the narrow channel and pulling even with Troy and Fran.

"Hey, what are you doing?!" asks Diana.

"Faster," he says. "We need to move faster."

Before the others can even adjust to what he's doing, Will tosses his pack into their canoe, right behind Troy.

"Will," says Troy, "you almost tipped the boat. What are you . . ."

"Hold on!" says Will.

He stands up in his boat then and leaps out of his canoe, holding his paddle above his head. It's not pretty, and he lands waist-deep in the water. Then, while Troy and Fran scream unintelligibly, Will manages to pull himself into the boat without tipping them over. His old canoe floats listlessly away into the grass, knocking against a rock. Troy and Fran are in shock.

"What the hell, Will?" says Fran. "How about some warning next time!"

"Three paddles will move us quicker," he says. "And we need to go quicker. So shut up and paddle."

He immediately starts digging through the water with his oar, and when his shipmates join in, they are indeed moving faster.

"Go!" he yells. "Go! Go!"

"What about us?!" you say, as the three of them start to cut a slightly faster path through the creek.

"You two need to keep up!" he yells.

You tell yourself not to look back again, but you can't help it. Before you start moving your aching shoulders, you turn around and watch as the spindly pines light up like birthday candles, the fire moving ever closer to the banks of the river. You close your eyes just for a second, then you breathe through your shirt and try to get in sync with Diana, putting your whole torso into the movement, the adrenaline powering you through.

Troy, Fran, and Will push ahead, but not by much. Your two canoes are within a couple of feet of each other as you move around a tight corner to the east. And in the distance to the north, you finally see something that looks like moving water. There hasn't been much of that since those first rapids. But you swear you can see a current taking shape.

"The Loop!" yells Fran. "That might be the Loop!"

The roar from the fire is noticeably louder, and she has to scream to be heard. After she speaks, she can't stop coughing. You give yourself a second to look, but you can't see the Loop as clearly as she can. You can only see patches of the white water throwing off mist and spray.

"OH GOD," says Troy, "NO. NO. NO."

But he does not stop paddling.

No one does. You can't tell if it's your imagination, but the heat seems to be rising at your back. This time, you don't look behind you. If the fire creeps up on you, you're toast, and it doesn't matter if you see it or not. The wind blows from what you think is the south, and suddenly, there's little oxygen to be found. You all fall into a coughing fit as you move closer to the rapids.

"Get down low!" says Fran.

And you all duck down, paddling with your backs hunched, trying to get under the smoke for a bit of air. Fortunately, the wind shifts again and clears out some of the smoke. You all take in huge lungfuls of air and fight with everything you have to move forward in the shifting gales. It sounds like a freight train is following you, and when you finally get close enough to see the beginning of the rapids, your body goes into a state of panicked shock. It's not just a strong current.

It's a waterfall.

Not the size of Niagara Falls or anything, but it's not nothing. Ten, maybe fifteen feet in the air. It seems to appear out of nowhere, cutting between two enormous black rocks and landing in more frothing rapids below. And the current is moving fast beneath your boat. These are not the relatively short rapids from the beginning of the trip. These rapids are wild. They're white and foaming, and any stick that gets drawn into their path is immediately sucked under.

Ahead of you, Fran is screaming. But the sound of the fire nearly drowns her out. There's not much time to think. If you keep going forward, you're going to be pulled into the path of the falls. If you jump out of your boat and swim to shore, it won't be long before the fire is likely to catch you. You can't really call what you're feeling a panic *attack*, because instead of going into alarm mode, your body seems to have shut down entirely. Diana's too. She's just looking forward, completely still.

What you expect to see from the boat in front of you is Troy scrambling to get out. What you see instead is Troy grabbing on to Will's shoulders. He's already decided: He's going to brave the falls. Your mind jumps to the quarry only for a moment, watching Sean dive off that cliff. He did it so effortlessly, flinging his body out into the summer air, completely ready for the plunge to come. You could barely make yourself walk to the edge to look down. How are you supposed to go over a waterfall?

There is still time for you to bail. You could try to outrun the fire on land. Maybe if you stay on the rocky surface, it won't catch you. Fire can't burn rock, right? You think about it, and your anxiety brain seems to already have made the choice to jump out, when an ache starts to build in your chest. You're not entirely sure if it's a pang—because you're not entirely sure what a pang is—but that's the best way you can think to describe it. It hurts, and soon enough you know why.

If you jump, you'll be sending Diana over alone.

And this time, you don't think you can do that. You already abandoned her once, and you know in that moment that you are not prepared to do it again. So you reach up and tap her on the shoulder. She looks back at you, completely horror-struck. But even in her bloodshot eyes and sunburnt skin, you see a flash of that person who climbed up a garage roof just to wish you happy birthday in what seems like another lifetime ago. She is the same person. Your only real friend. And whatever happens next, you have to face it together.

"HEY!" you scream over the din of fire and churning water.

"WHAT?!" she asks, her face tight with terror.

"HOLD MY HAND!"

She doesn't hesitate. She reaches out and grabs your cold fingers and interlaces them with her own. Then there are only a few seconds to brace yourselves for what's coming before the current grabs you. Behind you, you feel a wall of heat, like someone's chasing you with a flamethrower. The air goes dark as night. Then the raging water seizes you and the two of you go over the edge.

FORTY-THREE

It takes two seconds to drop. Maybe three.

But in anxiety-time, that's at least a couple of lifetimes. At first you're still in the boat, and you hold tight to the slick gunwale with one hand and to Diana's hand with the other. The sense of weightlessness sends a surge of adrenaline through your body and a sickening pit to your stomach. And then, at some point, your bodies separate from the boat and your hand unclasps from Diana's. Every muscle you have tenses for impact, and all you can see when you're airborne is water cascading around you. It sends up a mist that blinds you from what's below, so it's hard to tell just how far you're going to fall.

Diana hits the water first. You hit next and find yourself fully submerged in liquid ice too deep to see bottom. You flail around in the turbulent water, and when you open your eyes, you see the bright yellow of the canoe a few feet away. It's scraped and dented, but still mostly intact. You reach out a desperate hand and manage a grip on the side again. Then you clamp both hands on it and use the weight of the boat to pull your head out of the water.

You pop up, your ears ringing from the cold.

"DIANA!" you scream.

You wonder if you're going to have to go under to save her when you hear her voice from the other side of the boat, shaky but there.

"I'M HERE!" she says.

That's all you hear before you're moving again, shooting the next leg of the rapids while clutching your canoe, which jerks you through the water like an angry pet on a leash.

"Just hang on!" you say.

But you don't know if she can hear you, or even if that's the right thing to do. You look around frantically for the others, but you don't see any sign of them. A gust of wind kicks up behind you, and when you turn around, everything is on fire. The wind is hurling the flames forward, and you can see them burning through everything on the shore in real time. The rapids keep you just ahead of the fire, but the heat on all sides of you is growing unbearable. You duck your head underwater to cool off. You blow air out of your nose and mouth, clearing out the smoke and ash.

The current pulls you around a sharp corner, and your legs brush against some big rocks beneath the hull. You lift your legs up as high as you can. Although you can't see her face, you can see Diana's hand still holding tight to the gunwale on the other side of the boat. You just hope she's able to breathe. Between the wind and the rapids, it's getting harder to stay above water, and you find yourself holding your breath for longer and longer stretches of time.

Your feet slam into another rock, and this time it spins you and the whole canoe around so that you're going through the Loop backward. This is the moment when you're sure that you're not going to make it. You have no sense of where your body is in space, and the surging water has taken away most of your visibility. You plunge under the water again, and the glacial rapids engulf you. You stay under until your lungs feel like they're going to burst, and then suddenly you're not moving as fast. The current seems to have slowed, and before you can do it yourself, a familiar hand grabs you hard by the hair and pulls your head out of the water.

You sputter and wipe your eyes. Diana is looking at you with hair matted in front of her face. She pushes it back, and then screams:

"LOOK OUT!"

Hot coals and embers are blowing across the surface of the water. You've been spit out into a small lake, and there is fire burning all around you on the shore.

"The canoe!" you gasp. "Flip it over!"

You both grab on to the same side and pull, dumping any remaining gear into the churning lake. It's hard to tip it, but the burning refuse from the fire is good motivation. An ember lands on your neck and bites until you splash it with water. And when you finally get the boat over, you both swim underneath and come up under its domed roof. Your whole world is tiny and dark. You can hear the percussion of coals and debris hitting the hull, and the scream of the fire eating through everything around you. It heats the bottom of the canoe like a stove, too hot to the touch.

Diana reaches out and takes your hand again, and then you're in the middle of a lake, under your boat, trying to keep hell at bay. You can only hope that the others have created some kind of makeshift fire shelter on their own. But there's no way to look for them now without risking a severe burn. In the chaos that follows, you have no sense of time. You know you're treading water, moving your body to stay afloat, but you can barely feel your limbs. The patter above you sounds like a hailstorm. And you stay under your shell.

"The others . . . ," you say, trying not to cry.

"We can't think about that now," says Diana. "There's nothing we can do."

But a pinch in her voice tells you she is *very much* thinking about it now and wondering if she should risk looking for them. You both splash around for a second, attempting to stay contained in your little pocket of safety without drowning.

"Talk to me about something," says Diana. "Can you do that?"

Her voice echoes in your little cave, but you can't quite see her clearly in the dark yet.

"What . . . do you want me to say?" you croak, surprised you still have a voice.

"I don't care," she says. "Anything. I'm freezing and scared and I just need a distraction. Just say something."

You kick your legs, barely keeping your chin above water. Your clothes are getting heavy, but you couldn't take them off at this point without going under.

"Okay," you say. "Okay. I don't know what to say, so I'll just say that the answer is yes to your question from before."

Diana is silent.

"Do you remember . . ."

"Yes!" she says. "I remember. Just keep talking. What do you mean, yes?"

"Yes, it was guilt," you say. "That's what kept me from answering your calls after the funeral. It was a terrible thing to do, and I'm sorry!"

She doesn't say anything, which you take as your cue to keep going.

"I guess I thought maybe it was better if we just didn't see each other again. Like, it would hurt too much and it wouldn't help us heal. Does that make any sense? I don't know anymore if it does."

You're speaking quickly, and in the quiet that follows, a few embers glance off the boat.

"It does," she says. "But about the guilt . . ."

Her teeth are starting to chatter.

"Yeah."

"I'm just going to say it, Case. Because, at this point, there's nothing to stop me. Do you really think your brother died because we kissed one time in a kitchen? I mean, is that what you think happened?"

Her last words echo beneath the roof of the boat.

"I don't know," you say, swallowing a little water. "Maybe."

The outline of Diana's face is starting to form in the dark.

"I don't think it works that way," she says.

You look down into the water, which is largely still now. You can only see a flash of your kicking legs before the water gets too murky.

"It just felt so wrong," you say.

"Kissing me?"

"No," you sigh. "Being . . . in love with you. It felt like the worst thing I could possibly do. Like maybe it was so wrong that it had the power to destroy things. Even lives. That's how it felt to me."

She's still holding your hand, but she lets go for a moment to tread water more fully. Something large hits the boat and you both gasp, but it doesn't hurt you. It doesn't get in. Diana steadies her breathing.

"Man," she says.

"What?"

"That's just so sad."

"Which part exactly . . . ?" you say.

Her face comes into focus, her hair dripping around her.

"That's not what love should feel like, Case. You know that, right? It's not supposed to be a curse."

"I know," you say.

Only you're not sure if you do.

You've only been in love once, and that's exactly how it felt. Feels. Unrequited and impossible and dangerous. You reach a hand up to touch the canoe, and it still burns the tips of your fingers. The roar of the fire is dying, but it's hard to say if it's safe to open the lid yet. The fact that you can no longer truly feel the lower half of your body seems like a bad thing. Up until minutes ago, you thought you were going to be burned to death in a wildfire. Now you're starting to wonder about hypothermia.

"I haven't even felt like a person," you say.

She grabs your hand again and squeezes hard.

"Since it happened," you continue. "I haven't felt human. Like, when I think about myself, I see myself from really high up, like I'm not even totally in my body. My therapist called it disassociation, but I think it's something even more than that."

"Like you're just visiting," she says.

"Yes!" you say. "Like I don't live here anymore."

Diana dips slightly below the surface and comes up spitting out water. She takes a second to recalibrate.

"Hey, listen," she says. "Listen to me. Sean loved you more than anyone in the world. That doesn't just go away in an instant.

He would have forgiven you. He wasn't going to hate you forever. Maybe for a little while. But not for good."

She swims closer.

"Maybe," you say. "It was hard to tell what he felt."

"He never let you see who he really was. That's not your fault. He didn't do that with anyone."

"Not even you?" you ask.

"Not even me," she says. "I caught glimpses like you did, I think. But he kept a lot of the pain in. And then it came out in weird and dangerous ways. I don't know what we could have done about that."

You can see her eyes now, and they are right in front of yours.

"We didn't kill him, Case."

She closes her eyes.

"In some ways, we barely knew him."

She puts an arm around you then, and you see as she gets closer that her teeth are chattering uncontrollably. You press your head against hers. Her skin is freezing, and you're sure yours is too. When you kiss, your lips are cold. She kisses you back, and her breath is warm, but it only lasts a moment before the world around you comes rushing back in and you become certain of one thing: If you stay in this water much longer, there are going to be serious consequences for both of you. You don't have to be an outdoors expert to understand that.

"Shore," you say. "We have to swim for it."

"I think the canoe is too hot to move," she says. "We'll have to go underneath it."

"On three?" you ask.

She points to the water and counts you off.

"One. Two. Three!"

Under you go, back into the lake. You pull yourself through the dark water as best you can with your clothes on. You're not sure what you're going to find on the other side, but still, you come up, preparing for fire and brimstone. Instead, what you find is the calm of utter devastation. The wind has stopped. The fire is gone. And everything around you has either been scorched beyond recognition or completely devoured. It's a barren, black landscape of burnt matchstick-trees and volcanic glowing coals. Diana comes up next and stares in awe at the depleted land around you. She's speechless. It's shocking that you're alive.

"Let's go," you say.

You both move sluggishly toward a large rock sticking out from the bank. You don't think about whether you can make it; you just have to. So you propel yourself another fifty feet by way of a glorified dog paddle, barely staying afloat. But when you get to the wet rock, whatever fuel you have left disappears, and you have to inch yourself onto it with your elbows like a wounded soldier. Your whole body is convulsing with shivers. Diana's is too. You know you can't go to sleep, but that's what your body is telling you to do. It's only when you hear the quiet voice in the distance that you sit up straight.

"Is anybody there?!"

FORTY-FOUR

Your heart starts hammering.

"OVER HERE!" screams Diana.

She gets to her feet first, but neither of you can see anyone. There's still a thick pall of smoke in the air, and you can't even find the glow of flames farther to the north. The voice sounded male, but it was hard to tell whose it was. You walk across the burnt forest, the ground still sizzling and popping beneath your feet. The world around you looks so devoid of life and color, it feels like an unsettled planet, or maybe some kind of purgatory where you might linger for centuries awaiting your fate.

"TROY!" Diana yells. "WILL! FRAN!"

There's no answer this time, and you wonder if you actually hallucinated the voice you heard. The sound of Diana's chattering teeth is all you can hear, along with the low whistle of some whirring bugs who seem attracted to the burnt wood. A small fire burns what remains of the grass beneath your soggy boots.

The cold feels so deep in your body, you're not sure how you'll ever be warm again. But you know the first step is getting out of your freezing, wet clothes. As you walk, you start to peel them off, and Diana does the same. The air is warmer from the fire, but not warm enough to save you on its own. By the time you're both in your underwear and boots, you know you're going to have to do something more urgent or you won't be able to go on.

"GUYS!" yells Diana into the smoke. "WHERE ARE YOU?!"

No response again.

"Diana," you say through hiccuping breaths. "We need to get warm or we're not going to make it."

She kicks at the thin stump of a tree, and it shatters into uncountable pieces.

"I know," she says through chattering teeth. "But there's not much left to burn."

She's right; even though the fire moved through quickly, all the brush has been burned down to stubs and the trees are husks of what they used to be. As you make your way around the lake, searching for something that hasn't been completely swallowed, you eventually stumble upon a smoldering log, too big to burn in one go. You put your hands over it and find it still warm.

"Here," you say. "Help me with this. Maybe we can . . ."

You start kicking at it, and she joins in until the log rolls over. Then you begin to blow on the side that's still red. You don't have a lot of excess oxygen, but you use what you can spare until finally, a small flame comes to life in a single burst.

"I can't believe we're trying to create more fire," says Diana.

You keep blowing, and eventually the log catches in earnest, and then you get as close to it as you possibly can without lighting yourself on fire. Diana edges closer as well. The heat is not enough, but it's something. You huddle together around the small fire, trying to get some life back into your extremities. Your feet and hands are numb, and you don't know if you'll ever be able to feel them again.

You lay out your clothes where they'll dry, then you sit absolutely still, letting your body shiver until it finally starts to subside. You don't black out, but you're not sure if it's two minutes or two hours before the two of you can finally stand again. Your legs are tingling and painful when you do, but you have more sensation in them. Your compulsive shaking has faded too, but your body feels like it's been pricked with a thousand needles.

"The voice sounded like it was coming from this way," says Diana.

You put on your pants, which are now just a little damp, and follow her along the charred shore of the lake, swiping smoke out of your path with an outstretched arm. Once you've built up enough lung stamina, you scream again:

"HEYYYYYY!"

And this time, the response is a little closer.

"Over here!"

The words cut through the smoke and darkness, and you're able to follow the sound, more or less. Finally, you come to a crescent of sandy shore and you see two bodies standing absolutely still. Whatever happiness you feel at the sight of them is undercut by your immediate realization that somebody is missing. Then you see that they're looking down.

"He's been burned," says Will. "Really bad. And he's not conscious."

That's when you see the third body, Troy's, sprawled out on the ground. Fran is closest to you. She hugs Diana, and then puts a hand over her face.

"He tried to make it to shore too early," she says.

When you get closer, you can see that Troy is breathing, but he also has a wound on his forehead and one on his arm that looks reddish brown and blistered. His glasses are missing. He needs help, and he needs it fast. You pull one of the wet socks from your feet, and Will helps you rip it apart. A bandage has to be better than nothing. Anything else you had has been dumped in the lake. You bend down and gently begin to wrap Troy's arm. He's a skinny guy in the best of circumstances, but after days of little food, his limp arm in your hand seems like it's barely there. You wonder how much longer he can make it without wasting away. He twitches slightly when you touch him.

You remember him bravely going over the falls, and you don't allow yourself to think that this might be the end for him. But then, you also don't know how you're going to get him help.

"Fran, are we anywhere near the drop?" you ask with your last shred of optimism.

Fran is silent.

"What?" you say. "Did we miscalculate it?"

"No," she says, and points down to the sand beneath you. "You're actually standing on it."

Off to the side of where she pointed is some melted plastic you assume was once bottled water. There are a few scraps of cardboard too from other supplies. Everything else is ash. First your food was eaten by a bear, and now by a fire. You don't even feel much at this realization, just a kind of grudging understanding that there are so many forces against you that it seems pointless to try to beat them.

You lean down and put a hand on Troy's cheek. His body feels warm.

"We have to get him some care," you say. "We can't lose him. We just can't."

You look up at Diana. She avoids eye contact. And everyone else you see looking back at you is barely there. The fight they once had, even hours ago, to escape the flames and get to safety, is gone. Now you are all exhausted and hungry and in various states of hypothermic shock. It seems like there's nothing left, and you have no idea what to do.

Diana sits down by Troy and holds his hand. Fran sits next to her. And then finally, you sit on the other side of Troy's body and Will sits next to you. You get close enough to combine body heat, hoping some of it might transfer to Troy too. It took a few days, but the wilderness has finally stripped you all down to nothing. You have no supplies, no medication, no food. You have boats and wet clothes; that's it. Everything else is gone. Even the world around you has been stolen by the fire.

"We were never going to make it, were we?" asks Fran.

The sound of the fire is so far in the distance, you can barely hear it anymore. And with all the wildlife gone except a few insects, the quiet after she says this is all-consuming. No one says anything for a while, and you're starting to think that maybe no one else is going to when Will chimes in.

"It was kinda unlikely, I guess," he says.

The amazing thing is that no one sounds sad, exactly. Just resigned.

"Do you think . . . normal people would have done better?" asks Diana.

You so badly want to say no. That your mental illness has nothing to do with it. But it's hard, sitting in this charred wasteland, without any gear or hope for rescue, to imagine anyone doing worse than you. And once you admit that, the floodgates are suddenly open. All the things you've told yourself for years about your deficiencies come back like summoned ghosts. It's a greatest-hits album that includes such favorites as: "Nothing You Do Will Ever Go Right," "Self-Sabatage Is All You Know," and "Your Own Brain Hates You." Each song is more punishing than the last, and it ends with the epic power ballad: "You Were Probably Doomed from the Start."

In the midst of this spiraling, there's only one thought that gives you pause and keeps you from completely breaking down. As you imagine all the ways you screwed up on this trip, there is a difference between it and all your other anxiety-fueled tragedies: You were not alone.

It's something, and it seems worth speaking aloud.

"If I was going to fail at survival," you say, "I'm glad I got to do it with you guys."

There isn't a magic moment after this. No one stands up and claps or even says anything in return. But there are nods and grunts, and no one contradicts you. So maybe it's actually an agreed-upon thing. And for now, you are still together, and you huddle for warmth. Night is finally falling, and one by one everybody starts to drift off to sleep. It's the first time everyone has slept in such close quarters since the inaugural night at the lodge. But even though you're borderline delirious with infection and hunger, you force yourself to stay awake. To make sure Troy is breathing. To keep watch for predators. And to keep yourself alive for just a little longer.

It could have been so much better.

That's what you're thinking in the dark.

Not this trip, which obviously couldn't have gone much worse.

But your life with anxiety. If you had just found other people—people you could talk to about it, people who really cared about one another—maybe you wouldn't have needed this "adventure" in the first place. If you had just asked for a little more help from everyone around you, and, god, if Sean had done the same, maybe things would have turned out differently. Maybe you wouldn't be here, at the end.

Diana is slumped against Troy, and all you want is just one last chance to be with her outside this place. To go to Perkins again and sit there drinking bad coffee and laughing. The longing you have to be back in that terrible restaurant actually makes your heart hurt. But it also feels now like something that happened in another life. In order to get back there, you'd have to use a time machine or a magic portal. But you have neither. Just a blackened canoe.

You manage to stay awake for another hour or so, trying to ignore your hunger. Mostly, you worry about Troy. Across from you, his chest moves up and down. The rhythm of it gives you hope, but it also makes you drowsy. And gradually, your blinks get longer and longer. Even if Diana is right and falling asleep might take you under for good, you have little choice at this point.

And as you sit suspended in that place between dream life and waking life, you wonder if when you die—today or another time altogether—you will see Sean again. You're not a believer in much of anything beyond what's in this world, but you let yourself dream. Would it be possible to hug him again and say you're sorry? Would he still smell like himself? Chlorine and Old Spice deodorant. Could you ask him all the questions you never got a chance to ask? And what would happen from there? In this place, whatever it is, would you be able to stay together again? Would you both have perfect brains? Would you even want such a thing?

You close your eyes.

And you only open them again when you hear the humming.

FORTY-FIVE

At first you think it's in your dreams. It reminds you of the soft murmur of the bus's engine on the freeway when you first left for this trip. But when your eyes fully open to a sunrise just as pink as that first one, you are not on a bus. And you do not appear to be dead. You are sitting right where you nodded off, and the sound you hear is not coming from below you; it's coming from above. Somewhere above the blackened trees. You shield your eyes against the new morning sun and look up into the sky. The smoke has thinned, and only a light haze hangs in the air. The noise grows louder, until it sounds less like a hum and more like the box fan you used to keep in your window as a child.

You haven't even looked at the others yet. You just keep your eyes to the sky, and when you see a white-and-yellow blur slip slowly into focus, you wonder if you are really awake after all. It has two propellers and long rectangular wings, and it is buzzing lazily through the sky. It's an aircraft, but one you've never seen before—some kind of firefighting plane if you had to guess—and it is not that far from you.

You stumble to your feet, and you immediately start shouting and waving your arms before you even really know what you're doing. You follow beneath it as far as you can through the destroyed woods, even climbing up a small hill to watch as it dives down like a raptor and releases what must be at least a thousand gallons of water into the air from its tank. Then it ascends again, makes a tight turn, and disappears off into the distance.

"NO!" you shout. "NO! COME BACK! WE'RE HERE!"

You're not sure how long you're shouting, but eventually you're interrupted by a voice from down the hill.

"Case, what the hell is going on?"

When you look down, you see Diana standing with a hand shielding her eyes. She looks genuinely concerned about you. You motion for her to come up, but by the time she gets there, and you start rambling about what you saw, the plane is long gone. Still, you have her stand quietly and listen in case she can still hear its engine.

"Are you sure you haven't lost it?" she asks.

She puts a hand on your side, and for the first time in a while, you don't feel the urge to slip away.

"I'm not sure," you say. "It's a possibility, but I think it was real. It looked really real. And it was dumping water on the fire, which means it's likely to come back."

Fran and Will find their way to you and grumble as they climb the hill.

"What is it?" asks Will.

"Case hallucinated a plane," says Diana. "But on the off chance it's real, we need to figure out a way to signal to it."

The two of them stare back and forth from you to Diana. Their eyes are red rimmed, and it's hard to say what they think of all this.

"Okay," says Will. "What do we do?"

Will looks back down the hill to the burnt-out forest, and the resting body of his friend.

"Damn, man," he says, "Troy would know. There's probably a stupid Anarchist Vagabond episode about it."

Everyone quiets for a minute. Will is still looking at Troy, and he seems like he's going to cry. Somehow, he pulls himself together.

"Hey. The plane could come back soon," you say. "So what do they do in movies?"

The answers come quickly, without much thought. Send an SOS message (not possible; no radio). Build a fire for smoke signals (not the best strategy when everything else is on fire). Spell out HELP in rocks and branches (not bad, but there isn't an open space nearby). Scream and wave your arms (already tried). It's starting to look bleak, when suddenly Fran stares at something, and then walks over to Diana. She reaches for her pants, and without speaking, rips the belt out of Diana's belt loops.

"Fran!" says Diana. "What are you doing?"

Fran holds the belt buckle to the light. It's made of metal, and she toys with it in her hands. You can't really tell what she's doing until she steps into an opening between the dead trees and angles it a certain way. Then suddenly there's a small bead of light reflecting on her shirt. You remember playing a similar game with your dad's digital watch when you were a kid, making the reflected light bounce around the ceiling like a spaceship.

"Okay, look," says Fran. "I don't know if this will work, but maybe we can send a flash or something."

"Will the light go all the way up there?"

"I don't know," she says. "Maybe?"

She holds the buckle to her eye and aims it at the top of a burnt tree. It takes her maybe five minutes or so to get the light to land on the spot she wants, but it's barely visible.

"We need something shinier," says Fran.

She hands the belt back to Diana. From a distance, the hum comes again, and this time, you're not the only one who hears it.

"Oh my god," says Diana, cupping her right ear. "It's real."

"Are you sure the buckle doesn't work, Fran?" asks Will.

"I'm sure," she says.

"Maybe we can try screaming again," you say. "And jumping around because . . ."

"WAIT!" yells Will. "Wait a second."

He pauses only for a moment, and then he takes off faster than you've seen him move in days. It's like one last shuttle run. Only this time, he doesn't freeze or lose his cool. And you watch as he cautiously approaches Troy's body. He's saying something to Troy, but you can't hear what it is. You only see him reach into the pocket of Troy's pants and remove something. It takes you a minute to figure out what it is, but when he finally holds it aloft, you could almost cry.

The collapsible whisk.

The one your mother packed you. The one Troy wielded like an Arthurian sword. When it hits the sun, the light reflects off the stainless steel of its handle and lingers in your vision like a lens flare from a camera. Will reaches down and puts a hand on Troy's chest. He holds it there and says something else. Then he runs back to you, whisking at the air around him.

"He *still* had it?" you say.

"I knew he would," says Will. "Dude wouldn't let go of that thing, remember?"

"What did you say to him?" asks Fran.

Will runs a hand through his hair.

"I told him I'd bring it right back," he says. "And that his friends wouldn't let him down."

You all nod. But the sound of the engine is getting closer, and if you want to give this a real try, you need to find some room to get the light through the trees. Against all instincts, you start to run north where the fire was moving. It's the path this plane is likely to take. Will passes the whisk to Fran like a baton, and she cups it perfectly. You move through the desiccated forest like a herd of gazelles, using inexplicable energy to jump fallen trees and rocks. Until finally, you stand at the bottom of a small rocky cliff. It looms above you. The top looks treeless, and you know in your soul that it's the perfect spot to try the signal.

"Jesus," says Fran. "I can't climb that."

You look back at Diana and Will, and they both stare at the almost-sheer face. It's not a mountain. But it's mountainlike. And strength is running low.

"Give me the whisk," you say. "And tell me what to do."

Fran hands it to you faster than you thought she would, and you stuff it in your pocket. Then she breaks it down for you. She talks fast, but you catch the gist: Hold it to your eye. Try to aim it.

"How will I know if it's aimed right?" you say.

"You won't, really," says Fran. "You just have to try your best."

Before you can think carefully about any of this, you reach out and grab at the wall of the cliff. You find a foothold, and you pull yourself a few feet in the air. It's just like climbing up on the garage, you tell yourself. But you're already shaking. So you close your eyes, and in your head you start a conversation with the one person you knew who wasn't afraid of heights. Maybe, you think, he won't want to see you. But maybe, he won't be able to resist doing what he once did best: helping you through a tough situation.

Sean, you say. *I don't know if this is a good time, or if you even forgive me, but I need you.*

You look above you, and there seems to be another hold to reach for; you just don't know where you're going to put your feet. The engine sound is getting closer, and you've barely made a start.

I have to climb this cliff. But as you might remember, I'm not so good with heights.

You close your eyes and reach for the rock. You grip it with your palm, which still has some numbness. Then you move a boot up and press it against the rock. The rubber holds.

How did you do this so many times? Jumping. Diving. You were never afraid.

The plane is not yet above you, but it's making the fan noise again. The one that signals it's getting closer. You can't bring yourself to look up, afraid you'll lose your footing. So again, you reach, and this time, you find a stray root to grab on to. When you grip it, it holds.

Do you remember that time when we were kids, running through the backyards of the neighborhood, playing Capture the Flag? You climbed this tall chain-link fence and left me below. I was too scared to climb up.

You have to look down to make sure your foot is on an edge. Somehow, you're already ten feet in the air. Your stomach lurches. You want to let go and just drop. You wouldn't hurt yourself too badly yet.

I was little. Maybe six. I tried not to cry. And I looked up at you balanced on the very top. You looked so brave, surveying the neighborhood like it was your kingdom.

You decide not to drop. There isn't another hold directly above you, so you have to pull yourself sideways a little. This is when your foot first slips. Your stomach lurches, and you're sure you're done for, but then it catches again, and you manage to pull yourself to the side. Your friends are shouting things below, but you can't hear them. All you can hear now is your own heartbeat.

You looked down and saw me crying. And then you told me that I could do it if I just went slow and held on really tight to the links.

The next grip is easier, and there's a sizable shelf to put your feet on. It's over halfway, but it's also too high to allow you to jump down. You have to finish it now, or there's no good way to get to safety. You look up, and you know the plane is going to appear any minute.

I started climbing, just a rung at a time, like you said, wedging my shoes in the links. I made it halfway up, and then I just froze.

Some shouting from below cuts through your fugue. You wonder if it means that the plane has finally appeared. You don't look, though. Instead you stop for a second to get a breath.

I was going to die. It felt like I was leaving my body. And I knew suddenly that things were going to be harder for me. I had my eyes closed, and you told me to open them. When I did, I saw you next to me.

"You can't go down," you said.

You can't go down.

"You have to go up and over."

You reach up for the next hold. It's so small that only your fingertips can grip it. But you grab on anyway, and you pull your foot almost as high as your hand. You use all your remaining strength to push off with your foot. When you launch up, you don't stop. You grab the next edge, and with one more pull, your hand reaches the top of the cliff.

You pull yourself all the way up just as the thrumming of the engine is at its loudest. Miraculously, the plane hasn't passed directly over you yet. So you take out the whisk and hold it to your eye.

You locate the reflection.

You fiddle with the handle until you see the reflection bouncing off your shoe.

You aim toward your target.

The plane will be over you in seconds, but you know you need to create the signal before that happens, so you tilt the handle up, and you see the light hit the top of a tree. You keep tilting, and then, you have no idea where it is, or if it's going to meet the eye of the person who doesn't know they are your last chance at help. The only thing you can do is let the light hit you and try, however briefly, to throw a little of it back.

For a moment, it was just you and me at the top of the fence. There were people below, but they seemed so far away.

Below, at the bottom of the small cliff, your friends are cheering for you. They don't know if it worked, just like you don't. But they know you made it in time to try, and for a few seconds, that's enough. The plane dumps another massive amount of water on what you assume is a fire still raging. You watch it. And when it turns around, it looks so close you could touch it. You try the signal again, watching it inch through the sky. You can't hear anything but its engine. Your friends have gone silent.

"See you on the other side," you said to me, just before you dropped.

You all watch as the plane starts its journey back for more water, moving in a straight line toward whatever lake is supplying it. Then you continue to watch as it turns slightly off its route, just a little, then a little more, until, gradually, you see it turning back toward the fire.

Back toward you.

"See you," I said.

FORTY-SIX

Everything that happens next doesn't quite seem real.

First, a propeller plane lands on a lake, its fuselage skimming across the surface like a water strider. Next, it comes to a stop near the shore and a door flies open to reveal a tall, strong woman in a green flight suit, gray-blond hair spilling out of a tight black stocking cap. For a second, she just stares at you like you're ghosts. Then, suddenly, she seems to understand that you're alive and she starts moving very quickly. She hops back in the plane and drives it like a boat, as close as she can get to the shore. Finally, she comes running out with supplies, sloshing through knee-deep water.

"Oh my god!" she says. "Oh my god. What on earth are you kids doing out here?"

Before you can answer, she radios in that she's found you, and a far-off, staticky voice sounds just as stunned that people are still standing in the wake of this fire. Then the pilot has blankets. They look like they're made of tinfoil, and she hands them out, unfolding them and draping them over you, asking you rapid questions about your hypothermic symptoms.

"Look at me!" she says. "Are you slurring your speech? Do you have memory loss? Do you feel drowsy?"

She's talking so fast that you can barely understand her. By the time you've formed a response to one question, another one has popped up. Finally, you get space to tell her about Troy, and her face goes slack. She hands you each a drink. Then she sprints back to the plane.

You immediately open what you recognize is a warm bottle of Gatorade, fruit-punch flavor, and when you take a sip, it is undoubtably the best drink you have ever had in your life. For five seconds or so, you are wholly transported. You nearly fall to your knees. It activates taste buds you didn't even know you had, and you can't help yourself: You moan with pleasure.

But this pleasure is short-lived. Because immediately, the pilot, who tells you to call her Maddy, needs your help carrying something called a backboard. You and Will take the front, and Maddy takes the back, and in this way, you head to the place where you left Troy. On the way there, she finally asks what happened to you guys, and Diana tells her some details in a shaky voice.

"I wish I could say this was my first rescue for a troubled-teen program. But it's not. What kind of group was this? You only had *one* guide?"

Maddy stops talking when she reaches Troy's body, and you've never wanted anything more in your life than to find him breathing. You can't tell at first if he is, but then you see his chest rise ever so slightly. Maddy gets down and performs an assessment, paying close attention to his burns and bruises. And while she gives you instructions about how to help her load him on the board, she asks only one simple question.

"How did he get like this?"

The story, which Fran tells, is hard for you to hear. During the fire, Will and Fran made a shelter similar to yours with their canoe, wedging it against a rock near the shore. Quarters were tight with three of them under there, and when the temperature started to rise, Troy couldn't take it. He busted out of the fire shelter and swam the rest of the way to shore, only to be hit with burning debris when he arrived.

Maddy says he could be bleeding internally, and that you need to get him on oxygen in the plane as quickly as possible. When you ask point-blank if he'll live, she looks you dead in the eye and says:

"I don't know, honey."

Then, apropos of nothing, she wraps you in a tight hug. The kind your mom gives you when she hasn't seen you in a while. And for the first time, you fully realize that all of this really happened. There is an adult here. And this one actually wants to help you. She releases you from the hug and says:

"To be honest, I don't know how any of you are alive."

And when you bend down, she catches sight of your head wound and tells you to lie down when you get to the aircraft too. Which is how you find yourself on oxygen, lying next to Troy on an improvised bed made of blankets, with a bandage on your head and an IV in your arm.

Diana holds your hand. Will and Fran are holding Troy's hands. You are all headed toward a base where you'll then be driven to a hospital. These facts haven't totally kicked in yet. This rescue still feels like something you could wake up from any minute. There are fake-outs like these all the time in Choose Your Own Adventure books. You find yourself in relative safety only to recognize that you've been brainwashed and imprisoned in a mine.

Diana gives your hand a squeeze, and you feel like you could fall asleep for a thousand years. But instead, you look around the plane and you see that everyone is starting to zone out, staring off into the distance. They're already trying their hardest to disconnect from what happened. And you don't blame them. It's probably the healthy thing to do in this moment. A form of protection. But you also feel a strange preemptive sense of loss as you watch this happen. Not because you don't want this to be over—you very much do—but because when this plane lands, and everyone is eventually reunited with their families, that could be the end.

"Hey . . . ," you say, snapping everyone out of their trances.

They look toward you, concern in their eyes. You take a long pull of oxygen.

"Fear in a Hat?"

Nobody smiles. You're all too tired for that. But nobody tells you to shut up either. And after a brief and silencing dip of turbulence, Fran finally opens her mouth.

"That Troy won't wake up," she says. "That's mine. I didn't want to say it out loud, but if we had a hat, that would be in there."

You all look at Troy, his eyes still closed on the backboard, his body strapped down. You remember him waking up screaming on the first night, and you realize two things at once: that you love him and that he might never see Turbo again. But you swallow this down.

"I have another one," says Will, clearing his throat. "My fear is that it's all going to be the same when we land. Like: everything. Same as before. And all of this was for nothing."

You assume he means his situation with his dad, his sports

goals, and his loneliness. And you know that every one of you is thinking some version of this too. What if this experience has only made things worse? Or what if you've changed and the world hasn't?

Will's answer leaves only you and Diana left to share. She closes her eyes a second. Then she pulls her bruised knees to her chest.

"That I'll never forgive myself," she says.

She's not looking at you. Or at least, not *just* at you.

"I'm going to try. But I'm not sure I really know how."

No one asks her what she's referring to. Maybe they know. Or maybe you all have something you need to forgive yourself for.

You want to hold her then, but you can't move from your bed without disconnecting from your IV.

"What's yours, Case?"

"What?" you say.

She leans down by your ear.

"Your fear?" she says. "What's yours?"

You were never great at this game. But this time your sheet isn't blank. This time, there's something sitting there just waiting for you to speak it.

"That we won't be friends," you say.

There's a moment of silence and everyone watches you. The vibration of the plane is all you can hear, and it's making your ears ring. You try a yawn to unpop them.

"Why wouldn't we be?" says Fran.

Her voice is so soft, you can barely make it out over the propellers.

"Because it's hard," says Diana.

Everyone turns to her.

"When you've been through something really painful with somebody, then they can be . . . a reminder of that pain. Like, if this plane actually lands and you go back to your life and eventually feel better, seeing me might bring you back to that place of fear. It . . . it can happen. Even if you care about the person."

You feel Diana's eyes on you, and this time you meet them.

"It's not fair," you say. "But it's real."

The plane tilts to the left then, and suddenly you can see miles of forest out a nearby window. And all of it has been depleted. Aside from the blinding blue patches of lake, it looks like the wilderness you traversed was a charcoal drawing that someone put their thumb on and smeared. White smoke pours up from nearly every direction, and you wonder if everything you just experienced has all been turned to ash. And if it's all gone, where did the experiences go?

For now, they're still with you—you can see them so clearly— but how long will it be until your brain decides that the memories are harmful? How long until it erases the fish you caught or the way it felt hearing the embers bouncing off your canoe? The same is true, you know, of Sean. You've tried so hard to keep the memories you have with him alive, to play them out in your head like movies. But gradually, some of those will start to go too. And then, tree by tree, you'll lose him in pieces like the forest below you. You might lose everyone this way.

"It can't be over," says Fran, who is also staring toward the window.

"Why not?" says Will.

"Because," she says, "we're all connected now. Whether we want to be or not."

No one denies it. But no one jumps up to declare allegiance either.

"We magnified each other," she says.

She reaches out for Diana's hand, who hesitates, then takes it.

"It was dark out there, you guys. It almost got us."

You can feel the plane dip lower in the sky. And thankfully, this seems intentional. You're already starting your descent, heading back to earth, where everything you've discussed awaits you, whether you want it to or not. Fran still watches out the window.

"But we made one another brighter somehow," she says. "And I don't think even our fear can kill that."

FORTY-SEVEN

In the days that follow, you are mostly alone.

After an initial evaluation, you're all treated in different rooms and, eventually, different hospitals. Then you're interviewed separately by the police about Silas, and by the media for stories that die down as quickly as they flare up ("Worry Warriors of the North Found Alive!"). Your cell phones are lost to the woods, and by the time they're replaced, it's too late to exchange information, so you know little aside from a few basic facts. Will had severe dehydration. Fran got sick, presumably from lake water. And most importantly: Troy is alive but still unconscious.

Diana alone gets your number. She calls you as you heal from an infection, a bad case of cellulitis that laid you out for days, while intravenous antibiotics swirled through your body and you drifted in and out of consciousness. But this time around, you pick up the phone, still drowsy and dizzy from the infection. You chat mindlessly about hospital food and your new fame until the painkillers knock you out for the evening. Her grandmother won't let her leave the house, she says, or else she would visit.

This goes on for a few weeks. Your parents, who sobbed openly when they saw you, burst into tears anew every morning when they show up to your room. They thought they lost another child, and now they can barely take their hands off you when they're around. Your mother's hand has been in your hair for what feels like 70 percent of each day. Sometimes she sleeps there at the hospital. The love is real, and it's good, but one morning when they ask what they can do to make you more comfortable, you say, "Start talking about Sean," and your mom has to leave the room. When you wake up later that evening, they're sitting by your bed.

"We can try," says your dad.

Somehow, though, despite the real food, the warm clothes and bed, and the glorious medication, you can't shake the feeling that you're still trapped. Not in the woods, or even in the hospital, which allows you to go for walks outside now that you can make it to your feet without a dizzy spell. It's more like a prison of your own making. You can't quite adjust to being back, and when you finally walk out of the hospital for good one morning and return home to your old bedroom, you realize what it is: Your life cannot begin again when one of you hasn't truly returned.

Until Troy wakes up, you are stuck between worlds.

So as soon as your parents let you go outside unaccompanied (contingent on hourly check-ins), you find out where he is, and you make the journey to the suburban hospital that holds him. It's not until you finally make it there, shuffling through the long quiet hallway on the fifth floor, and open the door, that you see it's not just you who's been stuck. In the room, alongside Troy's parents, are Fran, Will, and even Diana, sitting cross-legged on the floor. They're nearly unrecognizable now that they're healthier, but you can kind of match your image of who they were before with what you see now.

"We were wondering when you'd get here," says Diana.

And from then on, that's where you meet.

Troy's fragile body, covered in bandages, lies in a bed in a small room that looks out onto the landing pad for the hospital's sole helicopter. Once or twice a day, there's a sound like a gas-powered Weedwacker as the copter revs up and goes off to find the next unlucky soul to deposit in the place. But the sound doesn't wake Troy. Neither does the TV you watch without really watching, or all the things they stick him with to keep him alive.

As the days pass—the number of days you were lost and then more—things do begin to change for others. Fran shows up with a new hair color—mermaid green this time—and a new girlfriend, Zooey, who is ultra-goth but has a disarmingly warm smile. Since Will is taking a break from tennis, you teach him to play chess and he soon becomes obsessed, playing twenty games a day online. In between being annihilated by eight-year-olds on the internet, he tells you that his father has agreed to let him see a therapist who specializes in intergenerational trauma.

So far, the experience of seeing everyone again is not making you relive the pain. Though it is strange. Meeting everyone now in a climate-controlled room, seeing them bathed and dressed in clean clothes, is like meeting them again for the first time. Sometimes you're not sure who they really are. Are they the people who screamed in despair in a clearing in the woods, or are they the people watching reality TV and eating snacks from the hospital vending machine?

This includes Diana. For all your talking on the phone, you thought everything would be comfortable again when you saw each other. But unfortunately, the old awkwardness has resurfaced, and you haven't yet spoken about the night under the canoe. The only saving grace is that she's started teaching you Serbian again. No swear words this time, but phrases you can repeat to Troy in hope that the strange sounds might awaken something in his brain.

"Molim te probudi se." *Please wake up.*

"Ti si lepa dusa." *Yours is a beautiful soul.*

"Tvoj veiner pas je tuzan." *Your wiener dog is sad.*

You all trade off engaging with him. Fran plays him hardcore bands she likes, cranking up the volume on her tiny speaker, as men who sound like Cookie Monster scream profane lyrics into the room. In between songs, she tells him about her new medication, and what it's like to taper off the old one. Will watches chess videos with Troy, staring with slack-jawed admiration at the confident nerds who lay out complex strategies he hasn't yet begun to understand. Diana whispers things that nobody can hear, and at times, when you leave the room, you think you hear her singing to him.

When your turn comes, you aren't sure what to do. It's hard to talk to him without crying, or just ranting about your problems. Panic attacks, those old friends, rear up again, mostly triggered by nightmares about your trip. You can manage them, but you wonder sometimes if they're here to stay. But Troy isn't your therapist. And he doesn't need to hear about your pain. If that's true, however, what does he need to hear about?

Eventually an idea comes to you, and from the moment you think of it, you know somehow that it's right. So one night when you go home, you climb back into the storage space above the garage and you find the box of books that you abandoned after Sean's death. You dig through the musty stacks until you locate

Journey Under the Sea. Then you start working your way through the book with Troy, each day choosing a different path.

"The choices you make are your own!" you recite from the intro. "One mistake may be your last . . . or it may lead you to fame and fortune!"

Some days you are attacked by a giant squid. Some days, it's a great white shark. Still others, you get the bends, or drown in a cave, miles and miles beneath the surface of the ocean. On day four, it's a giant poisonous sea snake whose venom has no antidote. But then, around day five or six, you choose a path that doesn't kill you right away. And as you move farther beneath the ocean, you discover a trail to an underwater cavern where the lost people of Atlantis have lived for centuries.

As you read aloud about this meeting, you notice that other people in the hospital room have started to gather around you. It's Fran and Diana today—Will is conspicuously absent—but they listen closely as the people of Atlantis give you the choice to become one of them. They can give you an operation that will allow you to breathe underwater, or you can decline. Everybody in the room has an opinion. Fran thinks it's a trap. A nurse who has come in to check Troy's vitals says they'll kill you on the operating table, or put you in their zoo of creatures from the surface. Diana stays quiet. She has an odd look on her face.

In the end, you decide to go for it. Everyone is hanging on your every word, but when you turn to page fifty-eight, something falls out of the book. You watch it tumble to the ground, a folded-up piece of notebook paper. For a moment, everyone forgets about the plot; there must be a look on your face. You set the book on Troy's bed and reach down to grab the paper. When you unfold it, you immediately recognize the handwriting as Sean's. At first you can't even read it. You just look at the blue-penned letters like they're decorative.

Then you see what they are: notes about his obsession with this book. All the paths. All the wrong turns. There are long streams of numbers that correspond to paths of pages. Routes through every part of the story, and which choices he made.

"What is it?" asks Diana.

You shake your head.

"I don't know for sure," you say.

You turn back to the book for a second, and while everyone listens raptly, you tell them about undergoing the operation to get the gills, and then about the life you lead underwater when it's over. It's a winning path in the book. You're alive for once. But then the last line of the chapter gives you pause. *You like it*, it reads, *but you regret that you will never again know the world above the sea*. Nobody says anything. You look back at Sean's scrawl. There are a few more notes at the bottom, seemingly about this page. You read them out loud.

"*You can win and still lose. You can't live a life fully under the surface. You have to find a way back even if it's hard.*"

The last words on the page stand alone, with some space in between.

"*You are not an Atlantean,*" you say.

You hear Diana's chair skid back, and then you watch as she gets up and calmly walks out of the room. Everyone watches her go. You stand next, but it's not until Fran says, "Go get her, dude!"

that you feel your legs moving and you too head out into the hall-way, where you find Diana looking at the bronze face of a man who donated to this wing of the hospital years ago. You walk up behind her, and she turns when she hears your footsteps. Her voice, when she speaks, is as clear and resolute as you've ever heard it.

"We have a choice, Case," she says.

The man on the plaque looks old and distinguished, like he lived a full life doing important work and giving to charities. You want to let Diana know that you remember what she said about Sean's last words. But she seems too determined, so you just listen.

"We can stay down here forever," she says.

The hallway is so clean, the floor gleams like the surface of a lake.

"In our grief."

You swallow and your throat is dry.

"We could stay all our lives if we wanted to," she adds. "We could live here."

"We already do," you say.

"Or . . . ," she says, "we could let ourselves come back to the surface. That's what he was trying to do. And I think that's what he would want us to do."

You've been especially attuned to sounds since you came back from the woods, and you hear so many of them now. The whir of hospital machines. A janitor's cart, rolling on a bad wheel. The hushed tones of patients' families. It's the complete opposite of the woods in every way.

You sit down in the hallway and lean up against the wall. The donor looms above you. Diana looks down at you, and then, after a moment of contemplation, she joins you, your shoulders touching.

"It's hard to remember who I was before," you say.

Diana stares across the hall into Troy's room.

"You were a kid all alone on a roof," she says.

You wish her depiction wasn't so accurate. But in a way, those hours before you met her were the "before." In your darker moments, you've wished that the two of you never met. But then you remember how alone you felt.

"I never asked you. Why did you climb up to see me that first night on the garage?" you ask.

She huffs out an uncomfortable laugh.

"I was drunk," she says.

You pause.

"Okay," you say.

"Ugh, I don't know," she says. "Maybe that's not it. You were alone on your birthday, on top of a garage."

"Oh," you say. "So it was pity . . ."

"No," she says. "That's not it either. I think when I saw you, it just felt like something I would do. It felt familiar."

"Being alone?"

"Yeah," she says. "But we don't have to be anymore, if we don't want to."

She leans against you, and you close your eyes.

And it's in that moment, one that you wish would last for an entire hour, that you hear the commotion from down the hall. The slap of the footfalls comes first. Then a door bursts open, and you see Will, sprinting like he did on that first day at the gas station, his eyes nearly closed with determination. Behind him is a red-faced male nurse. The nurse is yelling and trying to get a breath at the same time.

"Sir," he is saying. "Sir. I told you that is not allowed . . ."

He's not in great shape, the nurse. And it's hard to tell what his winded warning is in reference to until you get a better look at Will. He's back in a tracksuit, bright red this time. And he's holding something. Something that seems hard for him to grab hold of. Your mind races, but you can't for the life of you think about what kind of contraband he would be transporting through a hospital.

"Troy!" he screams. "Troy. I've got him. He's here!"

It starts to click then, and as Will thunders closer, you also see the short, flailing limbs of a terrified long-haired dachshund, better known to most people as a wiener dog.

"Oh my god," says Diana, and rises to her feet. "Oh my god."

"Secure the door behind me!" Will yells. "I repeat: Secure the door behind me!"

You get up too, and you don't hesitate for a moment. You and Diana are in lockstep as Will crashes into Troy's room, clutching Turbo. You take one look at the nurse, and you know you cannot let this man in the room. If you can survive a bear attack, this poor guy has no chance. And in this particular context, the consequences seem laughable. What will they do? Arrest you and send you to juvie, where you will be given an actual bed and prepared food?

You slam the door behind Will, and Diana and you brace yourselves against it, ready to move heaven and earth to make this reunion happen.

"Enough is enough, Troy!" says Will. "This dog is bereft, bro. You are his sole reason for living, and you need to wake up right now!"

He plops the dog on Troy's chest, where it seems stunned. Of course, nothing happens. And you chastise yourself for thinking there would be a miracle. The nurse pushes against the door, and it pops open a crack. But you push back and quickly close the gap again.

"I'm calling security!" says the nurse.

"Now what?!" says Will, and he looks on the verge of tears.

He kicks a chair across the room.

"It doesn't count if one of us doesn't make it," he says. "It doesn't count!"

And you know he's right. None of you need another absence in your life. You all have too many. There's no more room for absence and uncertainty. This, your therapist often said, was actually at the very root of your anxiety. The fact that life is always barreling toward you and always uncertain. And it keeps going until the second it stops. What you want—what every person alive wants—is to control it. But that is impossible.

Because no matter how much you try, you might find yourself in the middle of nowhere with no idea how to survive. Or stuck on a rapidly warming planet. Or in love with someone, entirely and aggressively against your will. Or trying to help a complicated person who can't find his way to accepting it. Or you just might find yourself in a hospital in suburban Minnesota, barricading a door while your new friend tries unsuccessfully to wake your other new friend from his coma with the use of a dog.

You don't have much time for revelations at this juncture. The pressure on the door is too great. And Will is starting to break down. But you know, if only for a second, that it's never going to stop. None of this. The absurdity and the peril and the absolute heartbreak of this life is going to keep going. But you also know with equal, fleeting certainty that you have to actually be there for it all.

Two things happen then in quick succession.

The first is that the door flies open, sending you and Diana to the floor. The nurse and two befuddled security guards stumble in, and you're not sure what they were expecting but it's not this. The second thing that happens is that Turbo seems to finally understand where he is. He takes a long hard look at the creature he loves most in the world, and then he proceeds to release the loudest, most mournful cry an animal has ever made. It is earsplitting and tragic and seems to contain the entire history of grief on earth in one canine bay. Everyone covers their ears and freezes in place as he howls again and again.

You look over then, and Diana is mouthing something to you. But you can't hear her. You move closer to her, and you take your hand off your ear for just a second. You feel her lips graze your ear, and when you turn toward her, you're surprised to see her smiling.

"We're here!" she says.

And then, it's as if something shifts in your brain. As all the mayhem unfolds around you, you feel like you're in a body again. *Your* body. And you are I.

Even though you know your brain will best you again, for now, there's a moment of total calm, and you hear each thought so clearly.

Yes, I am here.

And then I watch as Troy opens his eyes.

ACKNOWLEDGMENTS

When I was eighteen years old, I was diagnosed with anxiety disorder. It was a lousy birthday present, but I couldn't exchange it. And in the decades since, I've been working almost every day to keep my defiant and melodramatic brain from ruining a perfectly good time on this earth. I wrote this book for that teenage version of me who might have liked to read about others dealing with their equally vexing brain chemistry. Things are a whole lot better these days, and it all started when I asked for help. So, before I commence the roll call of book supporters and saviors, I'd like to give a heartfelt thank-you to those things that have helped me on this journey to relative calm. Here goes:

Thank you, therapy! Thank you, mood-regulating medications! Thank you, phone calls with hilarious friends, talks with supportive family, and strangers with British accents who make meditation podcasts! Thank you, writing! Thank you, moderate exercise! And thank you to anyone who has ever shared something about their anxiety with me. You made me feel less alone and more like myself.

But it takes a little more than guided meditations to get a book into the world. Fortunately, I am lucky enough to have a crack team of OG book champions who made the pages you just read possible.

Kirby Kim, agent/spiritual guide/confidant, everything starts with you. Thank you for your tireless work getting this book into fighting shape when it was punching below its weight class. You charged it with new life. Thank you as well to Eloy Bleifuss Prados and Lansing Clark, assistants extraordinaire, for your astute suggestions. And, of course, a big thanks to the whole Janklow & Nesbit team for taking such good care of me.

Alessandra Balzer, thank you so very much for believing in this book from the beginning, and for making it immeasurably better with your diligent editing and extraordinary instinct for turning a story. You care so much about everything you do, and it's contagious.

Thank you, also, to the All-Star Team at Balzer + Bray/ Macmillan, who each contributed an essential piece to this constantly shifting puzzle. Lavell Nero, Donna Bray, Bess Braswell, Teresa Ferraiolo, Molly Ellis, Kelsey Marrujo, Mary Van Akin, Shawn Foster, Kat Kopit, Celeste Cass, and Aurora Parlagreco. You turned this collection of words into a book.

Thank you to Ali Lefkowitz at Kaplan/Perrone for seeing exciting new opportunities in my work, and having faith in my stories.

Macalester College, thank you not only for employing me but also for providing world-class colleagues, brilliant students, and even some research assistants! Miriam Ruiz, your deep dive into Adventure Therapy programs was invaluable to this book. And Jizelle Villegas, your inherent understanding of character was a gift. In 2023, I met with a small cohort of two honors students in my office each Friday. One week, they kindly asked to see what their professor was working on, and I shared some of these pages for the first time. Hugh Gabriel and Ella Deutchman, thank you for making me an official part of the crew.

And now, a nod to those long-suffering people who read my early drafts and provided delicately phrased suggestions (oh, and some not-so-delicately-phrased suggestions). Tarik Karam, partner in crime, you're always a stellar, no-nonsense reader with the perfect joke to make the medicine go down. Your aim to make this book more exciting helped it go the distance. Matt Burgess, master of the seemingly innocuous question that changes the whole story, one of your queries brought the second half to life. Alex Albright, a conversation we had about therapy on a random patio one night helped me rethink its place in the book. Kristy Brecke, you told me all about your life as a wilderness therapist at a coffee shop and it provided a wealth of ideas. And, of course, Diana Josephson, you patiently answered every conceivable question I had about this world. Thank you for remaining a friend and for helping to shape my imagination.

Sarah Lindsey, our heartening sessions together help me understand what anxiety means in my life and, thus, what it might mean to these characters.

And finally, a thank-you to those folks who are obliged to love me through blood relation or marriage vows but who keep adding more to my life than they have any right to. Sal Bognanni, you didn't have the world's easiest 2025, but you still asked questions about my book almost every time you saw me. Where does this boundless solicitude come from? Kathy Bognanni, your willingness to sit down and find solutions to any writing or career challenge is inspiring. You are a dogged advocate (and a loving mom).

Mark Bognanni, you are saving the economy so I can still sell books. Much appreciated.

Roman, Nico, and Leo, you restore my faith in the future and gleefully take away most of my writing time. I wouldn't trade our hours together for anything in the world. I love the three of you so much it scares me.

Junita Bognanni—the last name on this list for a reason—you truly make this all possible. You analyze drafts, brainstorm ideas, talk me off the creative ledge, and buy me watermelons when I'm sad. I don't know what I did to deserve you. Your ideas, your care, and your profound and unflagging belief in me are on every page of this book.

Peter Bognanni's first novel, *The House of Tomorrow*, won the *L.A. Times* Book Award for First Fiction and was adapted into a feature film starring Ellen Burstyn and Nick Offerman. His second novel, *Things I'm Seeing Without You*, was published in four countries and is currently in development for television. Peter teaches creative writing at Macalester College.